PRAISE FOR
RETURN OF THE EVENING STAR

"What a delight to read a story populated with such characters! Noble, brave, and compassionate, Chloe and her heroic ensemble remind us that even in the face of loss and seemingly certain doom, it is our connections to those around us that will save the day. Diane Rios writes with verve, wit, and deep humanity, painting a portrait of a world very like our own, however fantastical it may seem."

—Alexis Smith, author of the award-winning *Glaciers* and *Marrow Island*

PRAISE AND AWARDS FOR THE FIRST BOOK
IN THE SERIES,
BRIDGE OF THE GODS

**2017 Moonbeam Children's Book Awards: Silver,
Pre-Teen Fiction – Fantasy
2017 USA Best Book Awards Finalist in Children's Fiction
2018 Oregon Book Award Finalist in Children's Literature
2018 Gertrude Warner Awards for Middle-Grade Readers
Shortlist**

Return

of the

Evening Star

RETURN

of the

EVENING STAR

A Novel

SILVER MOUNTAIN SERIES
BOOK TWO

by

DIANE RIOS

SHE WRITES PRESS

Published 2019
Printed in the United States of America
ISBN: 978-1-63152-545-2 pbk
ISBN: 978-1-63152-546-9 ebk
Library of Congress Control Number: 2018966189

Illustrations by Diane Rios
Book design by Stacey Aaronson

For information, address:
She Writes Press
1569 Solano Ave #546
Berkeley, CA 94707

She Writes Press is a division of SparkPoint Studio, LLC.

To my husband, Greg.

CYGNUS YAWNED, HIS GREAT JAWS STRETCHING wide as a groan escaped him. Nearby stars fluttered indignantly as he shook his massive head, knocking them from their orbit. Cygnus was ready to awaken. He had been sleeping for millennia, a celestial hibernation that might have lasted forever. But something had woken him up.

An ice-cold chill embraced him, and he felt his own stars shivering at the sound of a horrible, hissing voice coming from the deep, inky blackness of the sky.

"They will all die."

Cygnus whirled, scattering stars and small planets as he tried to see who had spoken. Another massive constellation towered above him, its fangs gleaming white against the black velvet of space. It was Scorpius, the snake. The giant reptile slithered his own stars and planets toward Cygnus, hissing his warning again.

"They will *all* die."

Cygnus was irritated. What in the gods was he talking about?

"Stop your nonsense, Scorpius." He growled menacingly. "You're just stirring up trouble."

"Oh, there is trouble all right," hissed Scorpius, undulating a line of meteors and small comets in the bear's direction. "But it is not of my doing. There is a war brewing in the land below, Cygnus."

"War?" scoffed the great bear. "What war? A human war? Why should I care if the humans go to war? If they all kill each other, that's no great loss."

"It's more than that, Cygnus," breathed the snake, his star eyes sparkling. "It's a war between the animals and the men."

Cygnus looked at Scorpius. He said nothing.

"Yes, and it is your loved ones who are at risk this time," said Scorpius with slithery satisfaction. "All of your children and cousins below will be vulnerable in this war. The humans have new weapons at their command."

"New weapons? What do you mean?" demanded Cygnus.

"They have made new weapons that move at incredible speeds, faster than any animal can run—even the fleet Awinita cannot outrun them. These weapons can be used to run down our people, to crush them, to mortally wound them, yet they are impervious to harm themselves. The animals have had enough, Cygnus, but they don't have any idea what they are up against. All they can talk about is a meeting on the mountain. They are ready to fight back."

"Fight back?"

"But they won't win," said Scorpius, hissing deliciously as he tasted the words.

"No, they won't win," agreed Cygnus sadly. He turned to look down at the world below, a small world but a beautiful one, and one that he loved very much. He said simply, "They'll need our help."

"*Your* help. *I* won't help them," Scorpius said disdainfully.

"Of course, *you* won't," answered Cygnus bitterly. "But I know who will."

"Who?" asked Scorpius.

"I will pay a visit to Silas," Cygnus said. "It has been a long time since I've seen my old friend. Together we will see what we can do."

"Silas?" Scorpius threw back his head and laughed out loud. A tumble of comets fell from his fangs and spun out into the darkness, lighting up passing meteors as they did.

"What can that old geezer possibly do?"

Cygnus was disgusted by the snake—Scorpius was always such an annoyance. Still, he had woken Cygnus when surely, Cygnus would have slept another thousand years and left his poor earth children to their doom. Ironically, it seemed he owed the snake a debt of gratitude—with this irritating thought, Cygnus shook his great head again and growled.

"You know as well as I do, Scorpius, that Silas the Stargazer knows the Evening Star. She could help, and he is the only one she will speak to."

"He is a fool," spat out Scorpius, flicking his tail angrily and knocking three planets off their orbit. "And she is a fool for befriending him!"

"You're just jealous," said Cygnus with a growl. "You know he loves her."

"Bah!" spat Scorpius in disdain. "Humans can't love stars."

"You know nothing about it, Scorpius," said Cygnus. "As usual. Now enough—I have an old friend to meet."

Fully awake now, the great bear constellation shook his magnificent mantle of sparkling stars, comets, and whirling galaxies and moved across the heavens toward the small blue-and-green planet.

CHAPTER ONE

"WILL YOU PLEASE ASK THE MARE HOW FAR we still have to go?" Lord Winchfillin gasped in pain as his mount Raja stumbled over another branch lying across the road.

The Artist laughed. "Ask her yourself! She can hear you perfectly well."

The two men were riding through the deserted streets of Tillamook Town. They had woken that morning at the Hotel Nell, and eaten a hurried breakfast provided by Faron the stable boy. After hearing the boy's account of what had happened in the town, they knew they could not stay. They must get out while they still could and continue the search for their young friend Chloe.

It wasn't just Tillamook Town—the entire countryside was in chaos. Only a few days earlier, fleets of flashing silver ambulances had suddenly appeared on the roads of the sleepy, rural communities, and begun terrorizing the population. Hurtling down the dirt roads at unimaginable speeds, these speeding "horseless carriages" deeply shocked the people of the land who had never seen anything like them before. Shock turned to horror when the drivers hopped out, their faces covered by masks—and began taking their loved ones away. If the "patients" struggled, the drivers placed masks—attached to silver canisters—over their faces. The victim's next breath would render them unconscious, whereupon the drivers would drag them to the waiting ambulances, shove them inside, and speed away—to where at first, no one knew.

Soon there were rumors of a new hospital in the west, in a small fishing village called Fairfax, and reports of multiple ambulances seen on the roads there. So far, the local police hadn't been much help—they were under attack themselves, and the most they had been able to do was to send increasingly alarmed telegraphs back and forth. Meanwhile the deadly drivers continued to comb the countryside.

As the men and horses rode out of town, they each reflected on the last two days, which had been the most frightening of their lives. The Artist thought for the hundredth time of that awful moment he had lost Chloe.

Hold on! he remembered shouting as Greybelle galloped for her life ahead of the speeding ambulance. The mare had been carrying the weight of two people and could not keep up the killing pace. The Artist had cued her to turn off the road, and he remembered the mighty leap she and Raja had made across a ditch and into the forest. That was when Chloe fell.

I failed her, the Artist thought morosely, tears welling up in his eyes. *If only I had felt it, if only I had known!*

Greybelle whickered softly as if she could read his thoughts. It roused the Artist from his sad reverie and he patted her shoulder. *She probably* can *read my thoughts,* he mused, half expecting the mare to agree.

His companion, patron, and old friend the Earl Lord Winchfillin rode behind on the old gelding Raja, a bleak expression on his face. The Artist heard the little lord mumbling to himself indistinctly, "New curtains . . . imported silk . . . *ruined.*" Lord Winchfillin sniffed loudly.

At the sound the Artist turned around in the saddle to face his friend. "Are you all right, my Lord?"

"Oh yes, yes. Quite all right." Lord Winchfillin wiped his eyes with a frayed lace cuff and recovered himself a little sheepishly.

"Forgive me, I am just waxing maudlin over my old possessions. Silly really. You know, it's a *very* good thing you discovered me when you did, my old friend!" he called forward. "If it hadn't been for you, I might have starved in that burned house, or gone crazy, or been attacked again—if those demonic drivers had found me first!"

The Artist nodded gravely and said, "Yes, it was very good luck that I found you when I did. I only wish I could have found Chloe, too."

"Yes, it is very unfortunate about the girl," agreed Winchfillin, sobering. "She was such a sweet child, and a very hard worker!"

"*Is* such a sweet child," the Artist corrected.

"Yes, yes—of course, she is!" Lord Winchfillin hastened to agree. "And I hope I thanked you both properly for doing such a wonderful job helping me prepare for my birthday party!"

A stricken look crossed Lord Winchfillin's face at the thought of his lavish birthday party and his magnificent home, both utterly devastated by the vicious ambulance attack.

"My beautiful party." He sniffed sadly. "And my poor guests! What do you think has become of *them*?"

"Nothing good, I'm afraid," said the Artist.

"We must try to do something for them!" said Lord Winchfillin, sitting taller in his saddle. His pale, dirty face gleamed for an instant with an uncharacteristically heroic light, and words tumbled from his mouth. "They are all friends of mine! We must find out where they have been taken!"

"In due time, my Lord," soothed the Artist. "We will look for them as soon as we are able. First though, I must find Chloe. She may need our help, she may be injured."

The little earl looked at his friend sadly as he said, "So many missing."

The men and horses continued silently through the eerily quiet streets. Everywhere was evidence of the horror the community had been through. Windows were broken, doors kicked in, and the horses carefully picked their way around debris in the streets.

The quiet was ominous. It was not the quiet of a town still sleeping, but an uneasy quiet of the fearful and the hiding. They passed the police station but did not stop. It was obviously deserted, the doors hanging from their hinges. A chair lay on the front steps as if it had been thrown there, or perhaps dragged from under someone who had been sitting in it.

The little group hurried along as best they could. Although still uncomfortable in Raja's saddle, Lord Winchfillin rode straighter and with greater ease now, having worked out most of the pains of the first day's ride.

They had a destination. They were traveling to the great mountain in the east. There had been rumors in the animal world of a meeting on the mountain. Whitestone the squirrel had told Greybelle the mare to go to the meeting with the men. It seemed that man was not the only one suffering from the ambulance attacks. Animals were being run down and killed by the hundreds, and many had had enough. It was time to do something about it. Whitestone told the mare that the animals might help them—for the greater good. It would be the only way to confront the speeding cars, for it seemed that neither man nor animal could do it on their own. And so the little group had turned their steps to the northeast—in the direction of the great silver mountain, Wy'east.

Once they had moved beyond the outskirts of town and entered the sparse forest, the Artist decided it was time to share with his old friend something he had just recently discovered himself. With her blessing, The Artist told Lord Winchfillin that the mare he was riding, Greybelle, could talk.

The earl didn't believe it and laughed loudly at his friend's joke.

"But it's true," Greybelle had said simply.

The look of shock on the earl's face at the sound of the mare's voice was comical. His cheeks drained of color, and his wide-open mouth shut up like a box.

Since then he had avoided the entire subject. Greybelle didn't speak again, preferring to keep quiet anyway, and they had ridden along in this way until the saddle began pinching.

"But . . ." Lord Winchfillin wheezed huffily, "I've never spoken to a . . . *horse* . . . before. How do I do it?"

"You just speak, of course!" The Artist laughed. "Just as you are right now! She can understand everything you're saying as well as I can!"

Greybelle said politely, "Yes, I can."

Lord Winchfillin looked a little sick. Gathering his courage, he took a deep breath and leaned forward in his saddle. "HELLO. I AM LORD WINCHFILLIN."

Greybelle whinnied, a bit indignantly. "I'm not deaf!" she said.

"Ah," said the earl uncomfortably. He cleared his throat and tried again. "Good morning, Miss Greybelle. So nice to make your, er . . . acquaintance."

"And yours, sir," answered the mare pleasantly.

A remarkable array of emotions crossed the little lord's face all in an instant—utter surprise, a pained distaste, a flutter of pride at the mare's respectful address, all of which he tried his best to conceal. He remembered his manners.

"Ah, *yes*, indeed. Quite right. Ahem." Lord Winchfillin cleared his throat and said politely, "Please, my good mare, could you tell me how far it is to this mountain?"

"I'd be glad to," answered Greybelle. "We should be there by nightfall."

"Ah! By nightfall, wonderful. Wonderful. Thank you. Thank you very much," said the little man meekly, sitting back in his saddle. His usual garrulous prattle was turned off like a faucet, and for once the earl seemed content to ride quietly, thinking his own thoughts.

The trail led through the foothills of a mountain range in front of them, the slopes dotted with scrub pines and strewn with large boulders. The horses spent the afternoon climbing the gradual incline, taking a moment here and there to rest in the shade of the trees. When the sun was high in the sky, the Artist called for a halt to eat what was left of the good pie Faron had given them that morning. The men dismounted and stiffly stretched their legs while the horses dropped their heads and began grazing on the thin grass growing in patches around the rocks. The splashing sounds of a nearby stream could be heard, and the horses and men drank their fill. Refreshed, the little group continued. As they climbed higher, the pines grew closer together, and the air became colder.

They soon came to a ridge that overlooked a valley and stopped in wonder at the sight that greeted them. The green lowland stretched ahead under the bright blue sky, and a great river sparkling with the light of a million dancing diamonds ran the length of it. At the end of the valley, like an enormous king upon a godlike throne, sat the mountain. The great Wy'east.

His ragged peaks were covered in snow, and a swath of clouds clung to the top like a crown.

The sheer size of the mountain made everything else seem very small.

"I sure hope the meeting isn't at the top," sighed the Artist, echoing everyone's thoughts.

A sudden cry and burst of movement made both horses shy violently, nearly dumping their riders. The Artist and Lord Winchfillin held on tightly to their plunging mounts as hundreds of enormous mountain ravens, the size of small dogs, exploded out of the trees. As they flew eastward over the valley, their rasping cries filled the air with a dark, harsh song. An ominous song.

Stunned, the friends watched the birds gradually disappear, and grimly made ready to follow. The trail down was not steep, and the horses had no trouble descending. They rode silently through the trees, each lost in his own thoughts about what they might meet when they finally got to this meeting on the mountain.

They were nearly to the bottom when they were again stopped by a strange noise. An unsettling whisper rustled through the undergrowth. What was it? It wasn't the wind, for just then there was no breeze at all. It wasn't birds, because it seemed to be coming from the ground. As they listened, the whisper became a vast rustling . . . and then more movement. All around them, the grasses, bushes, and low tree limbs began waving, and a light vibration could be felt beneath their feet. The horses snorted and stamped nervously. Suddenly the ground was alive.

Pouring out of the forest was a flood of small, furry bodies. Raja reared in a panic as the stream swirled over his hooves. Lord Winchfillin just managed to grab a handful of mane to avoid tumbling onto the moving carpet of . . . *mice*! Tens of thousands of mice were on the march, stopping for nothing. Like locusts intent on finding their next meal, the tiny creatures flowed around the horses, somehow avoiding their dancing hooves in their single-minded rush.

But a rush to where? they all wondered, and at the same time the answer came—the meeting. Just like the crows, the mice must be on their way to the mountain; there could be no other explanation.

Greybelle's ears pricked forward, and she looked baffled as she said softly, "Strange."

"What is strange?" the Artist asked the mare.

"*Seeds in her pockets*," said the mare. "Does that make any sense to you?"

"Not a bit," said the Artist, shaking his head. "Should it?"

"I keep hearing that phrase. Some of the mice are saying it: *seeds in her pockets*. I wonder what that could possibly mean."

Greybelle shook her head and started forward again, carefully stepping around the surging creatures, and they all made their way toward the mountain.

CHAPTER TWO

*C*HLOE ASHTON WOKE SLOWLY IN HER SNUG BED under the eaves, feeling better than she had in weeks. In fact, she had not felt this well since her father died, she thought sadly, stretching luxuriously under the covers. Indeed, she felt so good that she thought she must be still dreaming and lay still in the little bed for a moment, smelling delicious breakfast smells wafting up from below. A hazy memory flickered across her mind of Mrs. Goodweather and Brisco, and climbing a ladder up to a . . . *tree house?* Chloe's eyes snapped open.

She saw jewel-tinted light dancing on the wooden walls. She could see the tree limbs waving outside the windows. When she heard Mrs. Goodweather say, "Shakespeare dear, don't step in the syrup!" the dreamlike quality evaporated, and Chloe remembered exactly where she was, and why.

The girl sat upright and looked around, rubbing her eyes. It was no dream: she really *was* in a tree house, and Mrs. Goodweather really *was* making pancakes on the tiny black stove. She could smell coffee too, and even . . . orange juice? *How* did Mrs. Goodweather do it?

"Good morning dear!" sang out Mrs. Goodweather, a spatula in hand. "Come and have some breakfast."

Chloe's best friend, a white rat named Shakespeare, squeaked happily from his place on the windowsill. He was munching a tiny pancake from a miniscule stack Mrs. Goodweather had made him, syrup dripping from his whiskers.

"Good morning!" answered Chloe cheerfully, taking a seat at the table. Mrs. Goodweather set down a plate in front of her stacked high with blueberry pancakes. A small jar of maple syrup sat on the table, and Chloe drizzled it over the stack. Mrs. Goodweather sat down with her, a cup of tea in her hand.

"These aren't . . ." Chloe said, halting the fork that was halfway to her mouth, and looking suspiciously at the blueberries.

"Oh no, dear!" Mrs. Goodweather laughed. "Those aren't my *special* berries, don't worry! Those are wild blueberries, and quite delicious! I've always said wild blueberries are the best blueberries."

"They certainly look delicious!" Chloe took a bite, and reached for her juice.

"Where is Brisco?" asked the girl, happily taking another bite of what might be the best pancakes she had ever tasted.

There simply was no better cook than Mrs. Goodweather, she thought, munching.

"Brisco's gone to look around," said Mrs. Goodweather, sipping her tea. "He's scouting the hospital grounds, and as soon as he gets back, we'll talk about our plan." The older woman raised her eyebrows significantly. "Now you just eat your breakfast, dear, and then we'll be ready for whatever he has to report." Chloe was happy to oblige, and stuck another delicious forkful of pancakes into her mouth, sighing in pleasure.

Just then they heard Brisco's tread on the tree house steps. In a moment his smiling, mustachioed face poked in the door, followed by the rest of him.

"Good morning, ladies!" said the carpenter briskly, seating himself at the table.

"Good morning, Brisco!" they both said at once.

Mrs. Goodweather took another plate of warming pancakes from the oven and placed them in front of the carpenter.

"My, my! Aren't we the lucky ones?" Brisco said appreciatively, tucking a napkin into his collar. "Having good Mrs. G to cook us one of her world-famous breakfasts, eh?" He smiled at Chloe and rubbed his stomach hungrily.

Chloe giggled. There was just something about the handsome carpenter that made it impossible to stay worried. He was always busy, and always had a smile on his lips.

She agreed enthusiastically. "But we are also lucky that *you* are with us, Mr. Knot. Surely no one else could do the marvelous things that you do!" She gestured around at the tree house he had built the previous day, in no time at all.

"Oh, well. Pish posh, anything for a friend," said Brisco modestly, blushing just a bit under his mustache. "And do please call me Brisco."

"Brisco, then," said Chloe shyly.

Mrs. Goodweather sat down with her tea. "Tell us, Brisco, what did you find at the hospital?" she asked, her face serious.

"Well," said Brisco. "I've walked around the entire place, and there is only one way in, that I can see. All the windows are sealed, the roof has no access, and there are only three doors—the front door, the back door, and one side door on the west side. Two of them are locked. Only the back door is open and the only way to enter the hospital, as far as I can tell."

"The back door?" asked Chloe, crestfallen. "You mean the one the ambulances go in and out of? That will be impossible, won't it?"

"It won't be easy." Brisco looked at Mrs. Goodweather.

The older woman said softly, "Well, if we *can* get in, we have our little plan."

"Yes! The plan!" said Chloe.

"It's a dangerous plan," said Brisco. "I don't like it. And I don't like the thought of you two being in that place alone."

"It is not to be helped, Brisco," said Mrs. Goodweather. "We need you on the outside, as you know. Chloe and I can take care of ourselves . . . if we can get into the hospital unnoticed that is."

"That's a pretty big 'if,'" said Brisco. "Especially with only one way in."

"We'll just have to chance it," said Chloe. "My mother is in there!"

"Let's go over the plan again," said Mrs. Goodweather. "Now, it will be dangerous, there is no point in denying it," she admitted. "And I cannot guarantee it will ultimately work, even if we do manage to get to where we need to be. But, we must take the chance. We *must* get inside. If we do, and *if* we can get to the top people at the hospital—I'm talking about the highest of the high, the people who run the whole institution: the administrators, the decision makers, the leaders, the presidents—then . . . I think we could possibly *shut the whole thing down.*"

"Tell us how again," said Chloe eagerly. She loved this part.

"Well now." Mrs. Goodweather went to the counter of the tree house, and picked up a small paper bag which she brought back to the table. From inside she withdrew a large packet which she opened to reveal a quantity of large, ripe, juicy blueberries.

"I brought a few of my most special ingredients along with me."

They all gazed at the plump, perfect berries, and as a most delicious smell wafted up from the packet, Chloe and Brisco sniffed its syrupy sweetness appreciatively.

"Whatever you do, do *not* eat them," Mrs. Goodweather cautioned, closing the bag. "They are extremely powerful and are to be used very sparingly, and only by someone with experience. They can be very dangerous if used incorrectly, *very* dangerous indeed. So, promise me"—she looked severely at the other two—"promise that you will *not* touch these berries."

Chloe and Brisco both solemnly promised.

Mrs. Goodweather stowed the berries back in the cupboard, reminding them of the consequences. "When you eat a little, they heal whatever ails you. If you are in pain, the berries take the pain away. They give old limbs new life, they make old eyes sparkle, and in short my friends, *they make you younger*, which is why my customers love them so."

"But . . . eat too many of the berries and you will *continue* getting younger. And younger. And younger! Eat too many berries and the years will melt away, and along with them . . . so will you." Mrs. Goodweather's eyes grew serious, and their normally sunny depths sparkled with a mysterious glitter.

Then Mrs. Goodweather said in a voice that gave Chloe a shiver, "Keep eating the berries, and you will *become an infant*."

Brisco's eyes shone, and he clapped his hands in amazement. Mrs. Goodweather leaned forward. "I can bake these berries into pies, and if we can find a way to serve them to the heads of the hospital . . ." She trailed off meaningfully.

"They will become babies!" finished Chloe and Brisco together with a shout of laughter. Brisco pounded the table with his fist in glee.

"Shhhh! Not so loud!" shushed Mrs. Goodweather, smiling broadly. "But yes, that is the general idea!"

"Babies! They'll all become babies! Oh, it's perfect, it's positively *genius*!" said Chloe, laughing with delight. "Oh, oh! It's too funny! Hey! Maybe we could feed the pies to all the ambulance drivers, too!"

"Well, unfortunately I don't have enough for all of them," said Mrs. Goodweather. "If I could, I would bake a thousand pies and feed them to every staff member here, turn them *all* into babies! But there aren't enough berries for that. That is why we need to get to the *top* people, the ones who control the hospital and the drivers. Once we have gotten to them, the others will fall, or at least stumble, and then maybe we can find some help—surely there are still *some* policemen about?"

"But *how* will we get to them? The decision makers? The administration of the hospital?" wondered Chloe. They didn't know who ran the hospital, or even where they were. They could be anywhere inside that huge building. The plan became less funny by the second, the more she thought about it. Failure, after all, meant almost certain death.

Mrs. Goodweather sighed. "*That* is what we still must figure out. You said there were three doors, Brisco. The front, the back, and one on the side? What is the side door?"

"We can't go in by that door. No way," said the carpenter.

"Why not?" asked Chloe. "Is it locked?"

"No, it's not locked," said Brisco. "But we can't go in that way."

"Are you sure?" asked Mrs. Goodweather. "Why not?"

Brisco said nothing for a moment. Then he shrugged his shoulders and said, "It would be easier to show you than to tell you."

There was no lingering at the table after that; Chloe wanted to go straightaway to the side door of the hospital. The girl and the carpenter helped Mrs. Goodweather clear up the breakfast things, and they all left the little tree house, shutting the door and climbing down the steps to the forest floor.

"This way," said Brisco, leading them into the trees.

The three made their way along the back of the hospital, toward the western side of the building that looked out over the ocean. They came to a boulder surrounded by bushes, and Brisco motioned for them to stand behind it. From here they could see the side door of the hospital—an arched doorway illuminated by green lights. It was closed, but Brisco pointed to a wooden contraption, built from the door to the dock below. It looked like a long slide of some kind.

"What is that?" asked Mrs. Goodweather.

"I think it is a chute," said the carpenter.

"A chute? What is a chute? What is that for?" asked Chloe.

Just then, as the group watched transfixed, a loud *click* was heard, followed by a deep grinding sound. They all jumped as the door began to open. The three hiding behind the boulder held their breaths as the door slowly rose to reveal a moving belt that carried something large out of the hospital and onto the chute. It was a long box made of plain boards. The box was open, and they could see something inside it, covered by a blanket. The box rolled out of the door, slid into the chute, and with a rattle and a bang, slid swiftly down the hillside to the dock below.

There was a small tugboat at the dock. They could see two burly-looking men standing on the dock, who easily caught the wooden box as it came hurtling down the chute. The two men seemed well-practiced at their task, as if they had done it many times before. They deftly caught the box, picked up the contents, and stored them on the boat, then stacked the empty box to the side of the dock, just in time to catch the next box that came racing down the hill.

"*What* are they doing?" breathed Chloe.

"I'm not entirely sure, but I have a suspicion," said Brisco quietly.

The men on the dock repeated the routine repeatedly until the boat was full. They rang a bell on the boat, which seemed to be a signal to the hospital, for at the sound of the bell the boxes stopped coming. The same *click* was heard, and the grinding sound began as the green door slowly closed.

The three behind the boulder watched in silence as the tugboat cast off from the dock and moved away to the deeper ocean. It stopped where they could still see it clearly, bobbing up and down in the waves. After a few moments they could see the men come out on deck and lift a blanketed form. One of them shouted, and the sound carried clearly over the water.

The three watching from behind the boulder could hear the words as clearly as if they were still right below.

"Oy! Watch out!"

"You're dropping him!"

There was a dull thud as the form fell onto the deck. And then, "I *told* you!"

"Well help me pick him up then!" A small scuffle and then a splash.

Brisco turned to Mrs. Goodweather and gave her a significant look. Chloe looked at both of her companions, and choked out wildly, "What? What is it? What are they doing?"

Brisco cleared his throat and then said very softly, "It appears that they are dumping bodies into the sea."

CHAPTER THREE

SEEDS IN HER POCKETS. WHAT COULD THAT mean?

The last mouse had finally passed the men and horses, the grasses and brush stopped rustling, and all was still again. The little group carefully continued in the same direction as the mice, and the Artist turned this phrase over in his mind. Who was the "she" they were talking about? It couldn't be Chloe, could it? No, impossible. He shook his head sadly. For the thousandth time the old man wondered what had become of the child and hoped with all his heart that she was safe, wherever she was.

Greybelle and Raja stepped along, livelier after their drink at the stream. The way was more difficult now that the path had disappeared, and there were no roads in this remote area. The railway had not yet transformed this part of the landscape, nor were there any telegraph wires, nor outposts of any kind. This place was still wild, but both men and horses had toughened up quite a bit in the last few days, and their scanty diet had made them lean. They pushed valiantly on, nearing their goal as each hour slipped by.

When the little band reached the valley below, they traveled more easily. Here, protected by the surrounding hills from the strongest winds, the trees were still covered in colorful leaves, and autumn still reigned supreme. Flaming red maples and brilliant yellow larch trees mixed to create a forest of beautiful color. The two men and horses walked on the springy turf under the trees, feeling more hopeful than they had in days. The soft valley breezes, the riot of color overhead, and the sound of the nearby river soothed their spirits and distracted their thoughts from what might be waiting for them up on the mountain.

They arrived at the river and followed it toward the mountain, which seemed bigger than ever. After some time, they reached the foothills and stopped. The two men slid wearily off the horses, and everyone took the opportunity to rest. There was still a climb ahead of them, but for the moment they were satisfied to wash their faces in the river, to drink their fill, and to eat the few apples that remained in the Artist's big pockets. Lord Winchfillin noticed a patch of blackberries nearby, and picked enough to share.

The sun was beginning to sink toward the west, and the Artist wondered whether they should make camp here and start their climb in the morning. Before he could speak his thoughts, a sharp *chirrup* came from just overhead, followed by a rain of pine needles, and a gray squirrel jumped down to the ground beside them.

It was Whitestone, the squirrel who had told Greybelle about the meeting. He had been following them for some time, and now chattered animatedly at the mare, who pricked up her ears to hear.

Whitestone chittered and chattered, on and on, until the Artist gently interrupted, "I'm sure you'll translate for us, Miss Greybelle?"

"Of course," said the mare, cocking her head to catch the squirrel's last words. She turned back to her friends and explained, "Whitestone has been sent to accompany us to the meeting."

Lord Winchfillin looked at the Artist and guffawed. "A *squirrel?*" he said skeptically. "We need a squirrel as a guard? I find that hard to believe—" The little lord choked off his words at the outraged look he got from the squirrel himself.

Greybelle said somewhat reprovingly, "Whitestone has been sent by the Badger, who is an important leader in this area. We are lucky he was sent to guide us, we will need his introduction at the meeting. Without it we would never be allowed to go, and indeed"—she looked meaningfully at Lord Winchfillin—"without a guide—or guard—we would surely not even survive the attempt."

"Do you mean . . ." asked the little lord, his eyes wide.

"You would both be killed," Greybelle said simply.

A shocked silence followed.

Then Greybelle said gently, "Although technically the Badger has already invited you, you are still human and so must have an animal to vouch for you. Whitestone has volunteered to do us that kindness."

The Artist bowed his head in thanks to the squirrel respectfully. "You do us a great service, friend Whitestone, I thank you."

Mollified, Whitestone nodded his head politely at the Artist but gave Lord Winchfillin a final glare before jumping back up into the trees to wait for them.

"Whitestone says we should go on a little farther, but we won't be able to reach the high meadow tonight," said Greybelle to the men. "It's about a four-hour climb, so we'll have to make camp on the mountain. He will show us where to sleep tonight."

"Does he know this Silas fellow?" blurted out Lord Winchfillin, as they made ready to leave.

"Nobody *knows* Silas the Stargazer," answered Greybelle.

The Artist added, "I heard a song about him once, but I thought it was just a legend." He swung up on Greybelle's back, and Lord Winchfillin led Raja over to a fallen tree so he could mount the old gelding's back.

Greybelle said, "The old man lives alone, far up on the mountain, and speaks to no one except for the animal leaders at council, which doesn't happen often. This is the first time in anyone's knowledge that he has addressed all the animals at once. And let me warn you all—at the meeting, take care what you say." Greybelle stopped so Raja could catch up.

"The wild animals will be united for a time, but they won't be tame. It will be a large gathering of both predator and prey, all pressed close together. It will be a very dangerous situation at best, and I would not trust the peace to be kept, even in front of Silas. Try not to go out of your way to antagonize anyone."

The mare's gentle gaze turned on Lord Winchfillin, who swallowed fearfully. "I . . . I won't," he said meekly. "I wouldn't dream of it." He gulped.

❧

After their rest and light meal, the travelers continued more quickly. Greybelle followed the flashing underside of Whitestone's tail as the squirrel leaped through the trees ahead of them. The way wasn't too steep yet, the incline ascending gradually past stands of pine that grew closer and closer together until once more they were enveloped by forest.

"How much farth—"

A loud *crack* just behind them cut off Lord Winchfillin's question. The horses halted. A vibration in the earth traveled up their legs, a pounding, a drumming—what in the world was it? Raja whinnied and whirled in circles, nearly unseating Lord Winchfillin, who clung to the gelding's wispy mane and cried out, "Stop! Stop!"

A great herd of elk came through the trees. They were led by the most magnificent stag the Artist or Lord Winchfillin had ever seen. He was huge—at least ten feet high at his nose, with another five feet of antlers crowning his head. At the sight of the humans, the great elk stopped short, and stared at them, his huge black eyes shining. He silently looked them up and down, and the men felt he knew exactly why they were there, and that he did not approve.

The great elk lord, for he must be a lord judging how dignified his look was, how regal his brow—this great lord of the forest stamped his front hoof on the ground, producing a deep thrum in the earth. He blew out a loud blast from his flared nostrils, and at that signal the entire elk herd stepped out from beneath the trees. Ten, twenty, thirty, sixty—at least a hundred—elk stepped out and walked past the men, eyeing them distrustfully. They were each as large as the horses, some with racks of antlers towering above them, their sharp tines gleaming in the afternoon light. The men and horses froze in place, and waited for the great herd of elk to pass.

When the last one had moved by, the elk leader raised his nose into the air and blew a high, bugling cry. The sound carried far out over the valley and up the side of the mountain, sending shivers up all their spines.

Greybelle looked around at her companions. "We must go on!" she said urgently.

As Whitestone led the way, more and more animals joined them. They seemed to be coming from everywhere. Flocks of birds alighted on trees around them, and more filled the air. Families of rabbits, groups of squirrels, small packs of coyotes, and a large group of opossums all passed by the slow-moving humans and horses.

The Artist and Greybelle weren't very disturbed by this, having seen many odd things in their lives, but for Raja and Lord Winchfillin it was a different story. The poor old horse's nerves were stretched as tight as a wire, and sweating and blowing, he pranced like a colt. Lord Winchfillin slipped in the saddle and grabbed at the reins, muttering, "Consarn it you fool horse! Just stand sti—"

Raja suddenly shied violently to the side, nearly throwing him. Something—something huge—was moving in the bushes. The little earl gripped the gelding's scrawny mane as tightly as he could, his face white as he stared at the spot.

The bushes around them seemed to sigh. The ferns and bracken lifted and fell as one, as if they breathed. The next minute it became apparent that *many* large somethings were all around them. Even the Artist gasped and a small scream escaped Lord Winchfillin when a huge, square black head appeared through the screen of ferns.

Small, fierce golden eyes peered at them suspiciously. *Chuff!* came a powerful grunt of fishy breath.

An enormous black bear emerged into the little clearing. At the sight of him, both horses whickered in fear. As the strong scent of the bear filled their nostrils, it was all the men could do to keep them from bolting.

Behind their leader, eight more enormous bears stepped through the trees, their towering shaggy sides as black as night. For all the rustling of the bushes, the huge bears were remarkably agile and able to move quietly through the forest. Their smell was anything but subtle, however—the pungent scent of dead fish, old mud, oily hair, and a sickly-sweet undercurrent of honey was so strong that it made the men's eyes water.

The bears in turn could not see very well, which irritated them, and they were made further upset by what to them was the *very* bad smell of the humans.

Chuff, chuff! they blasted, tasting the mixture of scents on the air. Then, as if called by an invisible signal, the bears dropped to their four feet and moved off as silently as they had come through the underbrush. Before he too disappeared, the leader turned to give the men a final look. He raised up on his hind legs, as tall as a tree, and swiped the air with one of his massive paws. Growling a warning, he too dropped to all fours, and with a mighty shrug of his great black shoulders, followed his family up the mountain.

The little group sagged with relief at the bears' departure.

"No, indeed," choked out Lord Winchfillin shakily to Greybelle. "We won't antagonize anyone—especially them."

Whitestone chirruped brightly and leaped off in the direction the bears had gone.

"The world really has turned upside down," said Lord Winchfillin mournfully. "In the old world I would say that one should *always* go in the opposite direction of bears, but in this new, strange world we are going to follow them. To *meet* them. To *gather* with them! It really is too much, I tell you." Lord Winchfillin's teeth chattered from his fright.

"Don't you want to get your castle back?" the Artist asked him practically.

"Oh yes, yes I do." The earl nodded. "I most certainly do."

"Well, believe it or not, my friend," said the Artist, grinning at his friend. "Those bears might be the ones that help you get it."

"Now, I really do not see how that is possible!" snapped Lord Winchfillin irritably. "Do you *really* think that those . . . those . . . *predators*, those *carnivores*, are going to help me get my beautiful house back?" he demanded. "I think the road is finally beginning to get to you, my friend, you're stark raving bonkers. How could *bears* help me get my castle back? We could never control them!"

"Indeed not!" interjected Greybelle. "That is the very thing we are fighting against! The bears will not be controlled. They would never allow it, you must know that." She tossed her silver mane.

"*Are* we fighting then?" asked Lord Winchfillin woefully.

"In one way or another, I believe we will have to," answered the Artist softly.

Greybelle agreed. "I think you are correct. If this many animals are going to see the Stargazer, then I know they will demand satisfaction. They will not have come all this way for nothing. But I also know that we can trust the Stargazer to give wise council, whatever the outcome. If we are careful, I believe we will be safe."

"Nobody is safe in a war," said the Artist sadly.

CHAPTER FOUR

ODIES!" WHISPERED CHLOE, HORRIFIED. "You mean the bodies of *patients*? Patients who have *died*?"

"Or . . . patients they have killed?" whispered Mrs. Goodweather, aghast.

The same chilling realization swept through Chloe at the same time. This was the logical conclusion, once they'd seen the long pine boxes sliding down the chutes to the sea. There were too many for it to be a coincidence. The hospital was killing people.

A stunned silence surrounded them, broken only by the distant sound of regular splashes from the boat, as it dumped the boxes' contents into the sea.

"What . . . what if they've killed my mother?" sobbed Chloe quietly, her small shoulders shaking.

"Oh dear, oh dear, don't cry, Chloe." Mrs. Goodweather put her arm around the girl, giving her a firm hug. "We will find her. No matter what happens, we will do whatever we can to find your mother, and to help the others. Don't cry, my dear. We can't give up hope now!"

Chloe knew Mrs. Goodweather was right, and she dried her eyes. They could *not* give up hope. They *had* to stop the hospital. Everyone in Fairfax was in danger. Everyone in the land was in danger! Chloe felt a steely resolve flow back into her heart. She sat up and tried to smile. She made her voice steady as she addressed the others. She was ready. "We have to find out how to get inside."

Back at the tree house, they discussed what to do.

"What if one of us goes down and joins the line?" suggested Mrs. Goodweather. "We could chat with the people and see what they know. Maybe we can see an opportunity down there that we can't see from up here."

"I'll go!" said Chloe.

"*No*," said Mrs. Goodweather and Brisco at the same time.

"It's too dangerous for you, my dear," said Mrs. Goodweather. "What if your uncle comes by and sees you? You could be hurt, or at least our entire plan could be ruined."

Chloe nodded and gulped, thinking of what it might be like to run into her awful Uncle Blake again. She hadn't seen him since she had escaped the Hotel Nell with the Artist, and she was in no hurry to do so, especially alone.

"Why not me?" asked Brisco. "I think *I* should be the one to go, and you ladies can stay here, safe in the tree house."

❦

IF HE WAS COMPLETELY HONEST, BRISCO HAD ANOTHER reason for wanting to go down to the hospital. Very early that morning, as he was scouting the grounds, looking for any way to get inside, he had stopped to observe the line of people camped on the hospital's front lawn.

These were the loved ones of those who had been taken by the ambulances, in town and all over the countryside. None of them knew what was happening or why their loved ones had been so suddenly and viciously taken away and brought here. Many of them had been waiting for days for any word of their family members' fate.

At first a single line of people, the number had grown until now there was a small village camped out on the hospital steps and driveway. Brisco was shocked by how many people were waiting, and in what conditions they waited. The nights were very cold. Here and there were small fires that the people warmed their hands over, but there was no avoiding the bitter chill of the night.

Brisco's own breath came in white puffs as he crouched behind a hedge, taking in the miserable scene. He was just about to turn and start back to the tree house when a slim, dark figure detached itself from the line and walked toward the steps of the hospital. A woman in a faded and patched purple dress, wearing a thin shawl, stopped in front of the doors where he noticed for the first time a large white notice was posted. The woman appeared to be reading the poster. From his hiding place Brisco could not see what the poster said, and he was watching the woman's reaction for clues when she turned toward him, and he caught his breath.

She was beautiful. Her smooth, pale skin and large brown eyes plucked at the carpenter's heart. Her soft brown hair was tucked neatly under the hood of her cloak, but curled wisps of it hung free here and there, utterly beguiling him. As she read the poster, her beautiful brow knit slightly and she looked thoughtful, and even more beautiful, in Brisco's opinion. For a moment he forgot everything else—the plan, Mrs. Goodweather, even Chloe—and he almost jumped out of the hedge to introduce himself. Just in time Brisco came to his senses and blinked at his own stupidity, and near miss. What was he thinking? What in the world was wrong with him? Had his head *actually* been so turned that he would leap out of a hedgerow—in the middle of an important mission no less—just to meet a pretty woman? He would probably frighten her out of her wits anyway, leaping out of the bushes like that. Brisco remained where he was, and watched the beautiful woman walk back to the line.

The carpenter guessed that she must know someone inside the hospital and he felt a wave of anxiety that it might possibly be a husband. As the thin figure walked away, Brisco noted her worn dress that looked as if it had once been fine, and felt a resolve to help her, even if she did already have a husband. He promised himself he would not forget her and would try his best to find her again. First though, there was a plan to be laid, and the best thing he could do to help himself, Chloe, Mrs. Goodweather, *and* the beautiful woman was to finish his scouting and get back to the tree house.

❧

JUST NOW MRS. GOODWEATHER WAS REASONING WITH him at the tree house table.

"Now Brisco, an old woman will attract far less attention than such a handsome, strapping young man as yourself," she said wisely. "Why, that magnificent mustache alone will have

every young lady looking at you. I am *much* less memorable.
An old woman can get around virtually unnoticed."

Brisco thoughtfully twisted the ends of his mustache,
wondering if the beautiful woman he had seen would like it.

"I will wear my kerchief over my head and no one will be
the wiser," Mrs. Goodweather said briskly. "They will think I
am some poor old country woman who is looking for her husband and they won't suspect I'm really a *spy*." She winked at
Chloe, who giggled. "And then when I come back, we can
make the pies."

They all agreed that Mrs. Goodweather should be the one
to go down to the hospital. Then Brisco told them about the
sign posted to the front doors of the hospital that he had been
unable to read. He suggested she might try to read it herself—
it might be something that could help them. He did not mention the beautiful woman he'd seen.

Mrs. Goodweather tied her kerchief on her head. When
she had placed her basket over her arm, she looked exactly like
any old granny walking to market. No grannies were walking
to market today, but many of them were in the line out front,
and Mrs. Goodweather would fit right in. She left the tree
house and walked down the hill to the hospital. Brisco, Chloe,
and Shakespeare watched her go down the little path. When
she disappeared around the corner of the hospital, Brisco
brought out a pack of cards for a game while they waited.

CHAPTER FIVE

ON A BRANCH OUTSIDE THE TREE HOUSE perched a crow named Blackberry. He was a very surprised crow—he hadn't expected to find people in a tree. It was the stained-glass windows of the tree house that first caught his attention, flashing in the sun. Their colorful sparkle intrigued him irresistibly, and Blackberry had flown down for a closer inspection. That's when he found the tree house, and then he noticed the people inside.

Blackberry watched the people hold up sparkling glasses and clink them together, and his eyes glinted with desire. He wanted those glasses. They sparkled so beautifully, he would be the envy of all his brothers if he had one in his nest! While he thought about a way to get one of the glasses, Blackberry noticed that one of the humans was a child. A girl child.

The crow felt a tug at his memory, something important about a human child, what was it? Oh yes! He remembered now! There was an alert out for a child—his brother Poole had told him only that morning to be on the lookout for a girl child, a woman, and . . . Blackberry's breath caught in his throat. Was that . . . *Brisco Knot*! Oh, my goodness!

Blackberry jumped in surprise and almost fell off the branch. He began dancing along the tree limb with glee, kicking small bits of pine needles and bark to the ground, and squawking to himself. Imagine! *He, Blackberry* had found the girl that everyone was looking for *and* he had found the legendary Brisco Knot! He would report it to the Badger himself! He would be famous! More famous than his brother Poole, at any rate, which was the most important thing.

Brisco Knot was known and beloved by all crows. Though a quiet and humble man, he was famous in their circles far and wide, for a great kindness he had done their king years ago. King Cornix had been only a prince then, a fledgling who had toppled from his nest. One wing broken, the young prince lay helplessly on the forest floor, becoming weaker and weaker, and would have certainly died had the carpenter not found him.

The legend went that at first the two royal crow parents had attacked Brisco, taking him for an intruder. But the carpenter had understood their distress, and spoke gently to them, assuring the crows he would not harm their child—and then he had wrapped the crow chick in his large, soft handkerchief, and carried him home.

After a week of expert care, the chick's wing had mostly healed, and Brisco had carefully returned him to the nest, to the great joy of the parents. Prince Cornix grew strong and was able to fledge properly along with his siblings, and from then on was devoted to Brisco.

Grateful he had saved their king, all of the other crows and ravens loved the man too and would do anything for him. And Brisco had a curious effect on the crows—they became a bit silly in his presence. Many became quite besotted, cooing and cawing, and fluttering down to sit on his shoulder. He could often be seen with a crow or two following along, through the trees, or even hopping in a rather undignified way on the ground behind him. There was just something about Brisco—he had a quiet charm all his own. And of course, he had some mysterious abilities of his own as well—quite wondrous abilities.

Brisco could make anything out of anything. Blackberry himself had seen him once build a bridge across a river in three minutes flat, made only out of things he found on the ground around him. Unbeknownst to the crow, Brisco had also made an exact replica of the dangerous ambulances out of wood, which was how they all had escaped to the tree house from Mrs. Goodweather's cabin in the woods. And it was he who had built the marvelous tree house, again out of found items.

Brisco can do anything, thought Blackberry, with a sigh of adoration.

The carpenter returned the crows' affection, always welcoming them, feeding them some of his own dinner, and helping them whenever he could. As a result, he had become crow legend, and all crow and raven chicks were sung songs of Brisco Knot's great act of kindness to their king.

And he had found him! Blackberry was so excited about his discovery he completely forgot about the sparkling glasses he had coveted so badly only moments before, and with a final hop and a squawk the young crow flew off quickly to find his family, and to report his find to the Badger.

CHAPTER SIX

The Artist led the way up the mountain riding Greybelle, lost in his own thoughts. What a strange adventure he found himself on, one of the strangest in his long life, he thought. He reflected on the days that had led to this moment. It wasn't long ago that he had been driving Raja and the cart to Tillamook Town, on his way to his old acquaintance Mr. Nell's hotel. After an excellent dinner, the Artist had joined a poker game in a back room. He liked playing cards from time to time, and he had recently been paid for some portraits, so he was ready for some amusement.

There were two shifty fellows sitting at the poker table that night, and the Artist did not like the look of them from the moment he sat down. The one who called himself Mr. Underwood was a horrible fellow. Passing himself off as a "gentleman," while that word could not be further from the truth. His clothes spoke of money, but his demeanor was that of a wild man. Gaunt, greasy, and rude, he and his companion Bings drank more and more, and became wilder and wilder, and by the small hours of the morning had bet everything they had in the world. For his part, the Artist had been ready to call it a night then, and go to bed, and laid his cards down on the table to fold, only to find he had won it all.

That had wiped the leering smiles off the two men's lips. The Artist remembered how the table went silent, and how Underwood and Bings stared at the huge pile of winnings, the reality sinking in. With that one hand, the Artist had won all of their money, and their horse, and . . . the girl.

Mr. Nell, unbothered by the loss of a girl he had owned for less than twenty-four hours, had stood up and congratulated his friend.

"Well, Artist, you got yourself a maid." Nell roared with laughter. Never did someone need a maid less, than the Artist. "You can get her to clean your cart!" the little hotelier guffawed. "Come on then, time for bed, boys." He began straightening the chairs and motioned for a servant to clear the table.

Blake Underwood, Chloe's uncle—for that is who it was—and his driver Bings sat watching the Artist sweep the winnings into his hat. Gradually his bloodshot eyes focused, and Blake glared at the Artist. "You . . . you *artist*," he sneered. "You . . . *old man*, just watch yourself. You just better *watch*"—Uncle Blake tottered and grabbed the edge of the table to keep from falling—"*yourself*, that's all I'm sayin'!"

"Come on, now, sir," said Bings, as drunk as his boss. "Let's get to bed."

"Stupid old fool . . . better watch himself that's all I'm saying," burbled Uncle Blake as he staggered out of the room, leaning on Bings's shoulder.

I won a . . . child. The Artist felt ill. He hadn't even realized that Mr. Nell had bet a *person*—how despicable that she had been used as a commodity in this way. God knows what had happened to her thus far.

He had risen early the next morning. He had not slept well. The Artist knew those two men from the poker game wished him no good. He feared they might try to get back what they had lost. If he could make his departure before they woke up and bring the child along with him—then perhaps he could save himself, and her. And, hold on—hadn't they told him he'd won a horse, as well?

That horse was Greybelle, who he was now riding. And the girl, of course, had been Chloe.

After only three days together, the old man and the girl had become fast friends. The Artist loved the child dearly and wanted nothing more than to help her return to her family in Fairfax. Then the ambulances attacked, and now they were climbing a mountain to try to save her again. He shook his head sadly and rode on in silence.

They heard it before they saw it. The path had narrowed, and the sounds of gushing water grew louder and louder, until they turned a corner and were met with the sight of a waterfall carving its way through the boulders. The aqua-blue water frothed and churned over the rocks, widening into a mountain river. The icy waters rushed over fallen trees that spanned its width and roiled in eddies along the edges. Spray from the falls blew out over the gleaming rocks, turning everything slick and wet, and walls of green ferns clung to them, drinking in the nourishing mist.

The sound was deafening. As they stood there, staring at the churning water, the Artist had to shout to be heard. "Looks like there's no way to cross but to swim it!" he yelled at his companions.

"What? Swim that?" screamed back Lord Winchfillin.

Greybelle and Raja eyed the fast current apprehensively. It was true: the path ended on one side of the falls and picked up on the other. There was no way to cross the fast-moving river besides swimming it. But how? The current was so fast it would surely sweep the horses away, and it was *cold*. Straight from the heart of the mountain itself, the river was made of melted snow and fed from an ancient underground aquifer. The current was extremely strong and could easily hold one underwater until they drowned. There were logs in the river too, with branches that could hook clothing and hair. The little group stood on the banks, looking uneasily up and down for a better point to cross. Whitestone scampered downstream to scout for a good spot.

The Artist shaded his eyes and looked after the squirrel. Squinting, he could see two dark heads in the water, slowly pushing toward the far shore. Was it more deer . . . no, it was other horses! Two strange horses emerged on the other bank, shaking the water from their sides in great, shivery shakes. Raja couldn't help himself and whinnied at them.

The two horses lifted their heads in surprise and whinnied back a greeting.

"Those are not talking horses," said Greybelle.

"Maybe they're wild horses, heading to the mountain, just like we are," speculated the Artist. "And I think they've found the best place to cross. Let's follow their example."

They all moved down to where the other horses had entered the water. The river still looked deep and fast, but they could also see two shallow places toward the center where they might gain a foothold against the swift current.

The two horses on the far bank whinnied their encouragement.

"Well, here goes," said Greybelle, stepping carefully into the water.

The Artist held tightly to her sides with his legs. The water was so cold that it burned. He knew that if Greybelle stayed in it for any length of time, she would seriously weaken and then the icy waters would numb her body so that she couldn't swim. The mare went in deeper and deeper until, snorting, she touched the freezing water with her belly. Then she had to swim. The Artist gasped at the shocking cold of the water. Greybelle pumped her legs powerfully through the current, propelling them forward. They were swept downstream a little way before the mare's hooves touched a shallow spot and she was able to push against it. In this way she made it across and climbed out of the water, blowing hard.

Raja took his turn. He stepped gingerly into the water and then leapt in the air when Lord Winchfillin shrieked at the freezing water on his legs. Snorting and blowing nervously, Raja pushed on into the river. When the old gelding started to swim, the little earl bobbed like an apple above him, moaning at the cold. Raja struggled valiantly through the rushing water and then finally he too was across.

After they had all shaken off as much water as they could and caught their breath, the little group turned toward the two new horses who had been watching them with ears pricked forward. Raja sniffed noses with them and Greybelle did the same, all of them snorting gently and whickering under their breath at each other.

"They say they are from a farm," said Greybelle. "They

heard from a raven that there was going to be a gathering of animals, and they wanted to come. They have a hard life on the farm—all of the animals are hungry and overworked, and they thought perhaps Silas could help."

"Well, we're all headed the same way," said the Artist cheerfully. "We might as well travel together. Did they say their names?"

"The brown is called Ned and the black is Tinker."

"Well, Ned and Tinker!" said the Artist agreeably, spreading his wet arms out wide. "Welcome to our little group. Let us all travel to the mountain together! And as we walk, we will dry ourselves in the sunshine."

The group of shivering horses and men moved away from the river. The afternoon sun dried their coats and their clothing, making traveling easier. The little band of horses and men made their way up a narrow path, following Whitestone as he led them by leaping through the trees overhead.

The Artist, feeling very clean and merry after his dunking in the river, began to sing a song.

In 1803 we sailed out to sea
Out from the sweet town of Derry
For Australia bound if we didn't all drown
And the marks of our fetters we carried.
In the rusty iron chains we sighed for our wains
As our good wives we left in sorrow . . .

"I say, my good man!" broke in Lord Winchfillin. "Can't you sing something a bit more . . . cheerful? Optimistic? I don't want to hear words of drowning, fetters or iron chains, or sorrowful wives, if you don't mind."

The Artist laughed. "Forgive me, my friend!" he said with a grin. "I will sing something more *bolstering* to give us heart for whatever lies ahead."

"Much appreciated!" sighed the earl.

The Artist then sang another song—of a long-ago battle that was honorably and bravely won for king and country.

Heart of oak are our ships, heart of oak are our men;
We always are ready, steady, boys, steady!
We'll fight, and we'll conquer again and again,
Ready, steady, boys, steady!

Lord Winchfillin knew the words and sang along. The rhythm and uplifting tune helped them forget their worries for a little while, and the aching of their muscles.

The little group continued in this way for another hour until the sun began to set behind the trees and they were forced to halt for the night. Whitestone assured them that they would have plenty of time to get to the meeting in the morning, so the men dismounted from Greybelle's and Raja's backs, and turned them loose with the two newcomers, Ned and Tinker. The four horses moved off companionably together to graze, and the men made a small fire and put a kettle on to boil for tea.

Soon, the smell of the Artist's famous flapjacks wafted through the trees, and there was silence in the little camp while the men ate their dinner. After they had satisfied their hunger and the last pancake had been eaten, Lord Winchfillin pulled out a long, ivory pipe from a deep pocket in his coat and puffed it contentedly next to the fire, while the Artist softly sang a few more lines from the song.

We'll still make them fear, and we'll still make them flee
And drub 'em onshore as we've drubb'd 'em at sea:
Then cheer up, my lads! With one heart let us sing
Our soldiers, our sailors, our statesmen and Queen.
Heart of oak are our ships, heart of oak are our men . . .

The Artist trailed off, his eyes lifted to the heavens, and gazed back at the stars that stared down at him. *Heart of oak are the animals*, he thought. But I am a man. *Which side am I on?*

The stars shone brightly on the mountain, illuminating the trees around him, the grass on the ground and the forms of his companions, and it comforted the Artist with its quiet light.

A soft snore made him look at his companion. Lord Winchfillin had fallen asleep, his empty plate still in his lap. The Artist smiled to himself. His old friend had come a long way since that fateful birthday party. Tattered, bedraggled, and uncomfortable as he was, the little earl was showing a strength and courage he could never have guessed he had. And, the Artist thought gravely, he would need every scrap he could muster.

The Artist was very tired, his heart still full of worry. Until he knew Chloe was safe, he could not fully relax. And what would be waiting for them tomorrow, he could only guess. Whatever it was, he knew it would be difficult, if not deadly.

He sighed and rested his back against a tree. Finally, his snores joined that of Lord Winchfillin's, and the two men slept awhile. Around them the forest was quiet, the sky above was clear, and in its inky depths the stars reached out over the land, their twinkling lights pointing the way.

CHAPTER SEVEN

RS. GOODWEATHER HURRIED DOWN THE path toward the hospital. A siren could be heard approaching, and she waited behind some trees for it to pass on its way to the big doors. When it was safely past, Mrs. Goodweather emerged from the trees, adjusted her kerchief, and continued on around the corner of the building.

The sight that greeted her was shocking. The crowd of people outside the hospital had been waiting for days, and the evidence was everywhere. Trash and discarded items lay scattered about, people sat on the ground, or laid on the ground, babies crawled about, and children dashed back and forth, chasing each other while their parents stood in line. The parents, grandparents, and all the people in the line were grumbling. The tension in the air was palpable, and only heightened by the sounds of sirens.

Mrs. Goodweather walked alongside the line, and up to the front doors of the hospital where she plainly saw the notice Brisco had described. She went up the steps and read:

GRAND OPENING GALA

Welcome the new Fairfax Hospital!
A grand opening gala will be held on
Friday, November 28, 1908
7:00 p.m.
By Invitation Only

Mrs. Goodweather realized with a start that Friday, November 28, was the day after next! Could that be true? She thought hard, counting the days since she and Chloe had been on the road, two . . . three, yes—tomorrow was the twenty-seventh and so the gala was the day after tomorrow!

The woman almost skipped with joy right there on the steps before she could stop herself. This was *exactly* the opportunity they needed! Surely the head of the hospital would be present at the Grand Opening Gala. If they could only find a way to get into the kitchen, or better yet get close to the table where the hospital head was sitting, maybe . . . just maybe they could slip him the pies!

Mrs. Goodweather's heart was pounding with excitement, her head was full of promising thoughts and barely begun plans as she stood thinking of what to do next.

A shout got her attention and she snapped out of her reverie.

"What's going on in there?" shouted someone in the line.

"We demand to know what's happened to our families!" shouted another.

The crowd rumbled angrily. From somewhere a woman started chanting the words, "Let us in! Let us in! Let us in!" It was picked up by the people around her, and then more people down the line until the driveway reverberated with the words. "Let us in! Let us in!"

The noise grew and grew, the people getting more riled and angry with every second. The chanting had warmed them, and when one person had started yelling, it galvanized the entire group. They were sick and tired of waiting! They wanted action. Mrs. Goodweather stood nervously on the steps of the hospital as the crowd screamed in front of her.

A loud *chunk* came from behind her, followed by a scraping sound as a lock was turned. Mrs. Goodweather jumped back at the horrible *screeeeeee* sound the doors made as they slowly swung open. Two white-coated attendants stood just inside the doors, blocking the entrance. At the sight of the doors opening, the crowd roared and surged forward.

The line of people crowded up the steps and tried to jam their way through the doors. The sheer mass immediately overwhelmed the white-coated guards and even caught up Mrs. Goodweather, moving her up the steps and into the hospital. Painfully squeezed and crushed against the wall, she fought to get her breath. The crowd poured in through the doors, filling the entryway and spilling into the waiting room.

In front of Mrs. Goodweather was the main desk with a nurse sitting behind it. Mrs. Goodweather felt a gleam of hope at the sight of a woman, but her heart sank as she saw the nurse's grim expression. She would be of no help, that was certain.

The double doors leading from the waiting room into the hospital were padlocked. The only place the crowd could go from there was down the corridor to a desk with a red neon sign above it that said BILLINGS. Here the people were permitted to form a queue, a line of white-coated guards kept them organized, and Mrs. Goodweather could see white clubs attached to their belts.

Soon the angry crowd became nothing more than a second line, this time to the Billings desk. This reminded Mrs. Goodweather of still another line she'd seen that morning from behind the boulder—the line of pine boxes going out to sea.

This place was a regular factory, she thought with a creeping dread. It has assembly lines running all through it. Each of these three lines is part of the same diabolical puzzle. A line of ambulances delivering patients, a line of people paying money, and a line of long boxes going out.

Supply and demand, she thought bitterly. The hospital was turning a deadly profit.

She watched the crowd a while longer, hoping to learn any more details that might help their plan, but after realizing it could do no more, the crowd settled down, and the room of people became docile once more.

Mrs. Goodweather had seen enough and walked back to the entrance to leave. Outside the people were angrily talking to each other about what was going on in there and asking each other where the police were.

Mrs. Goodweather wondered the same thing as she quickly made her way past the crowd, and around the hospital to the little path up the hill.

Chloe, Shakespeare, and Brisco were watching eagerly for her return, and put down their cards as she climbed the steps to the little porch.

"It's every bit as bad as we thought," Mrs. Goodweather

said. "As far as I can see, they are admitting people only to extort them for money. I believe that is the cursed place's whole operation—abduct their victims and drain their bank accounts. And I'm sure that as soon as the families can't pay, their loved ones are . . . er . . . *disposed* of."

"Oh, how awful!" cried Chloe.

Brisco shook his head sadly.

Mrs. Goodweather went on, "However terrible that is, my dear, it *does* give me hope for your mother." She smiled at the girl, who looked confused.

"It is likely that your family is still able to pay for her care, you see," said Mrs. Goodweather gently. "And so, it stands to reason that she is most likely still alive! And my dear—we will find her! *I know how we can get inside!*"

Chloe and Brisco looked at the woman in surprise. Chloe felt a gleam of hope melt the misery around her heart, and she sat upright, the tears drying on her cheeks. "How, Mrs. Goodweather, how?" she choked out.

"There is to be a Grand Opening Gala for the hospital the day after tomorrow! It could be the perfect opportunity to slip the bigwigs our special pies. Isn't it remarkable? We could not have asked for more fortuitous timing!" She clapped her hands in glee, her eyes twinkling.

Brisco looked unconvinced. He leaned his chair back as he said thoughtfully, "That's all well and good, Mrs. G, but we still need to find a way in. It's still a huge risk."

"The day after tomorrow!" exclaimed Chloe. "That doesn't give us much time!"

Mrs. Goodweather said, "I've thought of that. What we need are disguises."

"Disguises!" said Chloe. "What sort of disguises?"

Mrs. Goodweather leaned forward and chirped, "Chloe and I can pretend to be servers!"

Her companions looked at her in shocked silence for a second, and Mrs. Goodweather went on, "That way we would be able to get to the tables where we could serve the pies to the proper people!"

"Genius!" gasped out Brisco, letting his chair fall forward with a thud.

"Perfect!" said Chloe, delighted. "But—how will we find disguises? They will have to look very convincing if we're to be undetected. How in the world will we . . . ?" she asked.

"Oh, no worries about that, dear!" said Mrs. Goodweather. "I could easily sew us a couple of uniforms, if we could find some fabric."

"Well that would be my department," said Brisco, standing up from the little table. "I'll look around for your fabric, Mrs. G. I'm sure I can scrounge up something," he said confidently.

"I'm sure you can!" said Mrs. Goodweather, chuckling. "Well that settles it then. We have found a light shining in the dark. You know, child—there's always *something* you can do, no matter how hard things seem. And once you do something, even something very small, it often turns into something big. Something that changes everything."

She squeezed Chloe's shoulders, adding, "Now, who wants some lunch?"

Perhaps it was the relief of having a plan, and the excitement of the preparation ahead that made them hungry, but suddenly they were all ravenous. While Mrs. Goodweather prepared another of her delicious meals, Brisco and Chloe and

Shakespeare played cards. Their game was much merrier for they all felt the energy of hope coursing through them.

It wouldn't be easy. There was a lot to do before the day after tomorrow—the disguises had to be sewn, and the pies had to be made. There were a lot of details they still needed to discuss. The plan had to be foolproof, for there would be no second chances.

For the moment they needed to eat, and they all tucked in to Mrs. Goodweather's delicious dinner of pot pie, creamed corn, and baked cinnamon apples. Brisco produced a bottle of honey mead from his bag and poured them all a small glassful. He filled a bottle cap with mead for Shakespeare, who tasted it and, finding it delicious, lapped it up as fast as he could.

"To us!" said Brisco, holding his glass aloft and smiling through his mustache. "To the courageous Chloe, the magnificent Mrs. G, and the chivalrous Shakespeare!"

"And to you, Brisco!" added Mrs. Goodweather, raising her own glass. "To the most masterful and cleverest carpenter the world has ever known!"

The three friends clinked their glasses and drank to each other's health. Though their plan would be difficult and extremely dangerous, Mrs. Goodweather knew they all had that emboldened feeling one gets when one *has* a plan, any plan, after a long period of not having one. And that now they had a chance, however slim, and with hard work and a lot of luck, they might even succeed.

CHAPTER EIGHT

ZZZZZZZZZ . . . ACK!" THE ARTIST WOKE mid-snore to a terrible tickle on his neck. It felt as if a very large spider had crawled on him, and he bolted awake, brushing violently at the spot.

Whitestone the squirrel leapt back, greatly offended by the man's flailing hands which had nearly slapped him on the ear. Whitestone regarded the Artist with great disapproval.

"Oh! It's you, Whitestone," said the Artist sheepishly, relaxing. "Sorry about that, but I've been woken by more spiders than squirrels. Did you have something to tell us?"

Whitestone remembered his message and chattered brightly at the Artist, who turned to Greybelle for translation. The mare said simply, "He says it is time to go."

Whitestone chattered agreeably.

"Let's be on our way, then," said the Artist, gathering up his things. "My Lord," he said, gently shaking the sleeping earl's hammock. The little earl came awake with a gasp.

"What in the name of God time is it?" he said crankily, trying in vain to arrange his hair.

"It's time to go to the meeting, according to our fuzzy guide," answered the Artist, nodding at Whitestone.

"Is there any coffee?" Lord Winchfillin croaked.

"I'm afraid we drank the last of it yesterday," answered the Artist, patting Greybelle's neck. "Go splash your face in the stream—that will wake you up, but be quick, I have a strange feeling we need to get to the meadow sooner rather than later." He nodded upward as a large flock of birds passed overhead, drowning him out with their cries. "We don't want all the best seats to be taken." He winked.

The three quickly packed up what little they had with them. Lord Winchfillin knelt by the creek to splash his face, and they mounted the horses again. Moving off from camp, they hurriedly followed Whitestone, who leaped ahead through the trees. They were joined by more animals just arriving at the mountain. Scuttling and scampering through the underbrush alongside them were mice, rabbits, voles, chipmunks, weasels, and even two badgers, all moving toward the meadow. It seemed that every creature within twenty miles was on its way to the gathering.

Several more bears passed them, unnerving them all, and a herd of deer bounded by. Greybelle and Raja snorted at the sight of two mountain lions padding by on silent feet.

"This is going to be some party," said the Artist, watching their twitching, yellow tails disappear up the trail. "I hope we can all stay civilized."

"*Civilized*!" squeaked out the earl, his face white. "I just hope we can all stay *alive*!"

Up and up they climbed, animal, bird, and man, until they reached a place halfway up the mountain. Here the dense forest ended abruptly, and an expanse of alpine meadow stretched in front of them, dotted with wildflowers. Surrounded by trees, the meadow was the perfect amphitheater in which to gather. Its open sky and soft carpet of grass was a welcome relief from the steep and wooded terrain they had climbed. The meadow stretched out in front of them like a green lake with a tumble of boulders at one end.

Over the pile of boulders loomed a towering rock wall. Above the wall were the snow-covered peaks of the mountain. The summit was hidden in a swirl of clouds. Wy'east's cap was white all year long, and in winter his sides were packed with snow and ice. But just now, the deepest snow had yet to fall and the meadow was in a protected hollow.

While the men and horses hesitated, other animals began to file in and take their place for the meeting. The first to enter the meadow was a shadowy pack of wolves that silently arranged themselves near the tumble of boulders. They stood watching warily, their eyes gleaming at the sight of the smaller animals. After the wolves, two bears strode defiantly out into the middle of the meadow and stood looking around, daring anyone to challenge their authority. Several groups of deer stepped nervously out of the cover of the trees, but wouldn't approach the rocks where the wolves were. Smaller animals began pouring into the meadow, arranging themselves in groups, and watching to see the carnivores didn't get too close. Group after group stepped out from the trees and found their places. Soon the meadow began to fill up and the animals were pressed closer and closer together. Nervous snorts and yips were heard as someone's tail was stepped on, or someone bumped someone else. Everyone was on edge. No one completely trusted this strange, uneasy truce between predator and prey. How long would it hold? How long *could* it hold?

The animals passing by the group of men wrinkled their noses at the man-smell. They glared at the sight of the men and the wolves growled, showing their teeth and giving the humans a wide berth. Lord Winchfillin whimpered and stood as close to Raja as he could. The old gelding was no happier and crowded Greybelle.

The old meadow had never had such a gathering before. Hundreds of animals crowded together on the grass, and though there was tension, there were no fights, and every animal waited as patiently as possible for the meeting to begin.

The sun rose slowly above the mountain, turning its crown of clouds first lavender, then pink. The animals were silent, sensing a change in the wind. Was it beginning? Was Silas going to come? Where was the Stargazer? The limbs of the trees all around the meadow trembled then, as if an electric current danced through them, and a shower of pine needles dropped to the forest floor as someone stepped out into the meadow.

A small, wizened old man stood there. His face was brown and wrinkled, as were his hands and his bare feet. From his head hung long gray braids, and braids adorned his gray beard and mustache. He wore a simple garment of buckskin, and though he looked to be very old, he climbed the rocks like a much younger man. Silas the Stargazer had come down from the mountain.

No one knew exactly where Silas lived; it was rumored to be in a cave, high up on the peaks of Wy'east. He was very seldom seen, and the younger animals had never seen him at all, but only heard the legends and stories about him. He was rumored to be over one hundred years old. The legends said that only the stars could summon the Stargazer, and if that were true, then this meeting was even more important than they thought.

The old man stood there silently, gazing out at the multitude of animals before him. A hush fell over the crowd as they waited for him to speak.

"Why, he looks like the Duchess of Cheeves!" Lord Winchfillin giggled, almost unhinged by his nerves.

"*Shhhhhh,*" cautioned the Artist, putting his fingers to his lips.

Silas was speaking.

"Welcome, my friends." The old man's voice was gentle, but strong, and carried far out over the meadow. The animals became completely still, thousands of ears tuned to every word.

"You have all come such a long way," said the old man. "There has never been such a meeting as this—but there has never been a threat like this, either. It is no small matter that brings us together now."

An uneasy murmur of agreement rippled through the meadow.

Silas the Stargazer's weathered face was grave. He breathed deeply and continued, his voice still gentle, but tinged with sorrow. "Things are not well in the world, my friends. This you know. This you have known for a very long time."

Growls and grunts of agreement greeted this statement.

"And now my brothers, my sisters, and my little mothers"—Silas smiled down at the field mice gathered in the grass below him—"I am sorry to say that a new evil has come to the land. I have seen it in the stars. And you have seen it on the roads."

Angry roars, bleats, chirrups, and cheeps came from those present who had indeed seen the evil themselves. Almost every animal in the meadow had had some friend or family member killed at the hand of man.

Silas held out his hands as if to soothe the raised hackles of his angry audience. "We have all suffered greatly these last years," he said sadly. "My own people are gone from the land. Only a few remain hidden away in the north, never to return to these sacred lands. Your people remain, but how many generations have been hunted, trapped, poisoned, and killed? And now, we are threatened by a new kind of danger.

"I saw the evil foretold in the stars years ago. There was nothing I could do about it then—it had not yet even begun. And when it did begin, I did not understand what its power truly was. It was hidden from me, because I am also a man."

An uneasy silence from the meadow.

Silas went on, "When the new men first came and began to cut the trees—we did not understand. We thought there was enough for all, and we allowed it. But those men took *all* the trees, leaving nothing but a bare, poisoned waste behind them. They took and they took, they took until there were no more trees, and the land was dead."

The trees were gone, the animals cried with anger. *The land was dead.* They roared and stamped their thousands of feet, making the meadow jump.

"And when they had taken all the trees, they began to take the animals," Silas said darkly. "Not satisfied with enough to sustain themselves, they took more animals, and more, and more—they killed my people and they've killed your people too!"

They took the animals. The creatures in the meadow were maddened with hatred at the memories. *They killed our people!*

The meadow erupted in rage. The mountain lions roared, the wolves howled; there were barks from the coyotes, grunts from the badgers, yips from the skunks, even a chorus of squeaks from the mice who had heard every word and were doing their best to be counted.

The sound was so loud it alarmed the bears and they rose high on their hind feet, chuffing in alarm and squinting their eyes to see better what was going on. The rabbits, panicked by the bears, stamped their feet on the ground and some bolted crazily for the trees. The elk raked the air with their antlers, and the white-tailed deer flashed their white flags of danger.

Silas raised his hands again to quiet the crowd. It took a long minute until the meadow was calm enough for him to continue. The animals kept their places, but emotions were high, and all felt the truce was being tested. Reason would soon fade before the more powerful instinct to fight or to run would take hold. Silas knew it was time for solutions.

The old man spread his hands out wide. He said so that all could hear, "But we are not alone!"

The animals quieted, turning their attention back to the old man. What could he mean?

"Look where we are standing!" he cried, opening his arms wide. "We are gathered on the very flank of the most powerful force in the land!"

He gestured slowly around, spreading his arms out to encompass all he could see. "We have a *mountain* on our side, my friends."

The old man's eyes, almost lost in the wrinkles that surrounded them, gleamed in the dim light.

He laughed softly, though every ear heard him. "Oh, ho, ho, we are the lucky ones!"

He held his arms out and proclaimed, louder, "We do not have to *move mountains* in order to achieve our goal, oh no!"

Silas leaned forward with a gleam in his eye. "Oh no, my friends. We don't have to do that, for the *mountain will move for us!*"

An excited whispering broke out in the meadow. "*What* did he say?"

"What was that?"

"He said the mountain will move!"

"The mountain will move?"

"What did Silas say?" squeaked the mice from below.

The old man pointed upward and said, "Behold our greatest ally!"

All eyes turned upward. The shining peak of the mountain was free of clouds and gleamed in the morning light, its icy peaks catching the sun.

Silas said proudly, "The Mountain Wy'east!"

The animals whispered again. "What does he mean?" "What can the mountain do?" "What did he say?"

"Quiet!" shrieked a rabbit, his voice piercing the air.

Silas explained, "The Mountain's spirit is generous, and his love for you is great. He is an old friend of mine, and of yours, although you may not know it. We have been speaking, he and I, and reading the stars together. The stars told us to hold this meeting. You may remember the legend of how Wy'east fought with his brother Klickitat and destroyed the Bridge of the Gods?"

The animals knew the legend well—it had been told to them by their mothers in nest and den, burrow and thicket for generations—and a murmur of ascent rippled across the grass.

"Alas, that was only a temporary solution," said Silas sadly. "The destruction of the bridge may have stopped men from getting to the north, but they continued their destruction of the south, and Wy'east agrees with us that it is time to do something about it."

"Fight them!" roared the bears.

"Claw them!" screamed the mountain lions, baring their yellow teeth.

"Kill them!" bugled the elks, shaking their antlers.

"War!" piped up the mice as loudly as they could.

"War! War!" other voices joined them.

"War! War! War!" the call swelled through the meadow.

Silas looked out at them all silently, and his old eyes glistened with tears.

When the animals saw their beloved friend weeping, their angry calls trailed off uncertainly.

Silas said softly, "You want revenge, and no one could blame you. You have been mercilessly hunted, your families killed, your homes destroyed. There has been poison laid down for brother coyote, traps set for sister rabbit, snares placed, and hooks made to catch our brothers the fish and yank them from their waters. You have every *right* to want revenge!

"But war is a *terrible* thing indeed, my friends!" the old man said. "And once released, is a very difficult demon to get back into the bottle. War means *destruction*, with no predictable outcome. If we start a war, we must be prepared to die for it, for die we certainly will, by the thousands."

There was a silence as all considered this daunting thought. Then a strange and unnerving vibration began under their feet. A soft thunder began to build as all of the animals began to stamp. It built and built until the mice were bouncing off the ground, and Lord Winchfillin clutched at the Artist's sleeve.

"Whatever is it?" he breathed fearfully.

Then someone called out, "There are men in this meadow right now!"

CHAPTER NINE

HE TREE HOUSE WAS BUZZING WITH
excitement as Chloe, Mrs. Goodweather, and
Brisco set to work executing their plans for the
gala. The first thing to make were the disguises. Mrs. Goodweather said if Brisco could find her some sort of fabric, any
kind—she could whip up servants' uniforms in no time for her
and Chloe. Nobody doubted she could do it, and the carpenter
set off early that morning to scout around for fabric she could
transform into disguises.

A half an hour later the carpenter's boots were heard outside, the door was flung open, and he stood triumphantly on
the tree house doorstep, holding up his prize with a wide
smile.

"Eureka!" Brisco beamed.

"It's a miracle!" cried Mrs. Goodweather, and Chloe squealed
in delight. In his hands were two perfect black uniforms, complete with white aprons.

"Brisco!" exclaimed Mrs. Goodweather wonderingly. "How
in the world did you . . . ?"

Brisco laughed sheepishly. "I couldn't find anything at first," he admitted. "I looked and looked for any scrap of fabric for Mrs. G to work her magic on, but there wasn't anything at all—not even a handkerchief. I was on my way back when I spotted a shipping blanket, on top of some crates, and would have nicked it, but just before I did, some workmen opened another crate and *these* were inside." He grinned and held up the garments.

"Why, you even took the hangers!" Chloe said, laughing.

"Of course!" said Brisco with a grin. "I couldn't leave two empty hangers to tell them these were missing, could I?"

Mrs. Goodweather declared there never was a cleverer carpenter and that she was relieved she would not have to sew them herself, they would blend in perfectly this way. She was somewhat dubious about the size when she held the rather slender dress against her ampler frame, but alterations would be simple, and Mrs. Goodweather was certain that letting out a few seams would do the trick. Chloe tried her uniform on and found it a bit long. Mrs. Goodweather sat down to shorten the hem, and while she sewed, Brisco told them more about his scouting expedition, and how many more people were in line now, and about the woman he'd seen crying.

Chloe only half listened. While Brisco told of scouting around to the front of the hospital, she remembered the horrible things they had seen from behind the boulder. She thought of those long boxes sliding down that chute to the boat, and in her mind, she heard again the splash when their . . . *contents* . . . were dumped into the water. She shuddered, and felt a cold dread about her mother, and while Mrs. Goodweather pinned up her hem, Chloe's eyes filled with tears.

Then she heard Brisco say something about a crying woman, and for a confused second thought he was talking about her.

"What do you suppose she was crying about?" Mrs. Goodweather was asking the carpenter. Chloe heard him answer that he didn't know, but that she just seemed heartbroken and he felt bad for her.

"Why, Brisco, I do believe you have a little crush," said Mrs. Goodweather kindly.

Chloe glanced at Brisco and saw that he was blushing bright red. Rather than saying anything to Mrs. Goodweather's remark, he took a big sip of tea.

Suddenly, Chloe froze. *Wait a minute!* What had he just said? The woman was small, had brown hair, a purple dress that was patched at the hem . . . a vision of Celeste Hart swam in front of Chloe's eyes. She had looked just like that when Chloe had seen her and her brother at the Cobbly Fair! Could it possibly be? But no, that would be impossible—the Cobbly Fair was far from here, and that description fit a thousand women. Why would Celeste Hart be here of all places? It made no sense, it couldn't be her.

Still . . . the hospital. She was crying, Brisco said. And she was alone. Celeste Hart *could* be here because an ambulance had attacked her brother like all the others! There were many people here that were not from Fairfax, all brought here by terrible circumstance. It made some sense. It *was* possible.

Chloe lifted her eyes and interrupted the carpenter. "I'm sorry, Brisco, but did you say she wore a purple dress?"

The carpenter looked surprised. "Yes, I believe it was, why? What's up?" Brisco startled as Chloe jumped up from her seat and stared at him.

She said, "I know it sounds crazy, but it sounds *exactly* like the woman I saw at the Cobbly Fair. I know it's a long shot, and it's probably not her, I mean—how could it be? But I just had the *strangest* feeling when you described her."

Chloe went on, "I want to see her, Brisco. I want to see if it's the same person. Her name was Celeste, and she had a very nice brother named Avery, and I'm sure they would help us if they could!"

Both Brisco and Mrs. Goodweather looked at each other in surprise, and Chloe could see they were doubtful. But she just had to know!

"Please, can I go look for her?" she asked. "I promise I'll be careful, no one will see me!"

Brisco looked at Mrs. Goodweather questioningly. The older woman drew in a deep breath and said, "Of course, you must go, my dear. But as you said, be very careful and do not be seen. Our plan might be ruined if we start any kind of an uproar now. We must do nothing to derail our plan because I have no more of the special blueberries to use. There is no starting over."

Chloe promised she would take every care and caution, and would return to the tree house immediately after she had seen if the woman was indeed Celeste Hart. Silently Brisco guided Chloe around the back of the hospital to the wall where he had seen the woman before. She was nowhere in sight this time, and they moved to another hiding spot, under the trees and closer to the middle of the line. From there they could see the line almost in its entirety, and they scanned it carefully, looking for the woman.

Finally, Chloe spotted the same brown head, small shoul-

ders, and kind face she remembered even in the dark of the
Cobbly Fair. It *was* Celeste Hart after all! It was all Chloe
could do not to run forward and embrace her. She felt like she
already knew Celeste very well, although they had only seen
each other that one time, in the dark.

Chloe whispered happily to Brisco, "It *is* Celeste! The
same woman I saw at the fair. I don't see her brother Avery
though. He must be inside."

Brisco's face lit up when Chloe revealed that she did know
the beautiful woman, after a fashion. Gleaning instantly that
he recognized Celeste too, Chloe teased, "Brisco!"

The carpenter's eyes jumped guiltily away from Celeste,
breaking his spell. The carpenter made a motion that they
should go back, and remembering her promise to Mrs. Goodweather, Chloe agreed and followed him back along the line of
little pines to the cover of the forest behind the great building.

Chloe was bubbling with excitement when she reentered
the tree house. She sat down at the table and Shakespeare
jumped onto her lap.

"It was her, Mrs. Goodweather, it was Celeste Hart!"
Chloe's eyes were shining. "I wish I could talk to her. I just
know Celeste would help us! And I'm sure she would do anything to help her brother. They were so kind to me. I *know* we
can trust them!"

Mrs. Goodweather said cautiously, "Well . . . I don't suppose there would be any harm in trying to talk to the woman.
We do have some time before the gala, and perhaps it would
make her happy to see that you are safe, child. And, maybe she
can be of help to us, after all. We don't have another uniform,
but she could be a good lookout for us."

Brisco needed no encouragement. He was all for going straight up to the beautiful woman right this minute and escorting her directly to the tree house, and he volunteered himself for this duty. Mrs. Goodweather laughed at the carpenter's obvious infatuation. She suggested instead they find a more discreet way of contacting Celeste. It wouldn't do to have a strange man approach the woman in front of all those people and just . . . escort her into the trees. It would be noticed, and someone might try to follow them. Chloe couldn't go, but perhaps Mrs. Goodweather could? They discussed the difficulty of getting the woman away from the line without being noticed themselves, but it didn't seem possible for any of them to get away with.

Chloe sat quietly petting Shakespeare when her eyes suddenly lit up. "I've got it!" she cried out excitedly. "We'll send *Shakespeare!*"

CHAPTER TEN

HAKESPEARE?" BOTH BRISCO AND MRS. Goodweather exclaimed at the same time. Shakespeare squeaked.

"Yes! He would be the perfect messenger!" said Chloe. Turning to the rat, she petted his head between the ears where he liked it best, and crooned, "We'll send you with a message for the pretty lady." She looked teasingly at Brisco.

Mrs. Goodweather clapped her hands. "Of course! How clever of you, Chloe dear! He, more than any of us, could get to her unnoticed. The only trouble might be . . . well, might she be afraid of a rat? It's quite possible, you know. She may not let him get anywhere near her, and he would be quite unable to deliver his message," she said. "Well, there's only one way to find out. Why don't you write out a note, Chloe dear, and we'll give it to Shakespeare, and we'll see what happens, hmm? If it doesn't work, no hard done, and we'll cross that bridge when we come to it."

Chloe agreed. She looked at the white rat. "You remember the lady, don't you, Shakespeare?" she asked him. "You saw her that night at the Cobbly Fair. She was the woman with the purple dress. You would recognize her again, wouldn't you?"

Shakespeare squeaked in the affirmative. Chloe knew he must be remembering the lady and her brother. He would not have forgotten that they had tried to help his mistress in that dark place. He would be happy to find the woman again and deliver the note.

Mrs. Goodweather reached in her bag and produced a folded piece of paper. She unfolded it and tore a small square from one corner, which she handed to Chloe for her note. Brisco surprised them all by inexplicably pulling a quill pen from one inside pocket and an actual inkpot out of the other. Chloe beamed at the carpenter. Wasn't that just like Brisco, to have just what was needed, at the moment they needed it? She sat down at the little table to write out the note to Celeste. Chloe wrote carefully so that the ink would not blotch:

Dearest Celeste,
I'm so glad I found you—this is Chloe Ashton, the girl
from the Cobbly Fair. I am hiding nearby. This rat is my
friend. Follow him to meet me. We might be able to help
you, and your brother.
With love, Chloe

She folded the note into a small square and tied it with a string around Shakespeare's neck. The white rat looked slightly comical with the package attached to his back, but he took his job seriously and stood at smart attention until his mistress dismissed him. When she did, the rat quickly scampered down the tree to the ground and ran off toward the hospital. They could see his small white form for only a few seconds before he vanished into the underbrush. Now they could only wait.

⸙

Shakespeare ran quickly through the bushes lining the hospital drive. He reached the end of the hedge and waited there to catch his breath. His sharp eyes scanned for a good place to hide along the wall, and when he spotted one, the rat dashed forward into its protective shadow. From the end of the wall he could easily see the line of people and made another dash to an urn holding decorative topiary. Shakespeare paused here a moment to catch his breath and to look for the woman he remembered from the Cobbly Fair.

He spotted her. In an instant the rat recognized the same slim form in a patched purple dress, and when she looked up, he saw the same small, pale face under the same worn hat. Luckily, she wasn't far away, just a few yards down the line. Shakespeare thought if he could just get to the next topiary urn, he might be able to get her attention.

Shakespeare looked to see that no one was looking in his direction and then took off for the next urn. Straight and true he ran, the package still tied tightly to his neck, and reached the safety of the urn's shadows. There he sat panting, watching the woman and wondering what the best way would be to get her attention.

He decided he would have to be bold. He would have to risk being seen by others. Perhaps if he dropped the note on the ground beside her, she would see it and pick it up. He would try.

Shakespeare gathered his nerve and stepped out onto the road. He crept slowly but steadily, not wanting to attract attention. He reached the hem of Celeste's skirts unnoticed and was just about to drop his note when the woman standing next to Celeste stepped squarely on the rat's tail.

Shakespeare shrieked in pain, and the woman jumped high in the air, drowning out the rat's shriek with her own horrified scream. Shakespeare was tossed in the air when she jumped and was caught up in her voluminous skirts. Fearing being trod upon again, he clung as tightly as he could to the wire hoop that held out the skirts, while the woman beat at her clothes to dislodge the rat. The people around them hurried away, and the woman hopped and jumped about, thumping on her skirts and just missing Shakespeare's head. When nothing was dislodged, or appeared, or fell from her person after a moment or two, the woman began to calm down, believing whatever it was to be gone. The line gradually re-formed as the people around her laughed off the startling incident and returned to normal.

Poor Shakespeare had been bludgeoned and bumped and bruised by his wild ride in the woman's hoopskirts. He waited painfully, still clutching the wire hoop until all was quiet before carefully dropping to the ground. He peered out from under the hem, and saw the note lying on the ground. It must have fallen off during his wild ride! He thought he might have to pick it up in his teeth to prevent anyone other than Celeste from finding it, but before he could do this, Celeste herself happened to glance down toward the ground . . . and her eyes met Shakespeare's.

Celeste Hart was not afraid of rats or mice or even of

snakes. As a girl she had spent so much time exploring her family's forests with her brother Avery that she held a deep respect for all animals. She was very pleased to see the rat was unharmed, and gave him a friendly look. Shakespeare crept out from beneath the other woman's skirt and pushed forward the note on the ground with his nose. He looked back up at Celeste who was watching him with wide eyes. What was this? A rat with a note!

Celeste quickly leaned down and picked up the note. Once Shakespeare saw that she had the note in her possession, he took a chance and dashed back to the shadows of the urn. One or two people saw the white rat running across the road and pointed after him saying, "There he goes!" The woman with the hoopskirt gave another scream and gathered her skirts again in horror, but Shakespeare was safely hidden.

He watched Celeste read the note, and he saw her gasp. She looked pale, but excited. The woman forced herself to remain calm and walked casually over to the urn where Shakespeare was hiding, and leaned against it.

"Are you there?" she whispered.

Shakespeare gave two low squeaks in reply.

"Can you take me to the girl? To Chloe?"

Shakespeare squeaked again. He scampered off, back the way he had come, pausing in the shadow of the hedge, waiting to see if Celeste could follow. Acting as if she were only stretching her legs, Celeste walked up the road along the line of people and then stepped over to the hedge and stood looking for the rat. She saw Shakespeare run around the side of the hospital and disappear into the trees. She followed, expecting at any moment for someone to ask her where she was going, but no one did.

Shakespeare led Celeste under the trees, where they were immediately immersed in another world. The sounds of the people in line dimmed, and all was hushed and peaceful. The white rat ran down the trail, jumping over twigs and rocks and around fallen logs and waiting for Celeste to do the same. Finally, they came to the clearing where stood the old oak that held the tree house.

Shakespeare immediately leapt up the stairs, expecting Celeste to follow, but when he reached the porch, she was not behind him. The rat looked down to see the woman standing still beneath the huge tree, gazing up at the tree house in wonder. Golden light glowed from the windows, falling on Celeste and illuminating the area in which she stood. Suddenly Chloe burst out of the door and joined Shakespeare at the rail. She squealed with excitement at the sight of Celeste and called out to her.

"Miss Hart!"

"My dear!" Celeste called back up to the girl happily. "Is it really you?"

Chloe laughed delightedly and ran down the stairs, followed by Mrs. Goodweather, and a somewhat bashful Brisco. Shakespeare watched his dear mistress run to Celeste who opened her arms to embrace the child. The white rat hugged himself with his small white paws as he watched their reunion, knowing he was observing the special understanding that happens sometimes between strangers, who have met only once before but instantly recognize a friend.

CHAPTER ELEVEN

*T*HERE ARE MEN IN THIS MEADOW RIGHT NOW!" A hair-raising chorus of outraged growls and roars, barks and shrieks greeted this statement, and all eyes in the meadow turned on the Artist and Lord Winchfillin. The animals closest to them drew back, snarling fearfully.

Lord Winchfillin pressed as closely as he could against the Artist's coat. Greybelle and Raja stamped their hooves defensively, prepared to defend their friends if necessary. One bear reached out his muzzle to sniff at Raja's flank, and the old gelding screamed in fear and kicked out, making the bear roar, and frightening more rabbits who veered crazily off into bushes at the sound.

Silas looked at them directly over the heads of the animals. "I have noticed these men," he said calmly.

"Do not threaten them, do not harm them," he entreated the animals who still would not stand any closer to the men, and who bared their teeth at them. "Not *all* men are evil. Am *I* not a man, after all?"

The animals could not argue with this and muttered amongst themselves.

"Let us allay our suspicions for the moment and see *why* they are here. Perhaps they are known to someone and can be vouched for. Is anyone here to vouch for these men?" Silas called out to the meadow.

A small but strong voice called out, "*I* will vouch for them!"

"And what is your name, pray tell?" Silas asked.

"Whitestone, sir!" answered the squirrel, coming forward.

"Good to know you, brother Whitestone," said Silas. "And tell us, how do you know these men?"

Before Whitestone could answer, another deeper voice said, "I sent them."

The flat black-and-white head of the Badger emerged from the grasses.

"Greetings, Badger," Silas said. "It is good to see you again. These men are known to you?"

"They are known, though not by me," said the Badger.

"How are they known?" asked Silas.

"They are friends of a child who is with a woman known to me," explained the Badger. "The child is also known, but from a different place. She only became known to me when her pet rat—"

"Pet rat?" interrupted Silas, surprised. "That is unusual."

"Yes, it is," agreed the Badger. "And he used the call to get help for her."

"Her pet rat used the call?" said Silas, leaning forward. "That is *most* unusual."

"Nevertheless, I felt that I had to answer it," said the Badger.

"Quite right," said Silas. "That is what the call is for."

He looked up at the crowd in front of him. "Will the men please step forward."

The animals in the meadow parted, creating a clear path to the boulder where Silas stood. The men and horses filed uneasily down this path, trying not to look at the ranks of unfriendly faces. Silas might be protecting them for the moment, but they did not know how long his protection would last. At any moment the animals might decide they didn't care to follow an old man's instructions and would rather these intruders be ripped to pieces and gobbled up. Raja pranced along in a cold sweat.

When at last they reached the boulder where Silas stood, the Artist removed his hat and held it respectfully in his hands. Lord Winchfillin didn't have a hat, but he bowed his head and stammered out a courteous, though quavering, "How do you do."

The animals around them laughed loudly and called out taunting remarks. A rabbit blew a raspberry and a young vole threw a pebble, which hit Lord Winchfillin on the shin. Raja whinnied shrilly when a jeering elk shoved him in the rump with his antlers.

"Greetings, my fellow men," said Silas. His words were welcoming, but his tone was not overly friendly. The old man's eyes were very steady on them; he exuded quiet strength, and it seemed to Lord Winchfillin that he could read every thought in their heads.

His simple clothes of soft, stained buckskin and his weathered hands, bare feet, and long gray beard all spoke of a life lived under the open sky. His attire may have been unremarkable, but there was nothing unremarkable about the power of Silas's gaze. His clear blue eyes beamed down on them from the rock, and it seemed to the three men that an electrical current flowed out of him, through his hands to the air and through his bare feet that gripped the rock as sure as any mountain goat. His eyes glittered, not with the warmth of a friendly candle flame, but with a cool, detached white light, much like the stars.

"You are welcome here, if you have come to help us," Silas said to the men.

"We would like to help you, Mr. Stargazer," the Artist replied earnestly.

"Did you come here with the express purpose of helping the animals stop this evil that has come to the land?" asked Silas, his blue eyes more piercing than ever. "Or did you have another reason? I know the hearts and minds of men, and there is always another reason."

Lord Winchfillin quailed under the gaze of those eyes, their hold like a truth serum, erasing all thoughts of dissemination. It would be impossible to even get the words out, he thought, if one *did* try to lie.

Luckily the Artist had no intention of lying, and he answered honestly. "No, sir. We didn't know what the meeting was about in particular, but we were led to believe that if we came and offered our services to you, you in turn might be able to help us."

"Help *you*?" said Silas. His eyes opened wide with surprise. "You have come *here*, to this gathering of wild animals, on the side of the great mountain Wy'east, to see what *we* can do for *you*?"

The animals screamed at this arrogance, and some begged

to dispatch these brazen intruders at once, as an example to all others. Every beast in the meadow and both men waited breathlessly for what might come next.

Silas looked at them incredulously, his lips slightly parted as though he were about to say the word to let the animals swarm forward to overtake the men, and then he just . . . laughed. The old man threw back his head and laughed a deep, rolling laugh that started in his belly and came up through his nose. He fell forward and slapped his knees and laughed harder. The Artist and his friends all smiled nervously and chuckled along, hoping that this was a good sign, and all would yet turn out well.

The animals in the meadow were confused and angry, and some still growled menacingly. They found nothing funny about this at all, and they were not surprised by the selfish intentions of the humans. It was to be expected, they whispered to each other, they were *men*. They always thought only of themselves.

Silas finally stopped laughing and looked at the Artist with genuine curiosity.

"My dear man, that either takes great courage or great stupidity. And something tells me it is most likely the former. You don't look like a stupid man. Tell me, *why* should we help you?"

"Because she is a human who cares about *all* of you, as much as her own kind," said the Artist.

The animals in the meadow fell silent.

The Artist hurried on. "And, she loves the forest like it was her own home. Believe me, Mr. Stargazer sir, Chloe is worth a hundred humans, and she is worth every effort we can make to find her."

Silas was watching the Artist's face. He said, "And you'll go to these lengths to help her . . . amazing."

The Artist said softly, "Yes, sir. I mean to do everything I can. If that means riding miles out of my way and climbing a mountain, and even putting myself in the path of wild animals to try to win their trust to do it, then that is what I simply must do."

"Your devotion is touching, my friend," said Silas in a warmer tone than before. "And you are correct—it is indeed that kind of person that we need on our side."

The animals grumbled, some still upset that men were present at their meeting at all, known or not. Others looked skeptical that humans could help their cause, others as though perhaps they could be convinced, and a few others agreed the men might be useful. All the animals trusted Silas the Stargazer, and they would respect his decision about the men, however strange it felt to do so. They knew he had their best interests at heart, and that he was powerful. And no one could deny that humans—even stargazers—were the best weapons against their own kind.

Silas turned back to the meadow, and said so that all could hear, "Tonight, after sundown I am calling a special council. I will meet with the animal leaders and these men and decide what to do. I advise you all to stay close, until we have come to our decision. We will all meet again here, tonight. That is all for now, my friends. Take your rest now, and we will speak again soon."

Silas turned and, in a surprisingly agile, fluid motion, jumped down from the rock. He motioned to the men to join him and walked behind the tumble of boulders to a smaller, grassy area. The Artist and his friends followed, and sat on a fallen log with Greybelle and Raja alongside them.

Silas picked up his walking staff where he had left it against the rocks. "I must go gather my thoughts. You can wait here until the council. Don't worry—you will be quite safe." He directed this last at Lord Winchfillin, who looked distressed at the old man's departure.

"Thank you, sir," said the Artist. "We will wait here."

Silas nodded and, just as silently as he had arrived, disappeared into the trees.

Alone behind the boulders the friends settled down to wait. The Artist patted Greybelle's neck and said, "I wonder where Chloe is right now."

Lord Winchfillin had no answer to that question. The Artist went on, "It keeps me awake at night. I worry she was picked up by the ambulance back there on the road, but I also know that she had little Shakespeare with her, and that rat is more resourceful than you or I know, I suspect. If we could only get going, I don't like waiting another day." He scuffed his boot in the dust.

"Don't worry too much, Artist," Greybelle tried to comfort him. "We are among the most powerful friends we could hope for. After tonight's meeting I'm certain that Silas will allow us to travel to Fairfax, and indeed I'm almost sure he won't send us alone. We came to find help and I think we'll get it."

"I hope you're right," said the Artist.

The day wore on into late afternoon. The Artist made a foray into the forest to hunt for blackberries. He brought back a hatful and they feasted on berries and some of the bread he had left in his pockets, which had some fuzzy lint stuck to it, but was still delicious.

At last it was dusk. The shadows lengthened over the

meadow as the sun descended behind the mountain. A lone wolf climbed to the top of the rocks and raised his muzzle to the sky. A thin, wavering howl rose over the meadow and was carried away on the evening air. It was a mournful, yearning sound full of the hardships and the joys of a life in the wild. Every animal that heard it knew its story well, for it was their own. When the last note of the wolf's howl died away, it was time for the council.

CHAPTER TWELVE

*C*HLOE AND CELESTE WERE EACH A BIT TEARY at the end of their embrace, and both tried to talk at the same time. Laughing, they tried again, until Chloe gave up and told Celeste to speak first, and to tell them how she came to be here, and where was Avery, her brother?

Mrs. Goodweather interjected, inviting them all back up to the tree house where she would make a pot of tea, and everyone could tell their story in comfort.

Celeste climbed the stairs to the little porch of the tree house and stood for a moment marveling. She exclaimed over everything—from the carefully shaped shingles on the roof, to the delicate wooden scrollwork around the eaves and sparkling stained-glass windows, to the tiny kitchen, dining table and chairs, and the three cozy beds. She concluded that it was the most beautiful little house she had ever seen.

Brisco's face turned beet red at the compliment, and for an alarming moment Chloe thought he actually might burst with pride.

Mrs. Goodweather, by way of introduction, declared that it

was all the work of their dear Brisco Knot, that he really *was* the cleverest man in all the world, and that he could make anything out of anything, in no time flat.

Celeste turned to the carpenter, saying in her gentle voice, "You are a very talented artist, Mr. Knot."

"Please, call me Brisco, ma'am," Brisco said shyly, twisting his cap in his hands.

"Brisco, then," said Celeste, smiling sweetly. "And you must call me Celeste."

Brisco said, his face still red, "All right . . . Celeste."

The kettle began to sing, breaking the spell, and everyone laughed and sat down for tea. Mrs. Goodweather filled their cups with the fragrant brew, and placed a plate of orange and current scones on the table. As everyone sat eating and drinking, and dunking their scones in their tea, Celeste began her tale of how she and Avery had come to Fairfax.

She began at the place she had met Chloe, at the Cobbly Fair. She told how after they had been run off by that awful man holding Chloe prisoner, she and Avery had gone straight to the police. She told of how they had returned to the Cobbly Fair, only to find the nefarious Quick Sell booth had disappeared. She described their return to Tillamook Town and how they had found out from the police there that there was an "Eleanor Ashton" at the hospital in Fairfax. Remembering that was the girl's last name, she and her brother Avery had decided to go immediately to Fairfax to make inquiries about Chloe.

"Eleanor Ashton—that's my *mother!*" burst out Chloe, unable to contain herself.

"Yes, my dear it was."

"You saw her? You saw my mother?!" Chloe clutched Celeste's arm.

"Yes, my dear, we saw her, but she was just like all of the other patients inside the hospital—unconscious."

"But she is alive! My mother is alive!" Chloe burst into tears. Celeste put her arms around the child and hugged her.

Then Celeste went on to tell the sad story of how Avery had fallen ill at the hospital and had been taken inside, not to be seen again.

When Celeste had finished her account, Chloe began her own. She told the woman how she had been sold by Mr. Malick to a hotel in Tillamook Town, and how her Uncle Blake had taken her there. She told about how she was supposed to begin work as a maid and servant at the hotel, but had been won in a poker game by the Artist, who had also won her uncle's horse Greybelle.

Chloe took a deep breath, drank some tea, and went on. She told about how the artist took her and Greybelle to Lord Winchfillin's house, about the birthday party and the ambulance attack, how they had fled on the horses into the forest and how she had fallen off and accidentally been left behind. Chloe told of how Shakespeare had saved her life by finding help, which turned out to be Mrs. Goodweather. Then she told of their meeting with Brisco at the cabin and their subsequent journey to Fairfax.

It was a fantastic tale that took some time to complete. So engrossed were they in each other's stories that they didn't notice at first a sound coming from the window. The sound became louder and a repetitive *crack, crack, crack* came from the glass, making them all turn in alarm.

A large crow peered in through the window, turning his bright eyes from side to side to see the people within. He pecked at the glass with his sharp beak. *Crack! Crack!*

"What in the world . . ." said Celeste.

"Why would it . . ." said Chloe.

"For heaven's sake! Let the poor bird in!" cried Mrs. Goodweather, jumping to her feet and rushing over to the window to open it herself.

Blackberry hopped in, landing awkwardly on the edge of the sink. He squawked at Shakespeare, who glared back suspiciously at the stranger. Then Blackberry saw Brisco Knot. The crow stopped shuffling and cawed softly at the man. Chloe could swear she saw a smile on the crow's face, and her mind raced back to that gull on the cliffs near home, so long ago . . .

Blackberry flapped across the short space to land on Brisco's lap. Brisco chuckled and stroked the crow's glossy black feathers affectionately. Blackberry's eyes closed, savoring the man's caress. For a moment the young crow forgot his mission entirely and went into a blissful trance on the carpenter's knee.

Everyone else sat dumbfounded, except for Mrs. Goodweather, who knew all about Brisco's special love for crows, and theirs for him, but finally she couldn't contain herself any longer. "Well, aren't you going to tell us why you're here?" the woman asked.

Blackberry opened one eye and looked her balefully.

Brisco said to him kindly, "Well now, friend crow. You've made it pretty obvious you've come to see us, now tell us what it is you want, and we will try our best to give it to you."

Blackberry shook his head, flapped his wings, and flew

back to the counter. He looked out the window, and made a mournful sound, motioning with his beak toward the trees.

Mrs. Goodweather opened the window again, and the crow hopped onto the sill. He looked back at Brisco and out to the forest again and began to caw.

Caw! Caw! Caw! The sound carried out over the treetops.

Caw! Caw! Caw! Blackberry called again. He jumped out of the window and flew to a branch high in the oak tree, continuing his raucous call.

The four humans and Shakespeare the rat went out on the tree house porch. Above them Blackberry continued to call as loudly as he could, the sound carrying far out over the valley below.

Then, from over the treetops and the surrounding hillside came an answer. Scattered at first, then gaining in number, distant *caw caw caw*s came back to their ears on the wind. Blackberry continued his call, and more crows joined the cry, and soon the harsh cries of hundreds of crows drowned him out, as they began rising out of the trees and taking to the air.

Soon there were thousands of crows joining the flock, creating a great black funnel over the hospital, and the sound of their calls was deafening. Everyone could hear it, all around the town. The people standing in line outside the hospital stood transfixed at the strange sight in the sky. They pointed to the funnel of crows and whispered in fear. Surely this was a bad omen. No one had ever seen the likes of this before.

Brisco stood on the tree house porch with a strange expression on his face. He watched the huge cloud of crows gather in the sky, and when he turned to his friends, his eyes were shining.

"I have to go," he said simply, shrugging his shoulders.

"What do you mean, you have to go?" cried Chloe, alarmed.

"They are here to collect me. I'm needed," said the carpenter.

"But *why*? Why are you needed? Where are you going?" demanded Chloe, upset. He couldn't leave them now, not when their plan was about to go into effect!

"It's something to do with . . . all of this." Brisco's face was serious as he waved down to the hospital. "It sounds like the crows might have a plan of their own. I think they could be a real help to us."

"But how long will you be gone?" asked Chloe sadly.

"Not long," said the carpenter kindly. "I'll be back in plenty of time for our plan, I promise. Now I must be off—the sooner I go, the sooner I'll return."

Mrs. Goodweather put an arm around Chloe's shoulders and gave the girl a comforting squeeze. "I'm sure Brisco knows best," she said cheerfully. "And don't forget, we still have a lot to do here."

Brisco got to his feet and grabbed his jacket. "I'll be back in time for the gala, I'll make sure of it—don't worry." The carpenter looked directly at Celeste and touched his cap. "Don't worry," he said again.

"Good luck, Brisco," said Celeste softly.

They all watched him climb down and cross quickly to where the ambulance was hidden. Brisco pulled the branches off the car and got in to the driver's seat. He looked up at the ladies on the tree house porch and doffed his cap in farewell, then backed the car out into the clearing, and drove off down the little road.

Chloe, Mrs. Goodweather, Celeste, and Shakespeare waved back as the ambulance drove away. Overhead the huge funnel cloud of birds whirled over the hospital, and then flew over the ambulance and to the east. Brisco's car followed in the same direction and disappeared behind the hillside. The huge cloud of crows flew with him, thinning out into a long, black line, becoming smaller and smaller until it too, disappeared.

CHAPTER THIRTEEN

*I*T WAS TWILIGHT ON THE MOUNTAIN. THE air was uncharacteristically still—hardly a breath of wind stirred, and the trees around the meadow were quiet. Overhead the sky was a soft rainbow of purples, pinks, and golds as daylight disappeared. A few stars twinkled in the east, with more and more appearing as darkness fell. It seemed the entire world was waiting for the council to begin.

The Artist and Lord Winchfillin gingerly took their seats at the edge of the clearing. Silas was the next to arrive, stepping silently out from the trees just before dark. His buckskin garment glowed pale in the dusk as he took a seat on a rock without speaking.

Following Silas came the same massive bull elk that they had seen on their way to the mountain. There was no mistaking him. His towering rack of antlers gleamed like a crown above his head, his huge eyes were black and fierce, and his wet muzzle steamed in the cold morning air as he greeted the Stargazer.

This was none other than Rae, the king of the elks. Ten

feet tall at his chin, King Rae was extremely powerful. His cloven hooves were razor sharp, and his sides were scarred from hundreds of fights won over the years. His magnificent ruff of dark hair on his neck was missing patches here and there, but far from making him look old and weak, these battle scars only made King Rae more fearsome. The old bull elk stepped proudly into the clearing, his head held high, his antlers flashing like knives, disdainfully eyeing the men. Taking his place to the left of Silas, Rae pawed the ground, and waited impatiently for the council to begin.

Thump. Thump. Thump.

The next arrival caused the ground to tremble and small branches to fall from the trees. An intense smell wafted into the little clearing, and every nose wrinkled at the pungent mixture of odors. There was no mistaking this guest, even before he emerged from the trees. *Thump. Thump. Thump!*

A huge, shaggy black shape walked heavily to the middle of the clearing, growling and huffing and looking about with angry red eyes. It was Auberon, the king of the bears. Older than anyone could guess, King Auberon had outlived every member of his family and now ruled supreme over his grandchildren, great-grandchildren, and even great-great-grandchildren. The animals gasped as the bear king rose to his hind legs, reaching twenty feet into the sky. Small twigs and several dead bees fell out of his fur, and the smell of fish was stronger than ever. Though heavy enough to squash a log, and powerful enough to break boulders, Auberon could move almost silently when he wanted to, like a huge black shadow. His black fur virtually disappeared in the dark, making him almost invisible.

With another earth-shaking thump, Auberon dropped

back to all fours and chuffed a grumpy greeting to Silas and to King Rae. To the men sitting huddled on their log, Auberon gave a wrathful glare, and grunted his displeasure, making their blood run cold.

A few moments passed with no other arrivals. The seconds ticked by uncomfortably, Silas remained silent on his rock, while Auberon became more agitated. The bear king was not used to being kept waiting, and the smell of the men so near was driving him mad.

Then without any sound, smell, or other kind of warning, a beautiful white doe slipped into the clearing. Almost as if by magic, she suddenly appeared, moving as gracefully as a breath of wind. It was Afra, a great queen amongst the deer.

Slender and pale, her large eyes dark and liquid, the white doe took in the scene. Stepping lightly and with a great dignity, Afra greeted Silas and the other leaders before she took her place in the circle. She had led her people for a very long time. Queen Afra was more than fifty years old, but she still looked like a young doe. Her ancestors descended from an ancient line of gazelle known as the Awinita who had special powers of insight. It was said that thousands of years ago the Awinita could see the future. Queen Afra had led her people well, using her insight to protect them and keep them hidden from man. But it was getting harder and harder to find a hiding place. The lands were crawling with men now. And even more disturbing, when Afra tried to see what the future held, she could only see darkness. This greatly troubled her. She was eager to see what wisdom she could glean from the others. The graceful queen stood next to Silas and waited quietly for the proceedings to begin.

Next came the wolf who had howled so hauntingly earlier, known to all simply as Mai. Mai the wolf was not a king, or a ruler. The wolves had long since ceased to designate a leader, not because they had no qualified candidates, but because the leaders never lasted long enough to lead. Tempers flared amongst the fierce wolves so quickly that anyone unlucky enough to be elected leader of the pack was eventually torn to pieces. After enough courageous wolves had lost their lives in this way, the pack decided to dispense with the position all together. They did a fairly good job leading themselves and didn't seem to need a higher command. For councils or any other meetings, they merely sent an emissary, a simple messenger, and one with no real power over the rest of them. Mai was a loyal wolf, and easy-going. He did not have great ambitions to rise to power within the pack, and so he was a very good choice as emissary. Mai nodded to the others and found a place along the side of the circle, sitting on his haunches and looking curiously about him.

After Mai came the legendary King Cornix, of the Rooks and Ravens. With him was Fay, Queen of the Crows. More than half a million crows, rooks, and huge mountain ravens made up their vast kingdom. The two great black birds circled the clearing, looking for a place to land.

As Cornix and Fay perched in the trees above the clearing, a broad black and white head emerged below them from the bushes. The Badger, who had no other name, was the representative of the burrowing animals. He was cranky as he took his place; he wasn't as young as he used to be, and his paws were sore after his long journey.

Finally, a small form loped up to the edge of the circle and sat nervously eyeing the wolf and the bear. It was Remington, a venerable old rabbit who had lived through twenty winters and never lost a fight. In his youth Remington had been the fleetest rabbit in the land. His speed was legendary, even outside of the rabbits' warrens. One story told of how he outran a pack of race horses, right in front of thousands of humans. Remington had been a young rabbit then, in his athletic prime, and one day he had not been able to help himself, but had joined a horse race at a country fair, leaping into the racing pack and burning down the track. Remington left the pounding horses in the dust, easily outrunning them and crossing the finish line far ahead of the leader. (The humans present that day had been completely disbelieving. *Had* they just seen what they thought they had seen? A *rabbit* had won the race? No, not possible! Ridiculous! Or so they had told each other. It must be the heat playing tricks.)

Not so fleet anymore, Remington was still a presence to be admired and feared, at least among the smaller animals. His ears were ragged and torn in places, and his long teeth were yellow and still very sharp. Remington looked at Silas, waiting for the meeting to begin.

The last animal leaders to join the council were Felix and Puma, the cougar siblings who ruled the mountain lions, and finally a small burst of color as Columbia the blue jay—and representative of the winged creatures other than the ravens and crows—took her place on a nearby branch. She cheerfully greeted her old friends King Cornix and Queen Fay.

Finally, it seemed that everyone was assembled, and Silas got to his feet.

"Welcome, my friends," he said to the circle, holding out his hands. All the animals became quiet.

"We are here to decide how best to defend our people."

The animals waited for his next words.

Silas took a deep breath and said, "Today, we have heard the call for war."

The old man's face was grave as he looked around the circle. The animal leaders shifted uneasily and murmured to themselves, waiting to see what he would say next.

"But we know that in a war there is no clear winner, and many terrible losses." Silas looked around earnestly, "First and foremost I believe that we must *avoid* a war, if possible."

At this, some leaders nodded their heads in agreement, but others protested. The predators wanted to avoid nothing—they were here for some satisfaction, surely? The cougars Puma and Felix growled and scratched the earth.

"We have to do *something!*" King Auberon roared, shaking his heavy shoulders in irritation and pounding his front feet against the ground. Bits of bracken and brambles and several more dead bees tumbled out of his fur. The other animals were frightened by the huge bear's angry display, but many agreed with him.

King Rae the elk angrily pawed the earth with his hoof and burst out, "We may not be predators, but even my people want revenge, Silas. And I know they aren't the only ones." He looked around at the other leaders. "You know it's true! You hear them talking in the meadow, they *all* want war, and I don't think I could stop them from going, even if I wanted to." The other animals murmured their agreement.

Silas spread his hands out entreatingly. "But consider this, what if by declaring war against the humans we start something so dangerous, so much bigger than we thought, that we can't control it and in the end . . . we *ourselves* are destroyed?"

A tense silence hung over the circle as the animals considered his words.

Silas went on more softly, "We love our babies, do we not? Our little kits"—he looked at the rabbit—"our cubs"—the bear—"our fawns"—the elk and the doe—"and our chicks and fledglings"—the raven, crow and jay. "We want to *preserve* the land that feeds them, and protects them, and teaches them the way of survival, now don't we? We can't start a war that would destroy the land and possibly our own babes in their beds, can we? At least without some discussion?"

The animals' eyes softened at the thought of their young. They did not want to start a war that might kill their own children. But . . . the men were doing that already, and it was only getting worse. King Auberon was right, they had to do *something*!

"We need to move forward as peacefully as possible," advised Silas.

"Peace won't stop those men!" called out Rae, his hooves tearing at the earth as he pranced defiantly in place.

"Peace might be the desired result, but it's no starting point in this case," agreed Mai the wolf, his voice soft but nevertheless cutting through the murmuring of the others. The shy wolf spoke so seldom that when he did, the animals listened.

"The men forfeited their right to peace when they first attacked us. We will have to stop them, somehow," the wolf reasoned.

"What do you have in mind?" asked Queen Afra quietly. She rested her gentle brown eyes on Mai, who shrugged, not having a ready answer.

"Mai is right, we need to stop those cars," Silas said. "If we can stop the cars, then we can stop the attacks. That is the first priority. From there perhaps we may find where they are coming from. How, exactly I am not sure yet. But we must try. I'm convinced that we can stop these attacks, my dear brothers and sisters—if only to create a more compassionate world." The old man looked sad.

"Compassionate? Humans? They don't exist!" King Auberon roared in the direction of the Artist and Lord Winchfillin, who shrank closer to Greybelle and Raja.

"That is too bad that you feel that way," said Silas sadly. "For in truth, there are many kind and compassionate humans in the world. It is just the bad ones that we usually encounter, and they make us think all men are alike. But they are not. And to prove it, we have these three examples with us today." All eyes swung toward the men.

Silas smiled at the Artist and Lord Winchfillin, but he was the only one smiling. None of the animals looked friendly, or even convinced they could be trusted. King Auberon sent a soft but menacing growl in their direction.

Before the atmosphere could once again become heated, Silas said calmly, "Come now, my friends. They have been vouched for. Let us make the proper introductions and be friends. Come here, dear Artist and Lord Winchfillin." Silas motioned to the men. "I think there is more to know about you."

The Artist took Lord Winchfillin's hand. "Come on, don't be scared."

The little earl moved forward, mumbling a prayer.

Silas said in a conversational tone, "Tell us first how you came to know of the meeting."

The Artist cleared his dry throat and said, "Well, sir, I guess it was the squirrel that first found us in the forest. His name was Nettle, as I understand it. He took us to a house where a kind woman had been helping our Chloe, but they had already left to escape the ambulances. Then later on another squirrel found us, and he told us about the meeting. Since we couldn't find Chloe, we thought we'd better come and see if we could get help . . . er . . . see if we could help each other that is, in our common fight against the ambulances. The country isn't safe, and the animals are right—something has to be done!"

"Tell us please, what is your name?" asked Silas.

"I am called the Artist," said the Artist.

"Ah, of course you are!" Silas beamed. "I am not surprised in the least. You have a sensitive soul, that much is obvious." Silas glanced speculatively at Greybelle.

"And I suspect you may have some hidden talents, as well," he said shrewdly. "Tell me also, Artist, how did you know that the squirrel wanted to bring you here? Did you understand him? Do you understand animals in general, dear Artist?"

The Artist answered carefully, "Well, sir . . . truth be told, I *do* understand some natural things, you know. My father taught me to listen to the plants and the animals and trees . . . but . . . well . . . that's not how I knew what the squirrel, what Whitestone wanted. I knew what he wanted because . . . ." He looked questioningly at Greybelle.

The mare tossed her mane and said aloud, "Because *I* told him."

A gasp went up from the animals. The mare could talk like men! She could speak the man's language! What did this mean?"

Silas himself looked shocked. He jumped down from the rock he had been sitting on and approached the mare. He came close to Greybelle and reached out his wrinkled hand to stroke her mane.

"Oh, my dear," he said, petting her soft gray neck. "You are from the north?"

"My mother is from the Valley of Bree," said Greybelle.

Silas said, "I know of it. I've never been there, but . . . your family still lives there, I believe."

"They *do*, truly?" Greybelle said incredulously. "Are you sure?"

"Oh yes, quite sure," said Silas smiling kindly. "I have been told."

Greybelle whinnied a happy whinny into the star-studded sky. Her family was alive! They still lived in the lands that she had only heard of from her mother. The mare turned to Silas with shining eyes.

"Is there any way I can get there?" she asked him.

Silas looked at her kindly. "Not at the moment, my dear. But who knows what miracles may lie ahead? We shall see."

The old man turned back to the council. "I am honored and delighted to have with us a child from the north. This is the mare . . ." He looked at her questioningly, and Greybelle answered, "My name is Greybelle."

Silas went on, "Her bloodlines lead back to the oldest lineage of horses, from the days when animals could speak to humans. This mare is proof today those days are not a myth. Let us welcome her as a representative of her ancient and honored people, and of all of our honored ancestors from the old world."

The animals stamped their feet and paws and hooves appreciatively, and a small huzzah went up from the birds. None of them had ever met one of the talking animals, a trait that legend said they all used to share. That such an honored mare should be traveling with these men made the animals look at the humans with a little more respect. Perhaps they could be trusted, after all.

The presence of Greybelle gave them all a new hope. She reminded them all of where they came from, and of a way of life that evidently still existed, not just in legend. Perhaps with the mare *and* Silas on their side, they did stand a chance of winning this fight. The circle buzzed with a new excitement.

After a few moments Silas lifted his hands again and quieted the group. He said softly, "And now, let us lay our plans."

The animal leaders leaned forward eagerly.

"Ahem." A polite cough came from one side. Then a gruff voice said, "Excuse me, Silas sir. But I have some information that might be of importance."

Everyone turned to see the Badger step forward into the middle of the circle.

"Of course, dear Badger," said Silas. "What is it?"

"A young crow called Blackberry just reported to me, sir. He has found the girl and the woman. They are traveling with the carpenter Brisco Knot."

A low gasp went up from the circle. All eyes swung up to the trees where King Cornix and Queen Faye were perched.

"It is true!" called down Cornix. "We have confirmed it. They are hiding far west of here, in a town called Fairfax, near the sea."

The tension in the air seemed to break. With this news

came the final credibility that the men needed to gain the animals' grudging respect. Brisco Knot was a name the animals knew well, because of the crows who never tired of telling stories about their beloved friend. They were on the same side.

At the Badger's first mention of "the woman and child," the Artist and Lord Winchfillin looked at each other in complete surprise. Could it be . . . ? It *must* have been Chloe! She was in Fairfax!

Greybelle whinnied her joy at the news and even Old Raja nickered happily. He was glad enough about the girl, but it also seemed they wouldn't be eaten now, and for that he *was* truly joyful.

The Badger cleared his throat again and said in his gravelly voice, "Blackberry found something else, sir."

"What else did he find?" asked Silas.

The circle of animals and men went quiet to hear what the old Badger would say.

"He found where the cars are coming from."

CHAPTER FOURTEEN

*I*NSIDE THE TREE HOUSE MRS. GOODWEATHER made a fresh pot of tea, and the three women sat at the table finishing the scones. Earlier Mrs. Goodweather had sent Chloe to gather handfuls of the fragrant mint growing just below on the ground, then shown her how to crush it, and steep it until it made a rich, stimulating brew.

Chloe blew on hers to cool it, and breathed in the sweet scent of the steam.

"'The steam is as good as the brew,' so my mother used to say," Mrs. Goodweather said, sipping her own tea. "There are healing qualities in that steam, my dear. Good for the lungs and good for the blood. Very healthy. Helps you keep your good looks—*obviously!*" she said fluttering her eyelashes.

Celeste laughed, and Chloe thought it a beautiful, musical sound. How happy she was they had found each other!

Celeste said to her new companions, "We were so worried about you, my dear, Avery and I—after we saw you at the Cobbly Fair! We tried to help you—but you had gone by the time we returned with the police."

So many times I wondered if they had returned to find me—and they had! For a moment Chloe couldn't speak, but could only grasp Celeste's hand warmly, in gratitude.

When the girl could talk again, she said, "I can't thank you enough for trying so hard to help me. And now, I hope I can help you, too." Celeste squeezed her hand back. They both had their dear ones inside that awful place.

Shakespeare squeaked for another crumb of scone, and as Mrs. Goodweather obliged him, she told of how the white rat had done his part—how he had called for help in the forest, and most likely saved Chloe's life.

Celeste looked admiringly at the rat, who had already impressed her with his note. "Why, you're a hero, Shakespeare!"

Shakespeare looked flattered and licked his whiskers agreeably.

"Well, I already knew he was very clever, and I'm not surprised at all that he could pull off this feat!" Celeste patted Shakespeare gently on his head. She asked Mrs. Goodweather curiously, "But tell me, how could anyone hear him, so deep in the forest?"

"Ah, but many *did* hear him," said Mrs. Goodweather. "Better ears than mine heard him, and they came to tell me about it."

"Better ears . . . whose ears?" asked Celeste.

"The animals' ears," interjected Chloe, unable to contain herself.

"Animals? The forest animals?"

"Yes, two squirrels to be exact," said Chloe. "Whitestone and Nettle."

"But how do you know their nam . . ." Celeste trailed off.

"They told Mrs. G," said Chloe. "She can understand them!"

"Well, not every word," said the older woman. "But after living in the woods all my life, I get the gist of what they say. And we look out for each other, the creatures and I."

"I see," said Celeste. "How wonderful!"

"And you should see Mrs. G's house!" gushed Chloe. She described the vast gardens that produced so many delicious fruits and vegetables, the large, comfortable kitchen that Mrs. Goodweather made her pies and cakes in, and the pretty upstairs room that Chloe had spent her time recuperating in.

"Your house sounds like one of the most wonderful places in the world," said Celeste. "I would love to see it someday."

"And so you shall," said Mrs. Goodweather. "We will have a feast, when this is all over. I will cook a magnificent meal for you and your brother, and your mother, my dear Chloe, and your friends the Artist and Lord Winchfillin when we find them, and it will be a magnificent party of celebration, you just wait and see!"

The three women smiled at the pretty thought, but just then a siren wailed from somewhere below. The siren reminded Chloe of the last magnificent party she had been to, and she told Celeste of Lord Winchfillin's unfortunate birthday party. First, she described the lavish decorations and her own part in helping the Artist paint the sets for Lord Winchfillin's play. Then she told of the terrifying attack that had left many guests dead or abducted by drivers that leapt out of the speeding ambulances. She told of how the mansion had been lit on fire, and how she and the Artist had fled on the backs of Greybelle and Raja. She told of the ambulance that chased them, and how she had fallen unnoticed, until Shakespeare had called the animals for help.

"At Mrs. Goodweather's house I thought I was finally safe . . . ," said Chloe.

Mrs. Goodweather finished the story for her. "And then the ambulances came again, and we just made it out in time. Thank goodness I knew of a cabin where we could hide, and that's when I called Brisco."

Chloe cast a quick glance at Celeste, whose cheeks turned pink at the mention of the carpenter's name. "He seems a very capable person," said Celeste simply, glancing down at her teacup. "But tell me," she said more seriously, looking up again. "How can I help?"

Chloe smiled. "That's easy, you can help us with our plan!"

"Tell me more about the plan!" Celeste said.

Chloe looked quickly at Mrs. Goodweather, who explained about the gala in two days' time.

"You see, very important people will be there. Our plan is to make up a batch of my special pies, which have some very . . . er . . . *surprising* . . . qualities, and serve them to these people. Of course, we will have to be disguised to get inside the gala."

Mrs. Goodweather got up and crossed the little room to pick up the two uniforms she had already altered to fit her and Chloe.

"We only have two of these, I'm afraid," Mrs. Goodweather apologized. "But we still need to *make* the pies, my dear, and you can certainly help with that."

Celeste nodded agreeably and asked curiously, "What exactly will the pies do?"

Chloe and Mrs. Goodweather looked at each other, and

Chloe giggled. "Turn the people running this horrible place into what they really are."

Celeste looked blankly back, and Chloe and Mrs. Goodweather burst out together, "Babies!"

At the look on Celeste's face, they dissolved into helpless laughter, all the fear and frustrations of the past few days melting away as they leaned helplessly on the table, laughing. Celeste joined in, after she recovered from her surprise. Finally, they calmed down enough for Mrs. Goodweather to explain to Celeste more clearly the effects of the blueberries, and how they planned to slip the pies onto the tables, for the heads of the hospital to eat.

"The batch will be very strong, so the berries ought to start working immediately. Once we have the directors under control, Brisco will step in and help us subdue the rest."

"But how will Brisco do that?" asked Celeste.

"Brisco has his ways," said Mrs. Goodweather. "I suspect he will build a great cage, or a trap of some kind, perhaps he will rope them all together and tie them to a tree. However he does it, you can be sure it will be quite handy, although still quite dangerous." The older woman mused quietly, almost to herself, "I only hope that one man is enough against all of those drivers. I can't quite believe he will be . . ." Her voice trailed off and then Mrs. Goodweather shook her head briskly, snapping out of her morose reverie. "Meanwhile my dear, you and I will have brought the police, and the crowd can help us surely, and well, there you are!"

"I wonder what the crows want with him?" Chloe said.

"Now that *is* a mystery," admitted Mrs. Goodweather. "But I'm sure they can be of some help, and I'm also sure that Brisco can charm them into doing almost anything."

While Chloe pondered Mrs. Goodweather's words, she offered Shakespeare a morsel of scone, and the rat held it daintily in his paws, turning it around and around as he munched. Chloe watched him absentmindedly, and then her face brightened.

"I've got it!" she exclaimed, sitting up so suddenly that Shakespeare dropped his crumb and stared at her in surprise.

"What is it? What have you got?" asked Mrs. Goodweather.

"I know exactly what Celeste can do!" Chloe looked excited.

"What?" asked both women at once.

The little room was quiet as Chloe outlined her idea. It would coincide perfectly with their original plan, if all went well. It would be dangerous of course, but every plan would be dangerous, and something told the girl that Celeste Hart was more than up to the task. She might be a gentle woman, of smallish stature and an unassuming nature, but there was a rod of steely strength running through her. Chloe knew she could depend on Celeste to be brave, strong, and true, and she could think of no one better to carry out her new idea.

The women spent the rest of the evening around the table, talking over details and waiting for any word from Brisco. They played cards and sang songs, and for a little while forgot their cares and enjoyed each other's company. The little tree house glowed with a warm light, and occasionally a merry peal of laughter could be heard coming from the windows.

Below, the hospital's windows also glowed, and shadows moved behind them. On the western side of the great building, the green light blinked, illuminating the wooden chute leading down to the sea. With a shuddering groan and scrape, the huge metal door slid slowly open once again.

CHAPTER FIFTEEN

"THEY ARE COMING FROM FAIRFAX," SAID
the Badger.

The animals murmured their surprise.
Fairfax, again!

"Blackberry says Brisco Knot and the other humans are planning to try to stop the cars themselves. They are going to break into the hospital."

Several leaders gasped in surprise at this bold plan. Even Silas looked amazed, and said after a second of shock, "We must reward the crow Blackberry, for what he has found may well be the key to our success!"

The old man was thoughtful for a moment, while the others whispered excitedly among themselves, and then said clearly, so that all could hear, "My friends, here is my advice. We must join forces with Brisco and his friends in the west."

A general noise of approval came from some of the leaders, while a few others looked skeptical, and waited for the old man's next words.

"We must travel as fast as possible. Once we are in Fairfax, we can gather discreetly, and meet with Brisco."

Silas continued, "When we know the details of his plan, we can coordinate our efforts. Agreed?" He looked around at the animal leaders.

King Rae of the elk answered, "Agreed."

"Agreed," chimed in Queen Fay of the crows.

Afra asked in her quiet voice, "Stargazer, tell us—is this to be a group of diplomats, or of warriors?"

Auberon had had enough. These men had been talking for too long. He did not care if Silas liked these men, he did not care about Brisco Knot! This gathering was for *animals*, not men! He, Auberon, King of the Bears, did not need the help of *men*!

The great black bear rose on his hind legs again, and swiped the air with his giant front paws, his claws cutting the air. The hair on his massive shoulders bristled as he rose to tower over the other animals around him.

"Enough!" he roared.

Every animal and man present froze. The instinct to flee before such a threat was strong in every heart, even the other bears. But the huge bear made no move to attack just yet, and they all held their ground.

"We bears don't need the help of man!" Auberon raged. "YOU!" He looked directly at the Artist, who looked surprised to be singled out by the bear. "You say the child Chloe is worth a hundred humans? What do I care for that? *I* am worth a thousand men! Ten thousand men! *We* will not wait to meet with *more* men before we attack! I will call my brothers and sisters and we will kill *all* the men in the land! If you can or won't do anything, then we will put a stop to men's evil *once and for all*!"

The animals trembled before the mighty bear's anger. They feared his wrath, but they all understood it. An unrest rippled through the council. Perhaps King Auberon was right. Perhaps they should ignore these men and refuse their help. Men could not be trusted. A dark doubt began to form in some of their minds. Perhaps Silas himself could not be trusted. He had said it himself, he was a man too, after all . . .

Silas sensed the doubt and the fear and the distrust and he knew it to be an evil seed that would only grow. He knew also that they would lose if they didn't work together. So, he held up his hands again and strode to the middle of the circle where all could see him and could see he had nothing to hide.

"My dear ones," he said lovingly.

Auberon growled and looked away.

Silas spoke softly, with soothing, gentle words, and it was as if the trees spoke with him, their leaves dancing gently along with his voice.

"It is not for myself that I ask this very great thing of you."

The breeze rippled through the leaves and gently caressed the animals' fur, ruffling it and soothing them as Silas continued to speak.

"Killing for killing's sake is not the answer. We are better than that. That is the way of those other men. That is not our way."

Some of the animals felt the truth of this statement, and the anxious fluttering in their hearts slowly began to quiet. Silas went on.

"We must temper our rage with wisdom. I have read in the stars that this battle is a critical one. And, it is made even more difficult because in order to win it we have to cooperate with those who we usually fear. And not only men, my dear ones. You must *all* work together!"

The animal leaders glanced at each other, understanding the old man. It wasn't normal for deer to cooperate with wolves, rabbits with cougars, or mice with bears. This fight would require all to dig deep and to dispense with ingrained fears and prejudices. It would not be easy.

Silas said, "I have seen in the stars that we will *have* to work together, or we will surely lose."

Though calmed, still not everyone looked convinced.

"This fight is not simply of animal against man, for there *was* a time when we understood each other and helped each other," Silas continued.

"Those days are long gone!" called out Remington, the old rabbit, surprising them all. Auberon growled in agreement, and for the first time that they could remember, the bear and the rabbit were of one mind.

"Perhaps not," said Silas. "And in fact, indeed not. We have the proof standing here before us." He indicated Greybelle. "This mare speaks the human's language. Just as all your own ancestors once did. She is the living proof that we once did live together in harmony, and she is the proof that we still can."

The animals still did not look convinced. Silas waved toward the Artist and Lord Winchfillin. Then he said softly, "These people are surely descended from my own people. They would not be here otherwise. They want to help you, they are not like the others. We all share an ancient history, from a more peaceful and powerful time. A more prosperous time, for *all* of us."

Silas turned slowly in a circle. "Long are the years that you and I have understood each other. And respected each other and even loved each other. And yet, I am one of them."

For all his secret strengths and abilities, Silas was indeed only a man, but even Auberon had softened slightly at the old man's words. His parents had loved Silas the Stargazer, and he had been brought up to love the old man too, and to respect him. Silas had lived on the mountain and among them for generations. He had always been a wise advisor and true friend to the animals. He was a man, it was true, but not a regular man at all.

The giant bear growled a softer growl and lowered his head in respect for the small, brown, wrinkled, and grayed human, standing in front of him in bare feet.

Silas gently caressed the bear's fur. Then he stood straight and addressed the others.

"Let us gather our people," he said decisively.

"Summon the crow Blackberry, we will make him our guide." The old man turned so all the animal leaders could hear.

"Let us send out scouts to act as eyes and ears for us! Let us meet with those waiting in Fairfax and put together a foolproof plan. I believe if we are very careful we *can* succeed. But first . . . King Cornix!" Silas addressed the huge black raven perched in the trees overhead. The bird turned sparkling black eyes upon the little old man and cawed loudly.

"Would you send your people to Brisco? Tell him to wait for us, he will need our help! And hurry, my dear Cornix, we don't have a moment to lose."

The raven king cawed again, and took to the sky, followed by Queen Fay. Up the pair looped, higher and higher, drawing more ravens and crows from the trees as they went, and then as one flew away to the west.

Silas turned to the lone wolf sitting quietly at the side of the circle. "Mai," he said softly. The wolf looked back at the old man affectionately, and a high whine escaped his throat.

"Dearest Mai," Silas said. "You are swift and silent. You have great patience and endurance. For these qualities I choose you as my head scout to follow the ravens to Fairfax. Once there, look for a place for us to gather, find out what you can, and wait for our signal."

Mai whined again and blinked his yellow eyes in response before disappearing silently into the trees.

"King Auberon!" Silas whirled to hail the great bear who stood shifting from foot to foot impatiently. He would play along with this so-called plan for a while. Then he would do whatever he wanted. This made Auberon agreeable, but inside the great bear relished the thought that he might still be able to kill a man before the plan was through.

"*Great* King Auberon," cajoled Silas. "You are our might. You are our greatest power."

The bear shook his head disagreeably but was pleased at the compliment. The old man was correct in this at least. He *was* their greatest power. It was simply a fact.

Silas continued his soothing flattery. "There is no one who can stand against you. We all know that you have the power to wreak vengeance on whomever you choose."

The great bear snorted as if to say, "Of course, and. . . ?"

Silas said sagely, "I want to *reserve* your great power, my friend. I want to keep it from the enemy until just the right moment. The moment when we can unleash it to its greatest advantage. For the moment when we are prepared to triumph!"

Auberon liked the sound of that.

Silas said to the bear king, "Your strongest bears will accompany us to Fairfax. They must go quietly, and not disturb anything until just the right moment. We can't afford to give the game away too early, you see."

"So, when *do* we get to give the game away?" growled Auberon, his eyes glittering.

"You will get a signal, my friend, when the time is right," said Silas.

"And what happens when the 'time is right,' Silas?" queried Auberon.

Silas looked at his friend quietly, and then said with a steely strength so that only the bear could hear, "Then you will be the hammer that comes down and crushes them."

The great bear's eyes sparkled. He was satisfied. He could wait a little longer for his revenge.

Silas touched the bear's shaggy shoulder tenderly and said, "I want you to understand. We need you. We could not do this without you."

Deep in his loyal heart, beneath the rage and desire for revenge, the bear had a fleeting vision of a better world, one in which his cubs would not be clubbed, their mothers not be shot and skinned, their fathers not poisoned. He thought of being left in peace to live and grow and play and sleep the winters away in the mountains, without fear. He thought of his bears all growing to be *old* bears, and not killed before their time.

Auberon grumbled a deep, rumbling growl that Silas understood immediately. The old man embraced the great bear briefly. When he came away, Silas had a large spot of honey stuck in his own beard along with several small twigs.

Then Silas addressed the circle once more.

"We have the beginning of a plan, my friends!" he called out happily. "King Cornix and Queen Fay are gone to meet with Brisco Knot and our friends in the west. The wolf Mai has gone to scout the area around Fairfax for a place for us to gather, and here at the mountain we will send a force of animals to Fairfax tonight."

The animal leaders looked from one another in agreement.

"Afra, my dear," said Silas to the white doe, who stood silently by. "Your people are the swiftest among us. Your task is to find a place where our numbers can wait, until they are needed. A clearing or meadow where we can all hide safely. And you'll have help. I'm sending Remington along with you to act as scout and messenger."

The old rabbit hopped up and saluted Silas. He respectfully bowed to the doe queen. "It would be an honor," said Remington.

"Then go, my friends, tell your people and get on your way. The crows and ravens will carry messages, and we will join you there shortly. Good luck and stay safe!"

Afra whirled on her long, delicate legs and flashed her white tail as a signal for her herd of does to follow her. The deer bounded in high leaps out of the thicket. Remington stamped his hind foot on the ground and was almost instantly surrounded by a band of fifty or more rabbits. He quickly communicated his orders, and in a flash the band of rabbits disappeared into the underbrush to follow the deer.

Silas said to the remaining animal leaders, "Those that are too old or infirm to make the journey or those who have young may return to their homes. Gather whoever is left and meet in the meadow in one hour. Courage, everyone, soon we march!"

The animal leaders dispersed back to the meadow to meet with their fellows and tell them of the plan.

Silas sank wearily back against the rocks and closed his eyes. He seemed suddenly frail. The Artist and Lord Winchfillin walked over to him.

Silas opened his eyes and smiled at them. "I am glad you are here. We needed people like you on our side. One day you must tell me more about your father and his gardening, my dear Artist."

"I'd love to," said the Artist.

"But first you must go west and help your friend Chloe." Silas looked kindly at the Artist. "You love her very much, don't you?"

"Yes sir, I have to come to love the little girl dearly. She is very special. We all want to help her, and her mother."

"Her mother?" asked Silas. "Where is the child's mother?"

"She is in the hospital, in Fairfax," said the Artist sadly. "She may have met the same fate as all the others. I only hope Chloe doesn't try to do anything until we get there."

"Are we leaving tonight?" Lord Winchfillin mustered the courage to ask.

"Yes, my dear sir," Silas answered. "You two will go west and send word back to me with one of the crows."

"Send word back to you?" Lord Winchfillin looked alarmed. "You mean you aren't coming with us? But . . . who will control the bears?"

"Oh, I will be there," said Silas consolingly. "But there is something I must do first."

"What could be more important than keeping us from being eaten?" muttered Lord Winchfillin under his breath.

"I can't tell you just what it is yet, but I can't do it alone," Silas said to them.

"Do you need our help?" asked the Artist.

"That is very kind of you, Artist." Silas smiled. "But there is only one here that can help me, and that is . . . she." He indicated Greybelle, who snorted in surprise.

Everyone was surprised. Lord Winchfillin said disbelievingly, "Greybelle? You need Greybelle's help? Whatever for?"

Silas answered quietly, "I need her to talk to a friend. I think she might be more persuasive than I."

Greybelle tossed her silver mane and nickered. Silas walked over to the mare and patted her neck. "Would you mind very much, my dear?" he asked her.

Greybelle said agreeably, "I will do whatever I can, if it will be of help."

Silas turned to the men again. "It is time to go. We won't be long and will join you in Fairfax at the soonest opportunity. For now, good luck to you, and may the Great Spirit be with you on your journey."

The Artist and Lord Winchfillin clasped hands with the old man in farewell, and as they did, they felt a strange sensation that ran through their fingers and raced up their forearms. It was like a current of energy flowing into their bodies during that moment of contact with the old man's warm and calloused hand. It faded when the contact was broken, but both men felt better afterward, stronger, and ready for their journey west.

In the meadow the animal leaders spoke to their people. Some prepared to return home with their young, and others took the opportunity to rest before making the journey west.

There was a sense of surprising calm, now that there was a plan. The animals were ready to get started, and the atmosphere was very different than at the start of the meeting. It gave the animals heart to know that Silas was on their side, watching over them, and that something would be done about the terror on the roads. They were now ready for whatever might come.

To the west of the mountain, Mai the wolf loped along easily under the trees, heading directly for Fairfax. King Cornix and Queen Fay had passed the wolf, flying over his shadowy form, and cawing down to him as they took the lead. Afra and her people ran swiftly west, and Auberon's people followed. All through the night the animals that could make the journey set out. A steady stream of hoofed creatures, winged ones, burrowing ones, both predator and prey, moved west toward what exactly, no one knew.

CHAPTER SIXTEEN

*T*HE SMASHED AMBULANCE SPED DOWN A country road, its engine whining, its dented silver sides flashing in the sun as it careened around a corner. The vehicle barely managed to stay on the narrow road as it raced toward Fairfax. Behind the wheel, Blake Underwood, Chloe's uncle, drove like the devil, his face smeared in motor oil, sweat, and blood. His foot was pressed down hard on the accelerator, and he forced the dented, scraped, and banged-up ambulance down the road at a breakneck speed, daring anything to cross his path. He glared furiously out the front windshield, his eyes watering and blinding him so that he could barely see. He swiped an angry hand across them every few seconds, further smearing the grime across his face.

Beside him sat his old driver Bings, his greasy cap pulled down over his eyes. Bings was attempting to sleep in the passenger seat but woke up with a shout when Blake yanked the car back from the edge of the road. Blake screamed with laughter and demanded Bings pass him a bottle.

Uncle Blake was filthy. He looked a far cry from the gentleman he had pretended to be not so long ago. He and Bings had been on the road for days, pillaging households and taking whatever was useful, or saleable. The backseat of the ambulance was full of things hastily shoved in—silver plates, candlesticks, a painting, a damask tablecloth, some velvet drapes. The two men had long since stopped taking patients back to the hospital, which too often resulted in personal injury. Even the old people could sometimes get a good scratch in before they could get the mask over their face.

Instead Blake and his cohort Bings used the ambulance to carry their hoard of stolen goods, to sell them on the black market. They ate and drank whatever they could find, which meant they were very drunk most of the time.

Just now they were headed back to Ashton House. After a week on the road, Blake wanted to clean up, eat, and get a good night's sleep before taking a trip up to Tillamook Town to sell their latest haul. He grinned to himself, thinking how fun it would be to frighten that uppity cook Mrs. Eames and force her to make him and Bings a real feast. He hadn't eaten a home-cooked meal in far too long. He could change his clothes and get out of this bloody ambulance driver's coat. Blake grinned again as he imagined the poker games he would enjoy after he'd sold his goods.

He worried a little about that pitiful woman that had visited Ashton House, and who he'd let get away. It was still possible that she could speak to the police and tell them about the booth at the Cobbly Fair. But who would believe her, with her ragged patched dress. Blake chewed a filthy fingernail as he drove, and worried that if the blasted woman did tell the police about the Cobbly Fair, it would only be a matter of time until they traced the booth to the vagabonds, and then perhaps back to . . . *no.* Blake spat out the nail. There was no way to trace Tuttie and the vagabonds back to him! Nobody knew that they had met in the middle of the forest to exchange the girl—how could they?

Blake felt somewhat satisfied until he remembered Hotel Nell. His blood ran cold as he realized that they could certainly trace the girl from Hotel Nell to himself, for he had delivered her there! Cursing his stupidity, Blake pushed harder on the accelerator, which accomplished nothing as it was already pressed against the floor. He gnashed his teeth. *Why* had he offered to deliver the girl to the hotel? Why hadn't he just left well enough alone and severed all ties at the Cobbly Fair? He would be free and clear if only he had! Blake cursed roundly.

Bings, dozing next to him, snorted loudly in his sleep. Blake, wanting to take his anger out on someone, punched Bings in the arm. Bings woke with a yell.

"Ow! Oy!" He looked at Blake who looked back at him, smirking.

"Whad'ya do that for?" demanded the little man.

"Because I wanted to, that's why!" hollered Blake. "And here's another!" he punched Bings in the arm again.

The car continued to speed down the road, the two men arguing inside. The ambulance swerved from side to side crazily, which made the men stop arguing, and start laughing. Drunk, they laughed maniacally as they nearly swerved off the road. Blake wrenched the wheel to the side to bring the car back on the road.

Bump.

"I think you hit a rabbit!" yelled Bings, holding on to his seat as the car swerved in the other direction.

Bump.

"There goes another one!" screamed Blake, laughing so hard he could barely breathe.

The ambulance careened down the winding road, narrowly missing the edge again and again. Certain death waited at every curve as their wheels spun over the edge of a deep ravine below. Blake glanced in the ambulance's rearview mirror. Staring back at him was a man who looked like he had been in a war. He glanced over at Bings and noted the same about his companion. Mud and blood-spattered, eyes white against their blackened faces, their manic smiles red and slavering, the lack of sleep, stress, and frequent gulps from various brown bottles made them look totally insane.

The ambulance sped toward Fairfax and Ashton House. It was just dark on the road now, and the only working headlight cut a single swath of light into the night, illuminating just a few feet in front of the car. Blake peered through the windshield and saw the yellow lights of Ashton House ahead.

"That's the ticket!" He cackled, anticipating his hot bath and dinner. He slapped the sleeping Bings next to him. "Wake up! We're here!"

Suddenly a *huge* black shape appeared in front of the car. Blake slammed on the brakes and screamed, "*What the . . .* !" Bings flew forward and hit the dashboard as the car screeched to a halt.

"What is *that?*" screamed Blake as something enormous and black and . . . *shaggy* reared up in the light from the car. A deep, rumbling roar shook the night as the . . . *something* . . . bared huge yellow teeth and swiped the air with its enormous paws that were bristling with long, black claws.

"YAHHHHHHHHHH!" screamed Blake and Bings together.

King Auberon, for that is who it was, stood on his hind legs and roared his rage into the night sky. How dare this . . . *man . . . machine* try to hit him? The giant black bear hit the side of the ambulance with his paw and scraped his claws against the metal, carving deep gashes in the side. The two men screamed again as Auberon reared up again to deliver another blow.

Blake, quaking with fear, threw the car into reverse and screeched backward, just avoiding the bear's second attack. Blake drove backward as fast as he could, and the two men watched in horror as the bear pursued the retreating ambulance. Blake could not maintain control of the vehicle and veered crazily off the road, crashing backward into a hedge that lined the drive.

"AHHHHHHHHH!" screamed the two men again as more black shapes crossed the road. There were bears everywhere. Huge, shaggy black shapes loped by the ambulance, looking curiously in the windows at the two terrified men. The first bear had halted its charge at the sight of the other bears, and stood defiantly in the driveway of Ashton House, huffing angrily in the direction of the ambulance. Its eyes glared red and even as Bings and Blake watched, it reared again on its hind legs and roared, flashing its long yellow teeth.

"Let's get out of here!" implored Bings, almost crying.

"What do you think I'm trying to do?" snapped Blake, wrenching the gears of the ambulance and gunning the engine. The car groaned and coughed, and something clanked as it reluctantly dragged itself out of the ditch and back onto the road. Blake turned the damaged car, which was now belching blue smoke into the air, back toward town, his hands shaking on the steering wheel. The car couldn't go very fast now, and he watched fearfully in his rearview mirror to see if any bears were coming after them.

"What in blazes was that all about?" he said to Bings, who answered that he had no bloody idea. Bears! Who would've thought it? What were all those bears doing there?

Neither Blake nor Bings had an appetite to try to return to Ashton House now, and headed back to the hospital instead. They would stash their stolen goods at the Mercantile, and drop off the damaged ambulance, claiming it had been wrecked in the course of their duties. They could get a good wash and some kind of dinner at the hospital, too. It wasn't ideal, but it was better than facing those bears.

CHAPTER SEVENTEEN

AUBERON WATCHED THE LITTLE METAL machine rumble away and smirked with satisfaction. He had scared those odious little men out of their wits! Chuckling to himself, he dropped back to all fours and joined his people moving through the trees. He would allow the men to escape, for now. There were more important things to do, but the great bear was certain he would see those two again, and finish his business with them. He would make sure of it.

Auberon stopped on a rise to sniff the air. He could smell the sea, and the rich, salty aroma sat on his tongue like a treat. He closed his eyes and flared his nostrils, drawing the sharp, briny taste of the ocean air deep into his lungs. He liked it here, he decided. Along with the delicious smell of the sea, his delicate nose picked up the sweet smell of huckleberries, and . . . ahhhhhh . . . *fish*.

The bears moved in a quiet black mass through the woods, flowing like a shaggy river through the trees toward the hills. They had crossed the country swiftly, adding to their numbers as they went. They skirted the small town of Fairfax, avoiding the light, and were silently joined by a large group of deer. As the bears and the deer paused momentarily to look at each other, no one made a sound. After a moment of recognition, both groups moved on together. There was no need to speak— they all understood the common goal. Black and white against the trees, the bears and deer moved past the town, and up the hill.

All of the animals were on the move, gaining members to their mobs as they moved through forest, field, and air. None of the people in the town or at the hospital had any idea of the migration happening in the shadows just beyond the street-lights. The townsfolk huddled in their huts and houses, oblivious to the racoons, beavers, rabbits, mice, and foxes that tiptoed just outside their frosted windows. The shivering line of people waiting outside the hospital were huddled together against the cold night, and did not see the shadowy forms moving just past the tree line. The hospital workers, busy with their ghastly work, had no inkling of the army passing just outside the thick walls.

"North."

"North of the hospital. Find the meadow."

"Find the meadow and wait for word."

"Silas is coming!"

"The Stargazer is coming to help us!"

The whispered call traveled far and wide, igniting fear and hope in every breast. The Stargazer was coming, and *that* had never happened before, in even the oldest creature's memory. This was certainly the most important call in all their lives, and there was a flurry of preparation as the news spread.

The bravest of them—the young rabbits and teenaged raccoons, the yearling stags and the adolescent foxes rushed forward, forcing their elders to restrain them, and scold them for being rash. The young did as they were told, but their eyes flashed in anticipation of possible heroic scenarios ahead. The elderly voles and shrews, the mother mice, and the very youngest chipmunks stayed behind, and worried they would never see their family members again. Hurried, tearful goodbyes were held in every den, burrow, and nest as families parted, but there was no argument—they all understood that it must be done. Silas the Stargazer himself was coming. Man had gone too far. The animals *had* to act.

Mai the wolf had found them a gathering place that morning. It was a high place, carved into the hillside by a meteor that had fallen from the stars millions of years before. The crater had since become a beautiful green meadow, surrounded by pines. As soon as Mai stepped into the grassy space, after his long journey from the mountain, he had barked his discovery to the crows circling overhead, and they had flown east to report back to Silas.

Afra the doe and her people joined Mai soon after, followed by Auberon and the other bears. The crows kept circling and sending messages throughout the day, and the creatures of the land began to respond.

As thousands of animals mobilized across the country, answering the call, Auberon's bears retreated higher, above the meadow to sit in the shadows of the pines there, while Afra's small army of white does stood along the tree line, waiting to welcome the first arrivals.

CHAPTER EIGHTEEN

SILAS LEFT THE COUNCIL AREA AND STARTED climbing. His bare feet were accustomed to the rocks and gripped like hands as he deftly pulled himself up the mountain to a favorite ledge, far above the valley. He needed to think. Then, he needed to speak to a friend.

Cross-legged on the ledge, Silas looked out over the forests and fields below. He scanned the horizon where the sky was a deepening indigo blue. The moon was just beginning to rise. A warm current coming up from the south turned the mountain breeze balmy, and it blew softly through the trees. Silas closed his eyes and settled back against the wall of rock. He made himself comfortable, and then spoke to the mountain.

"Wy'east," the old man murmured softly, placing the palm of his hand on the sandy rock beneath him.

The air was still again, and nothing moved. Then a slight vibration could be felt, a gentle flutter in the rock, subtle, but perceptible. The old man smiled. The mountain was listening.

"I think we'll need your help, old friend," the old man said quietly, knowing the mountain could hear him.

THE MOUNTAIN COULD INDEED HEAR THE OLD MAN clearly. He could always hear the old man. He had listened to that beloved voice as it climbed his peaks and valleys for a hundred years. The mountain missed the old people, and Silas was the only one left. He had the stars and the clouds for company, but the truth was that Wy'east was lonely.

He had lost his love, the beautiful mountain Loowit, when he fought the terrible battle with brother Klickitat, and Loowit had gone to sleep forever. Since then the new people had come and driven out the old people, and now Wy'east was alone. He didn't mind being alone that much—he was a mountain after all. He was made to stand alone, steadfast and solid, and he did so. But they had a special understanding, this old man and the great mountain, and Wy'east wanted to help him.

From deep within the mountain's heart, below the volcanic rock, below the layers of basalt, below even a river of fire and molten rock that ran a mile beneath the top crust of the earth, Wy'east called up his voice. Though he could roar so loud as to deafen any ear, the mountain could also whisper, so that only the Stargazer could hear. What might be only a subtle tremor to the most sensitive, to Silas it made perfect sense.

The two old friends began to converse, talking over what could be done. Silas had a proposal for the mountain. At first Wy'east refused it, but when Silas pressed his case, the mountain reconsidered. As the hours went by, the stars came out in full force, the constellations gleaming and moving slowly through their nocturnal dance, the moon made her steady track across the sky, and an understanding was finally reached. Silas knew what he had to do.

THE OLD MAN STOOD, LOOKING UP INTO THE NIGHT sky. The space was not a single, inky black but a mixture of every raven hue, a complex palette of onyx and indigo, peppered with dazzling stars. As Silas watched, the stars began to move. Swirling galaxies rotated silently in the sky, and one began to float toward the old man. It gathered stars as it turned, drawing toward it small planets and the edge of a nebula. The collection of celestial objects spiraled gracefully toward the old man. They hovered overhead, and then encircled the peak of the mountain like a halo. The bright objects illuminated the clouds around them, sending twinkling comets over the tops of the uppermost pines. Silas watched in wonder as the stars lit up the landscape in their beautiful dance, finally coming to a halt overhead. The glittering orbs hung in the air like a hundred chandeliers, bobbing gently in the atmosphere, and Silas sank to his knees under their glow.

"Stargazer," came a fluting tune, a silvery voice from somewhere else, somewhere entirely unknown to mankind.

"My old love," Silas whispered, with tears welling up in his eyes.

"I have missed you," answered the Evening Star.

Silas began to weep, suddenly powerless to stop the flow of emotions that coursed through his heart. It was the effect of the stars. The energy field around stars was intense enough to disrupt an earth-dweller's heartbeat, and any sudden movement in the heavens caused all kinds of feelings and thoughts to flow through human and animal minds. With the stars so close now, Silas felt waves upon waves of emotion crash over him. It was how he had fallen in love with the Evening Star so many years ago, when he had been a young man. She had utterly charmed him one night in his early stargazing days, but had disappeared one day, and he had missed her sorely ever since.

"Cygnus has warned us," said the Morning Star, her silvery voice causing small clusters of stars to fall around the mountain. "And now Wy'east has called us."

"We are fortunate to have such compassionate, powerful friends," said Silas humbly. "We will of course gladly accept any assistance you choose to give us, my dearest Evening Star. Just tell me what you need me to do."

All through the night the three friends discussed what could be done to help the battle brewing in the east. The old man, the mountain, and the Star wore away the hours while the country slept, oblivious to the dance of the stars overhead.

It was nearly dawn. The eastern horizon had a tinge of pink, and the smallest stars began to twinkle in alarm. It was time to go, daylight was approaching. Anxiously they signaled to the Evening Star to come along, it would not do to be there when Old Sol rose into the sky. The Evening Star twinkled her dimming light in farewell and followed her fellow stars back into the sky.

Silas groaned and stretched his stiff limbs. The old man had been sitting in the same position all night, and his hair and clothing were damp with dew. He shivered in the sharp morning air. Silas rubbed his hand together to warm them, and quietly watched the rosy glow in the east become a radiant mix of violets and pinks.

Silas got to his feet and rested a hand against the rock wall. "Thank you, my friend. I will go and tell the others."

Silas turned to go back down the steep trail to the meadow. When he got to a familiar outcropping of rocks, the old man halted. His old eyes were still as keen as an eagle's, and he peered into the distance, scanning the horizon. After several minutes of this, he finally saw what he was looking for. Out of the thin gray clouds in the west, a line of black shapes appeared. They were the crow messengers, returning from Fairfax. They would have news. Silas hurried down the path to the meadow.

CHAPTER NINETEEN

THE MEADOW WAS NEARLY EMPTY NOW, MOST of the animals having dispersed in different directions. The Artist, Lord Winchfillin, and the horses were still there, however, grouped around a small campfire. The meadow was a bit misty in the morning light, and the fire crackled cheerfully, spreading the comforting smell of home, and of breakfast. Breakfast was being served, in fact; the Artist just finished frying the last pancake and plopping it on Lord Winchfillin's plate when Silas approached them.

"Good morning, Mr. Stargazer!" said the Artist brightly, wiping his hand on his pants, and offering the older man a firm handshake.

"Good morning to all of you," returned Silas warmly, heartily returning the Artist's grip. "I trust you passed a pleasant night? Not too cold, I hope?"

"Not a bit." Lord Winchfillin laughed. "Considering we slept in the softest, warmest beds you could imagine."

Silas looked surprised. "Oh? Beds, did you say? And what beds were these?" He glanced around for evidence of such soft, warm beds, but could see none. He gave the Artist a shrewd look, suspecting that he might be the one to explain.

The Artist felt suddenly shy under the old man's gaze and looked down at the ground, twisting his hat in his hands as he said, "Well sir, those would be the beds that I . . . that is that they . . . I mean . . . well . . . that the trees made for us. Sir." The Artist halted, feeling foolish, but the old man was nodding as if he understood. He asked the Artist softly, "*Made* for you, you say?"

The Artist said a bit self-consciously, "Yes sir, you see I asked them if they would, and they must have said yes, because in the wink of an eye there were three snug hammocks in the branches, ready and waiting."

Silas's eyes had an admiring look in them now. He said softly, almost to himself, "Well now! A tree-charmer. How long has it been since . . ." The old man looked wistful, his eyes clouding with old memories, and then he shook his head, smiling broadly.

"How wonderful," he said to the Artist. "How perfect. Of course you are a tree-charmer, dear Artist! It takes a sensitive soul—as I said before. You are most welcome to our little crusade, my dear sir, most welcome indeed!

"It is a long-lost art, you know," Silas said, now sitting down next to Lord Winchfillin companionably. The earl offered Silas a cup of tea, and the old man gratefully accepted it. "There probably isn't another within a hundred miles who could do the same, if any," said Silas, sipping his tea.

The Artist looked bashful. "My father taught me how. His father taught him, or so he told me. He said his great-grandfather came from people who *all* knew how to do it, people from far north of here."

"Ah, I thought as much," said Silas, happily. "It is the old traits, the old ways, popping up yet again. A shadow of another time. But a shadow is cast by something of substance, after all. There is definitely something there."

He laughed, shaking his head. "And it seems that you aren't the only one with ties to the old north." He looked at Greybelle, who nickered back at him softly.

"This mare's dam and sire were from the Valley of Bree," said Silas wonderingly, patting her soft neck. "A place long-lost to most of us, unseen by humans for hundreds of years since the Bridge of the Gods was destroyed." He looked keenly at the little group.

"I have spoken to the mountain," Silas said.

The Artist held his breath and sensed that Lord Winchfillin was doing the same. What could Silas mean he had *spoken* to the mountain?

"Do you remember that at our meeting with the animals, I told all of you that Wy'east would help us?"

They looked back at him in silence. Then Lord Winchfillin said tentatively, "Erm yes . . . but, could you tell us *how*, exactly?"

"He will repair the Bridge of the Gods," Silas said, a broad smile on his weathered face. His blue eyes beamed intensely from within their network of wrinkles.

Greybelle surprised them all with a whinny. "Oh, Silas!" she cried, tossing her silver mane up and down. "Does this mean . . ."

"Yes, my dear," said Silas kindly. "Once the bridge is repaired, we will be able to go north again. You will be reunited with your family."

The mare reared on her hind legs, whinnying her joy, and

pawing the air with her front hooves in happiness. The Artist and Lord Winchfillin exclaimed at the news; although they weren't entirely sure what it meant, it seemed like very good news, and they were delighted for Greybelle nonetheless.

"Oh! Oh, my!" said Greybelle, prancing with joy. "Let us begin! Let us begin our journey north at once!"

"Journey?" asked the Artist, becoming serious. "What journey?"

"A journey to get the help we surely will need," answered the Stargazer.

"*More* help?" asked Lord Winchfillin nervously. "Do we really need more help? I've had quite enough with those dreadful bears already. I can't imagine what more might come out of the north to 'help' us."

"Oh yes." Silas's smiling face turned grave. "The brave and courageous animals we have sent west will do everything within their power, of course. They will fight valiantly, but . . . I'm afraid many will die. It is the inevitable cost of war. If I can make a trip north, I may be able to find the help we need to spare many lives. I must try, at any rate. However, before we go anywhere, we must see what our messengers have to say." Silas stepped back and turned his eyes to the sky.

Caw caw! The long line of crows flying in from the west had reached the meadow, and were circling overhead, preparing to land. The noisy flock descended into the trees, flapping their wings as they arranged themselves, squawking at each other as they fought for the best positions.

Silas addressed them politely. "What have you to tell us, friend crows?"

A large raven with a gray wing replied, "King Cornix

sends word that Mai the wolf has found a place to gather in the west. Afra and Auberon are there already, and others are arriving as we speak."

The crows all sent up a chorus of enthusiastic *caw caw*s! The men exclaimed in surprise to themselves. It was happening!

At that moment a sound was heard that made everyone freeze. It was an unnatural sound, and a sound that did not belong in the wilderness. The sound was rough and loud and coughed fire. It hurt the animals' sensitive ears, and a choking smell hit their noses. Closer and closer it came, making them tremble. And then they knew what it was, and their blood ran cold. It was the sound of an ambulance.

Two great beams of white light appeared at the edge of the meadow, blinding them all. At the same time the crows rose into the air with a great rush of wings and screaming calls.

Greybelle stamped her hooves warningly, and even Old Raja whinnied a challenge to the monster. He remembered the attack at Lord Winchfillin's house very well—the drivers had lit his poor tail on fire! Even now the tail was pitifully short, the hair burned. The old gelding angrily pawed the ground. This time he would get a few good kicks in.

The Artist shielded his eyes against the light, and Lord Winchfillin picked up a stick from the ground, though his knees knocked together in fear as he did so.

The blinding lights were suddenly doused, leaving the meadow once again in the dark. Nobody got out of it, and for a moment everyone stood blinking in confusion. What—*who* —could this be?

In front of them was a silver ambulance. Overhead the

crows seemed . . . *delighted*? The birds seemed inexplicably transported by joy. They swooped through the air, over the ambulance, and back up to the trees. Even the crows in the trees danced along the branches, uttering soft caws of delight, their black eyes shining.

It wasn't the only strange note to be struck at such a time. Even while the group of men and horses waited anxiously to see what climbed out of the ambulance, they noticed that something else was off. What was . . . was the car made of . . . *wood*? What was going on here?

The ambulance door swung open. A man with a mustache climbed out, looked around at the dumbfounded group, doffed his cap, and said cheerfully, "Brisco Knot, at your service!"

CHAPTER TWENTY

ILAS GAVE A GREAT LAUGH OF PLEASURE. Walking forward, the old man clapped the carpenter on the shoulder and shook his hand.

"Welcome, Brisco!" said Silas heartily.

"*Silas*! What a great surprise!" Brisco's smile was warm as he greeted his old friend. "I should have known you might be here. The crows insisted that I come, and now I understand why."

Brisco looked around at the others, his eyes twinkling as he took in the forms of the Artist and Lord Winchfillin, who looked back at him in wonder.

"How glad I am the crows found you, dear Brisco," Silas said fondly. "And as usual, your timing couldn't be better."

Brisco grinned. "Timing is everything, eh Silas? It's good to see you too. You're looking fit, I must say!"

"Well, for an old man, anyway." Silas laughed good-naturedly.

"For a hundred-year-old man, I'd say very fit!" Brisco laughed along with him.

The others waited impatiently for an introduction, which Silas quickly provided. "May I present Mr. Brisco Knot, master carpenter, and friend to the crows."

Silas gestured to the others. "And Brisco, may I introduce to you, the Artist, the Lord Winchfillin, the mare Greybelle, and the horse known as Raja."

Brisco's eyes twinkled. "I feel I already know you. For I know someone who *does* know you."

"Chloe?" The Artist clapped his hands together as the carpenter nodded happily.

They all exclaimed in joy, the little group bursting at this glad and unexpected news. Greybelle's whinny turned into an exclamation. "Oh happy day, the child is safe!"

"Chloe has been found!" sang out Lord Winchfillin, hugging Raja.

"Oh, my dear child." The Artist closed his eyes in relief. *Finally.*

"I'm sure she would say the same about *you*, if she knew you were here," said Brisco, laughing delightedly. "She's been very worried about you since her nasty fall."

"You'll take us to her, won't you?" asked the Artist.

"That's why I'm here," Brisco reassured him. "We'll leave as soon as you're able."

"We're able right now!" burst out Lord Winchfillin, eagerly eyeing the comfortable seats of the ambulance, which would be a huge improvement over the sharp backbone of Old Raja.

"Your choice of transportation is . . . interesting," said Silas, approaching the vehicle.

"Is it made of . . . *wood*?" asked the Artist in amazement, running his hand down the sides of the painted car.

"Why yes, it is!" said Brisco proudly. "And it works just like a real one! Drives like the wind, and those stupid hospital workers can't tell the difference." He patted the hood fondly.

"It is a most ingenious creation," said the Artist, walking around the ambulance admiringly, noticing the fine craftsmanship. Even Lord Winchfillin crept closer to look curiously at the car.

Brisco turned serious. "There are some bad goings-on in the country, as you know," he said. "Chloe told me about the attack at your house." He nodded at Lord Winchfillin. "It's a wonder you managed to escape."

"A wonder and a horror," said Lord Winchfillin morosely, plucking at his ragged cuff. "My house, ruined. My guests killed! Taken! I would have surely been caught too if it hadn't been for my dear Artist coming back for me."

The Artist patted Lord Winchfillin's shoulder. "You would have survived, old friend," he said soothingly. "You were doing just fine when I found you."

The little earl laughed. "Oh yes, just fine hiding in the curtains! Doing just fine scorched and scraped and all alone. No, dear friend, I'm quite sure you saved my life!"

Brisco said kindly, "I see you are quite in the habit of saving lives, sir. Chloe also told me about that poker game."

"That was a lucky chance," admitted the Artist. "In general, not much good comes from poker games, but that one made up for all the rest." He looked anxiously at the carpenter.

"You're sure she is safe?" he asked. "Has Chloe been home to Ashton House? Has she seen her mother?"

"No, the poor kid can't go home because of her stinking uncle," Brisco replied hotly. "He's a nasty piece of work."

"I remember," said the Artist.

"Chloe thinks her mother may still be in the hospital," said Brisco. "Although I have some doubts, because . . . well, because of something we found."

The carpenter looked at the others significantly. "We found out what they are doing inside the hospital. We found out why they are attacking people and taking them away."

The group waited, hardly daring to breath.

"They are killing them," said Brisco.

A gasp from the others, and the horses snorted angrily.

Silas looked disturbed, as he took a seat on a fallen log.

"Tell us everything," he said sadly.

Brisco told them everything he knew about the hospital, the ambulances, and what he had seen coming out of the west door. He told of the chute leading down to the dock, and the boat that took the bodies out to sea. He told how they had seen with their own eyes the ugly "system" the hospital had, and that they were keeping people ignorant of what was happening inside.

"But Mrs. Goodweather has a plan," finished the carpenter hopefully.

"What kind of plan?" asked the Artist.

"A brilliant plan, actually," said Brisco. He explained to the others about Mrs. Goodweather's powerful berries, and how she planned to bake them into pies to be served at the gala. He told them of the effects the pies would have, and how they planned to take control of the hospital.

Brisco turned to the Stargazer. "Your thoughts, Silas?"

Silas paused. Then he said, "I think that is a very good plan indeed. I know of the berries your Mrs. Goodweather is using—they are one of the oldest strains, and very hard to find. She grows them, you say? Interesting . . ."

The old man looked as though he were thinking of visiting Mrs. Goodweather someday to discuss her berry crop, and then he shook his head, and focused on the task at hand.

"Yes, Brisco," he said. "In fact, we have just held a meeting to form our own plan. It was decided at the animal council that they would go west, to Fairfax."

"Animals, Silas?" asked the carpenter. "What animals?"

"All of them," the Stargazer said.

Lord Winchfillin burst out as though he had never been frightened, "Oh yes, and not just any animals, we've sent *bears!*"

He looked so gleeful it made Brisco smile. He liked the little earl.

"The animals are gathering near your tree house even now, Brisco," said Silas. "We heard you'd been spotted, with the girl. She is known to the animals, as is your Mrs. Goodweather, and even you, dear Artist." Silas looked at the Artist fondly.

Brisco said, a triumphant light in his eyes, "Together, I think we're almost certain of success, no? We only needed more manpower—er, animal power, that is. Excuse me, figure of speech . . . The point is, we could only *hope* before, but it was going to be an enormous risk. Now, having met you all—and you, Silas—I feel we could possibly win it!" The carpenter looked around at the little group, his eyes shining. "Just think: *we could win this thing!*"

"It only takes a day to get to Fairfax by ambulance. If we leave now, we could be there by tomorrow," said the carpenter, getting to his feet and slapping his knees. "We should leave immediately." He laughed. "I knew Silas the Stargazer would have a few tricks up his sleeves."

Silas smiled. "One or two."

Lord Winchfillin and the Artist looked at each other and laughed a little. The old man certainly did possess some rather unexpected tricks—there would be time on the journey back to Fairfax to catch up completely, and explain what Silas had said about the mountain and the Bridge of the Gods.

The Artist still had questions about Chloe's plan. "Tell me, Brisco, how do Mrs. Goodweather and Chloe plan on getting *into* the hospital with the pies?" he asked.

"Yours Truly stole her some disguises!" Brisco replied. "Snatched two uniforms right off the back of the truck! She and Chloe are going to pose as servers, and with any luck, gain access to the right tables."

"Hmm . . . risky," said the Artist, thinking *I do not like the idea of little Chloe in such a dangerous situation.*

"Yes, but there is no plan that doesn't pose some risk," said Brisco reasonably. "And now with you all on board, I think we really stand a fighting chance!"

Lord Winchfillin cleared his throat and said casually, "About those berries, er . . . do you think, when this is all over, that Mrs. Goodweather might give me just a little tiny taste? Just a nibble—just so I can smooth out a few wrinkles? Hmm?"

Brisco opened his mouth to laugh, but realized the earl was serious.

"Well, unfortunately sir, I did hear her say there was only just enough."

"Perhaps in the future, then," said Lord Winchfillin, disappointed.

"Perhaps!" said Brisco agreeably.

The Artist wasn't listening; he was thinking of how happy

he would be to see Chloe again. He wanted only to hear everything she had to tell since they had been so violently parted,
and to tell her everything in return. He felt another rush of
gratitude that she was safe and unharmed. Suddenly he
couldn't wait another moment to go to her, and stood up,
brushing off his pants with his hat.

"Let's get going!" he said. "You say the gala is tomorrow
night, and it takes a day to get to Fairfax, so we can't waste
another minute if we are to be in time."

"I can easily fit four in the ambulance." Brisco got to his
feet.

"You will only need to fit three," Silas answered. "I have a
little errand to run before I join you."

The Artist chuckled, thinking Silas's "little errand" was
about as big an errand as there ever could be.

Silas was suddenly all business. Time was ticking by, and
there was much to be done.

"The animals are gathering just north of the hospital,
Brisco," the old man reminded them. "They will be ready when
you give the word. Use the crows as your messengers. I . . . will
join you as soon as I am able." Silas turned to Greybelle. "The
mare is coming with me."

Brisco opened the ambulance doors for the men. Just before the Artist climbed in, he noticed Raja standing a little
apart, looking uneasy. The old gelding didn't seem know where
to go. He couldn't ride in the ambulance, and Greybelle was
leaving with Silas. Was he to travel to Fairfax all on his own?
The horse whinnied sadly.

The Artist went to him. "On second thought, folks, I
might just ride to the party. Raja won't be able to keep up with

the ambulance, not with his old knees." The man patted the horse affectionately.

"I'll stay with you!" said Lord Winchfillin loyally, though he hated to get out of the comfortable car.

Silas said gently, "No. You all must hurry. Raja can come with us."

Greybelle whinnied to the gelding, and he answered her softly.

"I would be honored to have such a valiant traveling companion." Silas moved to Raja and patted his thin neck.

The gelding looked to the Artist for approval. The Artist said fondly, "Go, if you want to, old man. My guess is that you'll have quite an adventure! With Silas the Stargazer, you might see some sights that you may never see again, or that any horse has *ever* seen."

Raja snorted happily and trotted over to join Silas and Greybelle.

Lord Winchfillin and the Artist said goodbye to Silas and the horses and got into the ambulance. The earl sank back gratefully into the padded seats with a sigh.

Brisco started the car with a roar of the engine. The crows took off from the trees, *caw-caw*-ing at the racket, circled the meadow once, and flew away to the west, leading the way to Fairfax, where Chloe and Mrs. Goodweather were waiting.

CHAPTER TWENTY-ONE

*T*HE NEXT MORNING WAS GRAY AND COLD, and eerily quiet. No ambulances had come to the hospital that morning, Mrs. Goodweather realized with some foreboding as she made the breakfast tea. Although she was glad no new victims had arrived, it could be a sign that there simply were no more victims to be had.

Mrs. Goodweather shook her head as she poured herself a cup of tea and went to wake Chloe. The gala was tomorrow night. It was time to make the pies.

This was the most important thing to get right, for it was the pies that held the key to their plan. While Chloe dressed, Mrs. Goodweather gathered the last of the stores, and brought out the small packet of powerful blueberries. She poured them into a pot on the stove, added a few splashes of water, a small spoonful of sugar, and stirred.

"I will boil these down into a syrup, my dear, and while it is cooking, we can roll out the crusts. You can help with that!"

Chloe joined Mrs. Goodweather in the tiny kitchen where Mrs. Goodweather showed her how to mix butter and flour with a little salt until it became pebble-sized crumbles. Then she added a little water and shaped the dough into a ball. Chloe sprinkled more flour on the counter and Mrs. Goodweather plopped the ball of dough down to be rolled out.

Chloe rolled and rolled, sprinkling more flour whenever it began to stick. Finally, Mrs. Goodweather was satisfied, and they set to work cutting the crust into circles. Mrs. Goodweather said practically, "I wish I had my favorite pie tins from home for these, but since I don't, we'll make them turnovers instead, like small hand pies."

She brought the simmering blueberry mixture from the stove to the table, and a rich, jammy aroma filled the little kitchen. Bits of blueberries swam enticingly in the purple syrup, but neither of them was tempted to taste it.

Mrs. Goodweather showed Chloe how to carefully spoon the berries and syrup onto half of the dough circles and fold the other half over, pinching the edges together to make the turnovers. As they crimped and pinched the edges of the pies closed, Mrs. Goodweather thought out loud.

"Now, these are going to be served at a very grand party. They need to look as though they belong there. They need to look fancy, like they came from a catering company. Hmmm . . . *ah!* I've got it! Shakespeare, my dear, come over here. Now, wash your little paws, that's it."

Chloe laughed, watching her dear little friend wash his tiny white paws in the water and dry them on the towel Mrs. Goodweather offered him.

"Now, place your paws here . . . just so . . . and here, that's it! Now that looks very pretty, don't you think?"

Where Shakespeare pressed his paws were tiny marks that

looked very nice indeed. He repeated the pattern all around the edges of the turnovers. When he finished, Mrs. Goodweather added a final flourish of three quick slits on the top cut with a knife, then she brushed a bit of butter on top, along with a final dusting of sugar and cinnamon, and slid the tray of six pies into the little oven.

The little kitchen hummed with activity. A mouthwatering smell of baking pastry wafted out through the open windows while Mrs. Goodweather stood at the little black stove with an oven mitt on one hand, humming a song, gently poking the pies to see if they were done.

"Five more minutes!" she announced, and closed the oven door. She turned to the table where Chloe was busy rolling out more dough.

"How many more should we make?" asked Chloe, her sleeves rolled up and her face splotched with flour.

"Well"—Mrs. Goodweather looked at the pot of syrup —"We have twelve so far, and we can only make a few more because my berry supply is almost gone. I think we'll have fifteen in all."

Mrs. Goodweather read Chloe's thoughts: the smell of the pies was so delicious that Chloe was beginning to wish they had made a few extra with regular berries.

"No worries!" the woman sang out, reaching into a cupboard and pulling out a plate of ginger cookies. "I made these earlier. I thought we might feel hungry after making those pies!"

The three friends munched the cookies happily and drank tea while they waited for the pies to bake, and for Brisco to return.

The little tree house was warm and bright, and Mrs. Goodweather wiped her hands on her apron. "Shall we sit outside for a few minutes?" she said.

Chloe agreed, and the two friends went out to rest a few minutes in the fresh air. Mrs. Goodweather sat in one of the chairs Brisco had whipped up out of nothing and sighed contentedly. "Well that is a good day's work already done."

Chloe agreed. "Yes, and the pies look so good I don't know how the hospital heads can help from eating them. I know what they can do, and I can hardly keep from eating them myself!"

"Well, mind that you don't!" said Mrs. Goodweather. "I can't have my right-hand woman turning into a tiny baby!"

Chloe giggled. "No, and I don't fancy the idea of you changing my diapers, either!"

"Well come to that child, neither do I." They both laughed.

"I hope Celeste is doing all right," said Chloe.

"Oh, I'm sure she is," answered Mrs. Goodweather confidently. "Celeste Hart is a clever woman, and I'm sure she'll be back—eh, what's that?"

The sound of an engine coming up the road caused her to break off and look at Chloe in alarm. Looking anxiously over the edge of the tree house porch rail, Chloe spotted the ambulance. Her heart stopped for a split second—had they been discovered? But even as the thought crossed her mind, she knew who it was.

"It's Brisco!" she cried. "He's back!"

Chloe flew down the tree house ladder and ran to meet the car as it came to a stop. She bounced up and down eagerly, ready to hear everything Brisco had to tell about where he had been, and what he had done, but then shrieked with utter surprise as the Artist got out of the car.

"*Artist!*" Chloe stared at her friend in disbelief. Then she ran into the Artist's open arms.

"Oh, Artist!" she exclaimed, hugging him tightly. "How can you be here? I'm *so* glad to see you!"

The Artist embraced the girl, and then set her gently back, so he could look at her. His eyes were damp and he had trouble speaking, but finally he found his voice. "I am so very glad to see you too, child!"

The two dear friends laughed and hugged again.

Lord Winchfillin had gotten out of the car along with Brisco, and everyone stood watching the two friends reunite. Chloe finally noticed the little earl. "Why, it's Lord Winchfillin! You escaped!" she exclaimed. "Oh, I am *so* happy that you did!"

"Not as happy as I am, my dear!" The little man winked, rocking back on his heels. Then the little earl approached her and held out both hands to clasp hers.

"My dear!" Lord Winchfillin gently pressed Chloe's hands. "May I just say how *delighted* I am that you are also safe and well."

Touched by the little earl's sincerity, Chloe leaned forward and squeezed him in a quick hug.

"We can continue introductions inside," called out Mrs. Goodweather, turning toward the tree house ladder. "I'm sure you're all tired and hungry, so come in and sit down and I'll make us all something to eat!"

The men's noses sniffed the air appreciatively and Brisco said, "Something smells good, Mrs. G!"

❧

THAT DAY WAS A MERRY ONE. FOR THE FIRST TIME THE little group felt relatively safe, and very glad to be together. With the pies already made, and cooling on the counter, they spent the time catching up, and filling each other in on what had happened to them since they were last together. Chloe went first and told the Artist and Lord Winchfillin how Shakespeare had called the animals of the forest, who had in turn called Mrs. Goodweather, who had rescued her and taken her back to the farm. After she explained how they had fled into the forest and met Brisco, the Artist began to fill in his side of the story.

While the Artist spoke, Brisco leaned over to Chloe and, reddening a bit at the ears, asked in a whisper, where had Miss Hart gone? Chloe assured him that Miss Hart was perfectly well and would return, but here she was interrupted by Lord Winchfillin calling out for Chloe to tell the group how much she had enjoyed his birthday party, before the ambulances came of course, so Chloe had to leave it at that for the moment.

The Artist and Lord Winchfillin took turns telling about their own terrifying escapes from the ambulance drivers. The Artist told the tale of how he and the horses had been injured and had been forced to spend the night in the forest. This was when Greybelle had revealed her ability to speak.

Chloe was delighted that the mare had revealed her secret to her friends. The Artist said it was Greybelle that had told him to follow the squirrel to Mrs. Goodweather's house, where they had just missed Chloe. He then told of the journey to the mountain and of the meeting of the animals there. He told about Silas the Stargazer, and how he had promised to help them.

"Wait a minute," said Chloe. "Where is Greybelle? Where is Raja? Didn't they come with you?"

"They went with Silas, over the mountain," explained the Artist. "Silas said we needed more help, and he needed Greybelle to come too. Something to do with her family, across a broken bridge. He promised to join us as soon as possible."

"Well, I certainly hope he can join us in time," said Mrs. Goodweather. "Tomorrow is the day of the gala, and we can't afford to wait for the old man, no matter what help he may bring."

"I don't know much about it myself," admitted the Artist. "But I believe him, and I think if you had met Silas, you would believe him too."

"Well, we asked for help, and help has come!" said Mrs. Goodweather happily, getting up to fetch a bottle of her spiced cider to celebrate. She filled everyone's glass, and raised a toast. "To our friends, old and new! To our endeavor! To our success!"

"*To our success!*" said everyone together and they all drank the delicious cider.

As the little party continued, Chloe was quiet a moment thinking of everything that had been said. She missed Greybelle terribly but was very proud of her friend. And she was so relieved that everyone was safe and unharmed, and she comforted herself with the thought that soon she would see Greybelle again.

All the rest of that day they talked, laughed, and told stories, enjoying the sensation of being among friends, and of celebrating. But, as the afternoon grew long and turned into evening, they each fell silent as the weight of what they were to do the next day fell upon them. It was only a matter of hours now, and nothing could go wrong.

They discussed the plan, and then went over it again, but no one could anticipate the exact sequence of events. It would all unfold the following day, and until then they could do nothing more but rest, which seemed almost impossible.

After a good supper, Brisco surprised everyone by building another bed for Lord Winchfillin, while the Artist preferred to find a tree hammock near the tree house, where he could think.

Outside the night was clear and calm, and cold. The stars gleamed silently as the Artist made his way down the tree house ladder. He walked over to the rock ledge and gazed down at the hospital. He shivered, remembering the attack at Lord Winchfillin's castle. Visions of screaming party guests, falling on the lawn and being dragged back to the ambulances, flashed before his eyes, and he closed them tightly, trying to blot the images out. This madness had to end. Their plan *had* to work.

He shook his head and thought that whatever happened it would all be over in forty-eight hours. He pulled out his little wooden flute. The Artist stopped under a tree that he would soon ask for a bed and began to play a tune. The melody was tender, but it had an underlying tempo that quickened the blood. It was a song full of what was in the Artist's heart, and in the heart of all the creatures hidden in the forest around him.

Animals in their dens near the tree house heard the flute's tune and burrowed closer together. Birds in their nests heard it and shuffled uneasily, knowing what it meant. It meant the time for action was soon. Not tonight, for tonight was for resting, but it was the kind of rest that comes before a battle.

Afra the white queen, waiting patiently in the meadow, heard the Artist's tune. Her sensitive ears swiveled to pick up every note, and she knew that tomorrow would be the day. Her does were bedded down in the grass around her, resting, but not sleeping, waiting patiently for the night to pass.

King Auberon, pacing restlessly above the tree line, heard the Artist's notes wafting up through the trees and growled. His great family, waiting in the trees around him, all growled in response. Soon. They would be on the move soon. They would stop the men very soon. The huge black bears, invisible in the darkness of the trees, gnashed their yellow teeth.

They were ready.

CHAPTER TWENTY-TWO

HE TRAIL UP THE MOUNTAIN WAS JUST WIDE enough for Silas and the horses to walk single file. The air was cool and sharp, and they could see their breaths puffing with every step. The little group climbed for an hour, and the horses began to get thirsty. Raja's legs were very tired, and he was just about to tell Greybelle he could go no farther when they reached the mouth of a large cave. The opening was so large it could easily accommodate the horses, and when they walked through it, they were astonished by the tidy home inside. It was Silas's home on the mountain, and it was a beautiful place.

The floor of the cave had been swept clean. A comfortable bed was against one rock wall, its mattress made of soft moss and dried grasses. A fire pit in the center of the cave had a stack of wood next to it, ready to light. Woven mats hung on one wall, made of different kinds of grasses, in different soft colors. Another wall had a mural painted with colorful dye, depicting fantastic scenes of animals, plants, and stars. Still another wall was lined with shelves that held clay jars, baskets of food, and dried herbs.

Silas crouched at the fire and soon had a crackling blaze going, which cheered them all considerably. He brought dried grass to the horses from a large store he had at the back of the cave. He showed them where a trickle of a stream ran down the side of the cave in a crack in the rock and collected in a shallow basin before flowing down another crack and disappearing. While the horses ate and drank and warmed themselves by the little fire, Silas sat and ate his own light dinner of apples and nuts.

"We can't stay here long, my friends," he said to the horses. "After we have rested and eaten, we must press on, but it won't be too much farther now."

Greybelle lifted her head, a wisp of hay dangling from her lips. "We are ready when you are, Silas."

Another half an hour saw them all comfortably full and warmed, ready to continue up the mountain. Silas doused the fire with water from the little stream and picked up his staff.

"Shall we, my dears?" he asked. The horses followed him out of the cave.

The three of them kept climbing. They soon reached a pass below the summit of the mountain. The deep cut in the jagged rock was surprisingly sheltered from the hard winds that blew over their heads. They traversed the pass easily and came out on the other side, reaching another ledge that overlooked the valley below.

Here the wind found them again and blew hard about their ears, tossing the horses' manes and Silas's long braids. Stronger gusts struck them from in front, making it hard for them to catch their breath. The clouds gathered overhead, building tall, dark ramparts in the sky. Small specks of rain began to strike their faces. Silas surprised the horses by sitting down amidst all this and closing his eyes.

Greybelle and Raja huddled closer to the rock wall and waited, braced against the elements. They trusted the old man but were frightened to stand in such an exposed spot on the mountain. Silas continued to sit still while the wind and rain struck his face and his clothes. Rumbling clouds overhead turned white as lightning rippled through the sky. Another rumble answered from below their feet.

The horses trembled. The entire world seemed to vibrate around them, from the clouds to the earth. The rain stopped, but the wind continued, and Silas laid his hands upon the ground.

The clouds rolled past the mountain, pushed by the strong winds. The wind suddenly became warmer and softened. Here and there a beam of sunlight broke through to dapple the valley floor below in moving emerald patches. A light rain still fell here and there alongside the sunbreaks. The wide, misty swaths drifted away over the valley.

The thunder ceased, and the earth finally stopped trembling. The horses were greatly relieved when Silas opened his eyes. He got to his feet, smiling. "We must go down," he said, coming to the horses and patting them reassuringly.

"What has happened?" asked Greybelle.

"Wy'east has advised us to take cover."

"Take cover? Take cover from *what*?" asked Greybelle. Raja snorted fearfully—he did not want any more noise and frightening rumbles.

"Only from his great strength," said Silas. "But we will be safe, you will see. Come."

Silas crossed the ledge to where a narrow trail wound down among the rocks. The horses followed him with some trepidation, but having no alternative, they made their way carefully down the north side of the mountain.

After an hour of descending the narrow trail through the rocks, they came out in a place dense with pines. Here, Silas finally motioned for them to stop. "Only a little farther, my dears. Can you continue?" he asked.

Greybelle was nearly exhausted and Raja the same. Both horses felt the strain of the journey, but neither had any intention of giving up. There was far too much at stake. Greybelle nickered at Silas agreeably, and Raja surprised them both by bugling quite enthusiastically that yes, he was ready!

Silas laughed and patted the old gelding on his neck. "You're a good soldier."

They continued until they reached the edge of the trees. Here the man and two horses stopped short and took in the awe-inspiring scene before them. Below was a deep gorge, carved into the rocks over millions of years by the Columbia River tumbling its endless, ice-fed waters to the sea. The sides of the gorge were littered with enormous boulders, making even the banks of the river impassable.

Silas was silent, gazing north across the water. Greybelle looked too and realized with a small shock that she was looking at the lands of her ancestors. On the other side of the great gorge began the northlands of old, and beyond those distant hills, shadowed and purple, lay her family's birthplace, the Valley of Bree.

The gray mare felt a deep yearning well up inside her at the thought of her home, and before she could help herself, a long, tremulous whinny started somewhere inside her stomach and burst forth, sending Greybelle's longing into the void. She stood trembling as her own voice echoed across the empty space, ears pricked forward. But there was no answer.

"We must take cover," said Silas. "Come."

Greybelle turned reluctantly away from the cliff and followed Silas and Raja back under the trees. They stopped in a small clearing well away from the chasm. Silas advised the horses to stand firmly on the ground and not to be frightened, whatever happened. They would be safe; Wy'east would protect them.

"What's going to happen?" asked Greybelle nervously, looking around.

"Something wonderful," Silas said mysteriously.

Greybelle and Raja stood expectantly, waiting for whatever was so wonderful to begin. All was still and quiet around them except for the buzz of insects and the distant call of a bird. Then, as if hushed by the same command, all sounds ceased, and an unnatural stillness spread across the mountainside. It was as though everything on the mountain was poised for something—waiting, not knowing why—and before they could wonder any longer, it began.

A deep vibration tickled the bottom of every paw, foot, claw, or hoof on the mountain. The vibration became a rumble that they could hear, as well as feel. Birds flew off the trees with frightened cries and the horses snorted nervously, their ears laid back. They had had enough of this kind of rumbling of the earth!

"Don't worry!" called Silas to them. He was holding on to a young tree as the ground beneath him began to move,

threatening to throw him off his feet. "Just watch out for—"
Bits of rock and earth began to tumble past them, one striking
Silas on the leg. "Ouch!" he said, then added ruefully, "*Rocks!*"

The earth gave a tremendous groan and bucked underneath them. Greybelle and Raja were tumbled to the ground
where they lay awkwardly, their legs splayed, thinking it best
to stay down on this tossing earth rather than risk being
thrown about. They didn't know what the old man had been
thinking, perhaps he was insane after all, for this was *not* wonderful—this was not wonderful at all!

All around them the mountain was in motion. The stands
of pines swayed back and forth like dancers, waving their
limbs up and down as though they were cheering the mountain on. Bits of tree limb and twigs snapped and fell, raining
down on the forest floor. More rocks tumbled past the horses,
and a few frightened rabbits followed, dashing down the side
before taking refuge in the roots of a tree.

Now the great mountain seemed to rouse itself and lift its
shoulders into the air. The rumbling became a frightening roar
as piles of earth cascaded around them. Raja let out a scream
as a rock struck his hip, and Greybelle whickered back to comfort
the frightened gelding. It felt to both horses as if the forest
was shaking itself apart, and the noise was deafening. How
could Silas say they were safe? They were anything but safe on
this crazy mountain!

Silas called to them from his tree, "It's moving away from
us now!"

Sure enough, even before he was finished speaking the
rumbling lessened a bit, and the moving earth calmed beneath
them. They could hear trees falling and rocks tumbling some-

where below them, but their own patch of earth had quieted; the worst of it had moved away, toward the river.

Silas pulled himself to his feet and stood shakily holding the tree. He said to the horses still lying on the ground, "Stay here."

The old man held on to trees for support as he carefully made his way back to the edge of the gorge, where he could see the river.

Thinking she might be able to stand now that the earth had stopped moving, Greybelle tried out her trembling legs, and Raja, showing the whites of his eyes, did the same. The old gelding limped from where he had been struck by the rock, but it was only a bruise. Though they could still feel the rumbling of the earth, it was apparent that the worst of the upheaval was safely away from them now, and the horses made their way to where Silas was standing.

A giant mudslide had ravaged the side of the mountain. To their right, where they had come from, nothing was left except rivers of fallen trees, wet earth, and tumbled boulders. Even as they looked at the wide swath of destruction, more earth moved past them, cascading to the river below. A huge boulder crashed down, and another. The man and the horses watched the boulders fall.

But what was that? There was movement—something was alive among the rocks down there. What was it? The horses strained their eyes to see.

It was bears. A group of black bears were there, moving about among the tumbled rocks. The horses did not understand what they could be doing. They were not running from the falling boulders; they did not even seem surprised that the mountain was shaking, and the earth falling. The bears seemed to be taking *positions* along the river. And then Greybelle and Raja could not believe their eyes.

As the boulders fell, the bears rushed forward to meet them. They placed their huge shoulders against the rocks and rolled them. Together in teams of two and three, the bears worked to move the boulders together. They pushed and rolled the huge rocks on top of each other, and then the horses understood—the bears were building.

The bears were building a bridge.

Finally, the mountain began to calm itself. The earth gradually settled, shifting and groaning, and all the trees stopped their violent swaying. The boulders stopped falling, and after a few moments the mountainside and ravine were quiet once more.

Silas smiled. "We're still here!" he said cheerfully, dusting himself off. "I told you Wy'east would keep us safe."

Below them the scene was utterly transformed. The rocks had fallen into great piles along the river, and the bears were hard at work. As the little group watched, they organized into a highly efficient team and soon had the feet of the bridge repaired. All the materials they would need the mountain had given them, and the great bears were finishing the job.

"Is it the Bridge of the Gods?" Greybelle asked Silas breathlessly.

"It will be, once again," said Silas, emotion in his throat as he watched the great bears do their work. "A new version of it, anyway."

The stone bridge was rough but solid, the boulders piled higher and higher, until the final layer of rocks were rolled into place, their tops fitted smoothly together. It was a monumental bridge, the work of the mountain, the Stargazer, and the bears of the north. The Bridge of the Gods hadn't been crossed in three hundred years, and as the little group watched, the first bears began to cross it.

"Come, my dears," said Silas to the horses. "We must go and meet them."

When they reached the south end, Silas halted. The group of bears crossing halted too, and observed him. One bear broke away from the group and came down the rest of the way, to meet Silas at the edge.

This bear was even larger than King Auberon. He bent his huge head down and growled softly at the old man in greeting. "Stargazer."

"I am honored," said Silas humbly, bowing his head in greeting.

"I am Arthur," said the bear. "And it is *I* who is honored. I know it was you who spoke to the mountain."

"And it was you and your people that rebuilt the bridge," said Silas gratefully.

"We did our part," answered Arthur. "But we needed the mountain." The great bear shifted from foot to foot. "I have family in the south, that I want to see."

"I know them well." Silas smiled. "King Auberon is a great friend of mine. In fact, that is why we are here, Arthur. Your brothers need your help. Even now, Auberon and his family are waiting for word to go to war. And, I'm afraid that it is war they won't win, in the end, without your help. It is why I am here."

"What can we do, Stargazer?" asked Arthur.

"Gather what animals you can, and come with us," said Silas. "Spread the word that the bridge is open and get as many northern creatures to cross it as you can."

"Can you send word to my family?" asked Greybelle, gathering her courage to speak directly to the huge bear.

"Where is your family?" asked Arthur.

"They live in the Valley of Bree," answered Greybelle. "Can we go there, Silas?"

"It is too far for us to go and get back in time to Chloe," Silas said to the mare. "But we will send messengers."

Silas cupped his hands around his mouth and made a clear, low whistle. He repeated the call, and in a few moments several large mountain ravens flew up to land in the trees overhead.

"My friends!" called Silas to the ravens. "*Now* you will do *your* part! I and my friends have done what we could, the bears have rebuilt the great Bridge of the Gods, and our friend Wy'east has done his job masterfully. Now it is your turn! Fly! Fly to the north! Spread the word that the Bridge of the Gods has been repaired! *Now* is the time to come down from the hills and take back the land! Tell all who will listen to come to Fairfax! Tell them we have an army, an army of animals! Rally them to our cause, my dear ravens! In the name of King Cornix and Queen Fay, in the name of all the old ways and, in the name of the north, fly! *Fly!*"

The black rooks screeched and rose into the air. Wheeling overhead, they flew off across the river, over the great bridge of stone, and into the shadowed purpled lands to the north, cawing out the news as they flew. The little group watched the crows disappear, and then Silas knelt where he stood, and placed his hand on the ground.

"Thank you, my friend," he said to the mountain.

Then the old man got to his feet and turned to the horses. "Now we must travel back to our friends, as fast as we can."

Silas climbed aboard Greybelle's back. He bade goodbye for the time being to Arthur, who promised to follow with his people. The mare understood they had no time to waste, and moved off at a brisk trot, with Raja following. Silas the Stargazer, and the two horses traveled swiftly westward, to Fairfax.

CHAPTER TWENTY-THREE

*T*HE MORNING OF THE GALA DAWNED BRIGHT and clear. Chloe had gone to bed the night before certain she would never sleep, but the next thing she knew Mrs. Goodweather was rattling the teapot.

Now Chloe sat at the little tree house table in front of a large stack of pancakes Mrs. Goodweather had just placed in front of her, but she wasn't hungry. Nerves sat in the pit of her stomach like rocks. *Tonight is the night. Tonight is the night.*

Mrs. Goodweather read the girl's thoughts and reached across the table to gently squeeze her arm.

"There, there child. Don't fret. It will be all right. The worst they can do is discover us, and throw us out, eh? And they might not even do that. Cheer up, now, I won't let anything happen to you."

Chloe smiled back at the older woman gratefully, though she wasn't entirely convinced. If they were discovered, well . . . the hospital might very well do *more* than just throw them out.

It was early, and there wasn't much to do but wait. The Artist and Brisco had left the tree house before dawn to scout around the hospital. The pies were cooled and packed neatly in the basket Mrs. Goodweather would carry down to the hospital that evening. The two uniforms hung neatly on pegs by the door. Thanks to Mrs. Goodweather's sewing skills, the fit of each was now perfect. The black dresses, white aprons, and caps were fresh and crisp, and looked professional.

"I can't wait for Brisco and the Artist to come back." Chloe sighed.

Lord Winchfillin was still in bed. He had stayed up too late the night before, and now he sat up, rubbing his eyes.

"Is there coffee?" he croaked.

"Good morning!" Chloe said brightly.

Mrs. Goodweather chuckled. "There's a fresh pot ready for you. I'll get you a cup."

Lord Winchfillin sat up carefully, arranging his bedraggled lace and smoothing his hair, and when Mrs. Goodweather came over, accepted the proffered mug gratefully. Chloe came over to sit by his bed.

"Did you *really* meet bears?" she asked, curiously.

"Oh yes, I certainly did," answered Lord Winchfillin. "And I hope I never meet another one! However, the way things are going, I fear that may be unavoidable." He took another sip.

Chloe said excitedly, "I think they are so *majestic*, don't you?"

"It isn't the first word that springs to mind actually, no," answered Lord Winchfillin dryly.

Shakespeare jumped onto the bed next to the earl, frightening him and causing him to spill his coffee.

"My goodness!" Lord Winchfillin gasped. "A rat!"

"That's only Shakespeare," said Chloe hurriedly, blotting at the spilled coffee with a napkin. "He's my best friend!"

"*Is* he?" said Lord Winchfillin tentatively, straightening slowly back against his pillow.

"Oh yes," said Chloe, scratching the rat gently on the head. Shakespeare closed his eyes in pleasure.

"You see?" she said, continuing to scratch. "Once he decides he likes you, he'll do anything for you. He's extremely loyal."

"Well, well," said Lord Winchfillin nervously, reaching out to the rat. When it caused him no harm, the earl took courage and carefully scratched behind Shakespeare's ears, just as Chloe had done. Shakespeare surprised them both by hopping onto the little lord's lap and settling in for a good ear rub. Lord Winchfillin obliged him, only a little nervously.

The sound of feet on the ladder outside announced the return of the two men. Brisco and the Artist trooped in, greeted the others, and sat down at the little table. Mrs. Goodweather placed another platter of pancakes on the table. The little tree house smelled deliciously of maple syrup and firewood, coffee, and a hint of the sea that the new arrivals brought in with them.

Mrs. Goodweather hung her apron on the back of a chair and sat down. "Now, just to make sure we all know what we're doing, let's go over it one more time?" she said, looking around the table, and they all agreed.

The Artist began. "Brisco and I go up the hill and find the animals that Silas sent from the mountain—Brisco says he knows where they are."

He looked at the carpenter, who nodded back. "The crows will lead us."

"And, once we find the animals, we wait for your signal," the Artist concluded.

Mrs. Goodweather picked up the thread. "Right. Meanwhile, Chloe and I will get into our disguises, and take the pies down to the back door. Hopefully, we can blend in with the other workers, and find our way to the dining room. Then we will serve the pies. That's when we'll send the signal."

"That's when I will send it, you mean!" said Lord Winchfillin, seeming delighted to stay in the tree house to play his part. "You will wave the white tea towel, and I will send the crow to Brisco and the Artist!"

"That's it," said Brisco.

"And then we bring the animals down," said the Artist.

"Yes, you bring the animals," said Mrs. Goodweather.

"Will we be able to control them?" asked Lord Winchfillin.

"No, of course not," said Brisco. "That is the whole point. They won't be controlled, but don't worry—we will be safe. Animals for the most part are far more loyal than humans. They know we are on their side. We have nothing to fear from them."

Lord Winchfillin looked skeptical but said nothing.

Chloe said softly, knowing it made all the difference in the world, "We are known."

They all looked at each other silently. That was the plan, and beyond that, there was no planning. Nobody could know what would happen after that.

"Keep in mind, Silas ought to be arriving any time now," said the Artist. "I don't think we should think too far ahead or worry too much . . . yet."

"The worst part is waiting," said Chloe, feeling the butterflies in her stomach.

"Agreed," said the Artist, wiping the last of the pancake

crumbs from his beard with a large handkerchief. "In fact, I think it's time for us to get moving?" He looked at Brisco. "Don't you?"

Brisco nodded and rose from the table. "Yes, it's time we got up the hill and found out what's going on up there, if there are any messages yet from Silas. But don't worry, we will be ready when the signal comes. And you can send a crow with any messages, any time. But we do need to get going."

The two men put on their coats again. Chloe jumped up and hugged the Artist tightly. "Be careful, dear Artist!" she said.

"Of course, dear child," said the Artist, hugging her back. "And you do the same." He added, "I would worry more if you weren't in the best possible hands. Mrs. Goodweather will look out for you. And you for her, I'm sure!"

"I'll see you soon," promised Chloe. "And just think, we'll see Greybelle again soon, too!"

The Artist shook Mrs. Goodweather's hand, slung a bag of provisions over his shoulder, and went out the tree house door. Chloe and Mrs. Goodweather went out on the porch to watch them go.

Outside, Brisco looked up to the sky and whistled. A crow appeared and landed on the carpenter's arm. Brisco said something to the crow, and it squawked before rising into the air, and flying off toward the north. The carpenter doffed his cap in farewell, and the Artist waved, then they turned to follow the crow.

For those at the tree house, the day wore on tediously. Waiting to do something difficult can be more difficult than doing the task itself. Those left behind busied themselves with jobs they had already done. Mrs. Goodweather checked every stitch on the uniforms and packed and repacked the pies in her basket. Chloe watched the back of the hospital and called out the arrival of every new van or wagon with gala supplies.

Lord Winchfillin spent the morning snacking on cold pancakes and sharing them with Shakespeare, who had taken a liking to the little lord. After they'd eaten all the pancakes, the earl and the rat went for a stroll around the base of the tree house together, Lord Winchfillin stopping here and there to point out different flowers he knew to Shakespeare, who rode companionably on his shoulder. It was almost like old times when the rat used to ride in Chloe's pocket through the gardens of Ashton House.

Finally, the long afternoon came to an end, and shadows fell across the ground. Chloe, Mrs. Goodweather, and Lord Winchfillin sat on the tree house porch and watched with growing nerves as a long line of wagons arrived at the back of the hospital to begin unloading party supplies. A host of delivery men began bringing in food, and people moved freely in and out of the big back doors.

It was time to get dressed. Chloe and Mrs. Goodweather went into the tree house to put on the uniforms. Though their hands shook, they zipped each other up and stood back to admire the effect. Mrs. Goodweather picked up the basket full of pies and draped a fresh white towel over the top.

"Well! If we don't look like we belong there, I don't know

chamomile from a chameleon." She nodded at Chloe in satisfaction, and they went back out on the porch.

Below, the hospital was also transformed. Lit by a hundred candles twinkling from the windows and lining the drive, it looked like a different place entirely. No ambulances were in sight now, being hidden away for the occasion. Earlier that day the hospital staff had hastily erected a wooden barrier that shunted the people waiting in line aside, hiding them from view. It would not do to have the disheveled bunch visible to the arriving dignitaries—nothing could disrupt the magnificent events of the evening—so the hospital hammered the wooden wall into place and covered it in festive bunting. A brass band was placed at the doors to cover any noise the crowd might make. Now, just before the gala was to begin, the hospital looked magnificent, dressed for a party, and not at all the place of horrors it had been only hours before.

Wagons were still arriving at the back doors as Chloe and Mrs. Goodweather prepared to descend. A cart of black-coated musicians arrived, and they climbed out with their instruments, and went up the steps into the hospital. Another cart with a stout chef and three sous-chefs pulled up, the first chef shouting at the others in French.

Chloe watched all this with her heart in her throat, thinking *What if I ruin this somehow? What if I let everyone down?* She couldn't bear that. She took a breath and gathered her courage. The plan *must* succeed, but it wouldn't succeed if they didn't get started.

Mrs. Goodweather gently touched Chloe's elbow. "It's time to go down, dear."

CHAPTER TWENTY-FOUR

*T*HE ARTIST SAT ON A FALLEN TREE HIGH ON the hillside. His legs dangled over the massive root system that rose like a wall from the forest floor. He shifted his seat, trying to get comfortable. It had been a very long day. Tired of waiting, he and Brisco were in the middle of a checkers game. The board was scratched into a piece of bark and the checkers themselves were rocks and pinecones. Brisco cackled triumphantly as he jumped three of the Artist's pinecones and took them.

The Artist complained, "That only happened because I'm distracted."

"But it happened," answered Brisco, grinning.

After the two men had left the tree house that morning, they had followed the crow, and had no trouble finding the clearing on the hill where the animals were gathering. It wasn't that far of a hike, and they began to see signs before they reached the clearing.

As they approached, they were surprised by the sight of a large white deer stepping out of the trees to greet them. It was

Afra, come to escort them to the clearing. She could not speak to the men, but they remembered the white deer from the animal council, and after a wordless greeting, followed her to the meadow.

Waiting there was a gathering that looked very much like the meeting on the mountain. Wolves, bears, foxes, herds of deer and elk, several mountain lions, a handful of lynx, and hundreds of smaller animals waited uneasily in the clearing. Flocks of crows, jays, robins, starlings, and finches perched in the trees, nervously rustling their wings and shifting about for space. Several dozen hummingbirds buzzed their wings anxiously, annoying the others by asking repeatedly where they should go.

There was nowhere to go just yet. Brisco explained the plan to the crows, who conveyed it to the other animals. The time to attack would come at the *end* of the dinner. That was when the pies would be served. They had to wait for the signal. And they were all waiting for Silas the Stargazer, but no one knew when, or if he would come. The clearing and the forest surrounding it was filled with tension as the animals continued to wait, their nerves stretching to the breaking point.

As afternoon deepened into dusk and the light began to fade, the rustlings and murmurings increased. A feeling of fear began to flow through the meadow as the animals worried the word would never come.

❧

BRISCO AND THE ARTIST HAD LONG SINCE FINISHED their checker game, and they stood together, watching the sky, waiting along with the rest, for the signal.

Suddenly Brisco shouted. "*There!*"

A crow was coming. It was King Cornix, who landed on a tree and cawed down to them urgently.

Brisco listened intently, then turned to the crowd in the meadow and called out, "My friends, we have just heard from King Cornix himself—*Silas is on his way!*"

A great cheer came up from the meadow. Silas was on his way! Silas was coming! Soon now, it would all begin. How long would it take him to get there? Would they wait for him before going down? The chatter in the meadow grew, but no one had the answers. They looked to Brisco, who conferred with King Cornix.

Brisco waited a moment for the noise to subside and called out, "If the call comes before Silas gets here, we must be ready to move without him!"

An uneasy rumble broke out from the crowd. What did the man say? Not wait for Silas? But they needed him, didn't they? He was bringing help. Without Silas, were there enough of them to do the job? Confusion broke out in the clearing, which threatened to turn into a nervous panic, as the animals growled and barked and roared at each other. If the call came, they did not want to wait. Why should they? Why should they listen to *this* man, at all?

Brisco hurried on, raising his hands to calm the crowd. "We might fail without Silas, it's true! But we will *surely* fail if we miss the signal, so we must be ready to move, with or without the Stargazer!" he called out urgently. "We've come this far, we have to follow through! We can't wait—it is up to us, my friends. Silas will come, help will arrive to fortify us—but we may need to move out before they get here, that is all."

The animals stopped grumbling; there was sense in what he said.

"Now, tell me," said Brisco, knowing they needed unity in this important moment. "Are you with me?" He spread his arms wide. "Are you ready to do what you have to do to protect your lands? Your families? Are you ready to fight?"

The assembly of animals responded with an overwhelming explosion of noise.

They could understand this. They did not *want* to wait. They were ready—it was why they had come! The rabbits shrieked, and stamped their back feet on the ground, the foxes barked, the mountain lions roared, the crows squawked, the jays screeched, and all two dozen hummingbirds rose high in the air, buzzing in circles, delirious with excitement.

King Auberon drowned them all out with his roar, rising to his full height, his shaggy fur dropping pieces of pine, ferns, moss, and more dead bees as he swatted the air with his huge front paws. The other bears joined him, and they made a truly fearsome sight. As they stood on their hind legs and moved from side to side, a throbbing hum seemed to rise from the bears as they started to growl deep in their chests. Then, growling, swaying, and beating a rhythm on the earth with their huge feet, the bears began to dance. They formed a circle and touched front paws, moving from side to side. Eerily, the huge bears danced together, gracefully, growling their deep, wild song.

The other animals were transfixed by the bear's dance. It

was a war dance, and it spoke about the ancient things—birth, death, the earth, the rain, and the sun. The bears' dance shook the ground as the bears' feet pounded it, but it made the animals' hearts light. After a few minutes of this, the bears dropped again to all fours, and the meeting was adjourned.

Everyone felt a renewed sense of optimism and excitement. They would go when the crow came. Now that they knew Silas the Stargazer was on his way, each animal felt a surge of new hope. Big or small, bear or mouse, mountain lion or hummingbird, each creature felt the strength and alliance of the others, and the importance of what they were about to do. It was a question of life or death, there was no doubt about it. And they wouldn't give up without a fight.

CHAPTER TWENTY-FIVE

CHLOE FOLLOWED MRS. GOODWEATHER DOWN the tree house stairs. They had waited so long for this moment, and it was finally here. She had expected to feel terrified, but as soon as her feet touched the ground, the girl felt a strange sense of calm. She followed Mrs. Goodweather down the little path toward the hospital, with Shakespeare safely hidden in her pocket.

Lord Winchfillin watched them go from the tree house porch. Chloe looked back at him once, and he lifted his hand in a small wave. She waved back, and then turned to hurry down the path behind Mrs. Goodweather.

Pausing at the edge of the trees, Mrs. Goodweather adjusted Chloe's collar, and straightened the towel on the basket, and they both took a deep breath before stepping out into the road. Walking briskly to the back steps of the hospital, they mustered as much professional poise as they possibly could, trying to look as though it were perfectly natural to be walking out of the trees holding a basket covered with a tea towel. No one took any notice of them.

Several wagons were pulled up near the doors, parked along the back of the building, and at least a dozen people were helping unload them and take the goods inside. Chloe and Mrs. Goodweather had no trouble joining the group and made their way quickly up the back steps. As they stepped through the doors, a sharp voice caught them.

"*You!*"

Chloe and Mrs. Goodweather froze.

A tall, thin man stood behind them. He held a clipboard and a pen. "Are you from Belhorn, Buddly, and Batts?" he demanded, peering at the clipboard, and then at them.

Chloe gulped. Mrs. Goodweather answered for them both. "Yes sir, that's right," she said. "We're here for the gala."

The man ordered, "Well, take that basket into the kitchen and report at once to Mrs. Harold, the cook. Hurry up, you're late, the dinner is about to begin!"

Chloe, who had been certain they had been discovered before they could even get inside, could not believe her ears. *He believed them!* In her relief she barely remembered to nod politely at the man, but Mrs. Goodweather steered her firmly to the left, following another worker carrying a bundle of bread loaves, toward the kitchen. Weak with relief at passing this first test, Chloe hoped fervently that the cook wouldn't ask too many questions. Suddenly it seemed the plan was more complicated than she had anticipated, and the goal—the dining room—was still very far away.

Happily, Mrs. Harold was so busy and overwhelmed in the kitchen that she asked no questions at all, and merely set the two to work chopping vegetables. And they worked hard. For the next half an hour, Chloe and Mrs. Goodweather did whatever they were told. They carried food, crates of wine, set out dishes, and polished silverware. After that Mrs. Harold ordered them to chop up a pile of apples. Mrs. Goodweather winked at Chloe as she picked up one of the long silver knives and began to chop so expertly the cook stopped by to praise her work. Chloe giggled. If only Mrs. Harold knew who she was praising!

The pies were safely hidden in their basket, stowed in a corner, under a table. Mrs. Goodweather kept a lookout for a spare silver tray on which to serve the pies. All of the food being served came out on the same silver dishes, and they would have to have one for the pies. The trouble was, there were none. All the silver was kept in a locked room, opened now for the dinner, but guarded closely. Each piece was counted as it was used, and there were no spare trays lying around. Mrs. Harold had told the footman exactly how many dishes were needed, and he would have to request her permission to hand out any more.

Mrs. Goodweather finished each task the cook set for her in record time, but Chloe could tell that she was becoming distracted by the problem of the silver tray. While thinking over the matter, Mrs. Goodweather forgot herself momentarily, and absentmindedly carved an apple she was chopping into an exquisite rose. Chloe cleared her throat warningly as Mrs. Harold approached, and Mrs. Goodweather, realizing her mistake, quickly chopped the rose up into small pieces. It would not do to attract unwanted questions or attention—it could derail their entire plan.

Inside the dining room the dinner was beginning. The first courses were being carried out, but Chloe and Mrs. Goodweather worked on in the kitchen for Mrs. Harold. Finished with chopping, she gave them the task of setting the servants' table, where after the party ended the workers would gather to eat leftovers from the feast, a rare treat.

As Chloe and Mrs. Goodweather laid the long wooden table with dishes and cutlery, they had to pass the pantry where the silver was kept. A sharp-eyed footman guarded the door. Mrs. Goodweather suddenly had an idea.

She said to Chloe under her breath as they carried glasses to the table, "The next time we come in here, drop something. Break it."

"What?" asked Chloe, startled. "Why?"

"You're creating a distraction, child. Make sure it breaks."

"But—" Chloe started to protest.

"Don't worry dear, I'll do the rest," Mrs. Goodweather assured her.

They went back to the kitchen for the rest of the dishes, and when they passed by the silver pantry, Chloe did as Mrs. Goodweather said and dropped one of the china cups she was holding. It shattered, sending shards of glass all over the corridor and causing the footman to cry out in dismay.

"Idiot girl!" he barked at her, coming forward and seizing her arm. "What's wrong with you? That will come out of your pay! Clean this up immediately!"

Chloe sank to the ground and meekly began picking up the pieces of glass. Mrs. Goodweather joined her, apologizing as she did. "Sorry sir, she's new, sir. I'll help."

The footman angrily kicked glass out of his way, and told them to hurry up, they would create an obstruction in the corridor. Already other servants were hurrying past them, crunching over the broken glass.

Mrs. Goodweather kept sweeping the floor, all the while inching closer to a stack of trays she spied just inside the silver cupboard door. When the footman bent to sign a bill brought by an errand boy, his attention was momentarily distracted and quick as a wink Mrs. Goodweather snatched a tray off the pile and hid it under her apron, returning to her sweeping just as the footman turned around and glared at her.

"Aren't you finished yet?" he barked.

"Pardon, sir!" said Mrs. Goodweather humbly, bowing her head. "I was just cleaning up the glass, sir, so you wouldn't cut yourself, sir."

"Well get out and get back to your duties!" barked the footman, turning away.

Mrs. Goodweather and Chloe returned to the kitchen, chuckling triumphantly. It wasn't much, but they finally had their tray on which to serve the pies. Now they just had to wait until the dessert course, and then find a way to slip into the dining room. The hardest part was still ahead of them, but getting the tray had been critical, and they both felt greatly encouraged. Now if they could only get the tray of pies to the right place, at the right time!

CHAPTER TWENTY-SIX

*T*HE DINNER WENT ON AND ON. CHLOE and Mrs. Goodweather were set to washing dishes the minute the first course was over, and they were kept busy. As quick as they were filled and carried up the stairs, empty dishes began to come back to the kitchen, and the piles grew higher and higher. The two scrubbed as fast as they could, but after the fifth course they began to despair that they would ever have the opportunity to slip out of the kitchen, and into the dining room.

After the eighth course was served, Mrs. Goodweather looked at Chloe and said with a steely determination, "We must find a way in."

"My feet are killing me!" A harsh voice made them both jump. A maid was sitting nearby on a bag of potatoes, her face red and perspiring. She had pulled off her shoe and sock and was examining angry blisters on her toes. "I don't know how I'm going to go in there again, carrying those heavy trays!"

This was her chance and Chloe leapt upon it. Wiping her hands quickly on her apron, she turned to the maid and said brightly, "You sit here. *I* would be happy to serve for you!"

The maid looked at Chloe in surprise for what seemed like a long time, and the girl grew afraid. *Did the maid just notice that I'm only a child? Have I just made a fatal mistake?*

Chloe's heart started beating again when the maid answered gratefully, "That would be wonderful, thanks!"

Before she knew it, Chloe was being handed a fresh white apron and given a silver tray covered with iced biscuits to take up to the dining room. She and Mrs. Goodweather looked at each other with wide eyes, unable to say all the words they wanted to. Mrs. Goodweather could only whisper to Chloe as she joined the others, "Look for the main table, so we'll know where to put the pies!"

There was no more time to speak as Chloe joined the line of servers moving up and down the stairs leading to the dining room. Coming out of a swinging door behind a line of other serving girls, she suddenly found herself thrust into a world of light, color, smell, and sound.

All around her the great room was sparkling, alive with music and full of the delicious, savory smells of the magnificent dinner which had finally been eaten. Chloe hesitated, looking around her in wonder. She stumbled a bit on the edge of the thick carpet, and the girl behind her hissed angrily, "Watch it! Hurry up!"

She moved forward, holding her tray as steadily as she could. It would not do to spill the biscuits and get sent downstairs again. She might never find a way to come back up. Chloe carefully put one foot in front of the other and at the same time tried to see which table her target with the pies would be.

It wasn't hard to spot. At the far end of the room was a long table set up on a dais. Sparkling gold candlesticks and enormous urns of fruit marked it as the most sumptuous table in the room, and obviously set for the most important people at the gala, and the people sitting around it announced their supreme importance with their expensive clothing and flashing jewels.

Surely that is the one! thought Chloe.

By this time of the evening, everyone was full of rich food and drink and were feeling quite expansive. The men lit up cigars and leaned back in their chairs to give their bellies more room; the ladies drank sherry, fanning themselves to deflect some of the cigar smoke.

The level of noise in the hall rose as the diners finished their dinners and pushed back their chairs in anticipation of dessert. Chloe placed her tray of iced biscuits down on a sideboard where the other girls put theirs and where huge silver urns holding hot coffee stood waiting to be served. The room was hot with so many people and foods, and the air had a blue haze from the cigar smoke.

The orchestra played on, and the music swelled along with the laughter of the guests who were drinking large goblets of sweet port wine. Candles sparkled everywhere, burnt halfway down, melting wax onto the white tablecloths that bloomed with baskets of fruit and flowers. The walls were hung with garlands of pine that added their aroma to the air. Chloe felt light-headed from all the sensations around her. Horrified, she felt a wave of nausea rise as she breathed in cigar smoke and the sweet smell of flowers. She shook her head, trying to clear it. She had to get the tray of pies from the kitchen, now!

Chloe jumped when the head footman ordered her to go back downstairs and get another tray of food. She hurried to the door of the hall and descended the stairs to the kitchen, looking wildly about for Mrs. Goodweather.

"*Ahhh!*" Chloe stifled a scream when someone grabbed her by the shoulder, and pulled her out of the busy corridor.

"Shhhh! It's only me!" Mrs. Goodweather was beaming at her, and holding the silver tray with the pies arranged neatly.

"Quick! Now is our chance!" She handed it to Chloe. "Do you know who to serve them to?" she asked anxiously.

"I think so," whispered Chloe, her teeth suddenly chattering. Her nerves were beginning to fray, and she struggled to get control of herself. She bit down on her tongue to stop her teeth from chattering and forced herself to focus. There was no room for error. She had to get this right!

"Good girl," said Mrs. Goodweather, pushing her gently toward the dining room door. "Now go get 'em. OH!" Mrs. Goodweather broke off as a man stepped in front of them.

"Just *what* do you think you're doing?" demanded the man angrily. "*You're* blocking the passage"—he glared at Chloe—"and I don't think *you're* supposed to be here at all!" This was directed to Mrs. Goodweather, whose apron was still dripping wet from the sink.

"No sir!" said Mrs. Goodweather, bobbing her head and retreating. She gave one meaningful look back at Chloe as she hurried back toward the kitchen.

"Get going, girl, into the dining room with those."

Under the footman's outraged glare and finger pointing the way, Chloe walked through the dining room doors, and moved steadily toward the table at the end of the hall. It was now or never.

CHAPTER TWENTY-SEVEN

LL AROUND HER THE WORLD THROBBED with sound and light. Chloe could barely hear it through the pounding of her own ears. Amidst the wild revelry, Chloe walked with measured steps toward her goal. The room echoed with talking, pierced occasionally by the laughter of those already deep in their cups of wine, but to Chloe it was as if all sound had been muted. She heard nothing, knew nothing of what was being spoken, as she gripped her tray and made her way to the table on the dais.

And then she was there. She halted, her heart pounding, next to the chair of a large, red-faced man in a black tuxedo who was waving a huge cigar in the air and telling a story. Chloe felt as though she were in a dream as she forced herself to bend forward and carefully place the tray upon the table.

Through the haze her ears caught the words ". . . grabbed him, gassed him, and threw him in the back! That was the last time he ever said 'please'!"

The company erupted in raucous laughter, and Chloe's heart pounded. Taking a step back from the table, she felt as though she were underwater. Everything was moving in slow motion around her. The scene was surreal, and the people were like laughing clowns—the big man's mouth was a horrible red hole as he opened it to laugh, spraying little pieces of food as he laughed. Chloe felt nauseous. For a horrified moment she thought she might faint, and gulped some air, trying to steady herself. She must *not* faint! She stood staring down at the two neat rows of pies.

"Eh? What's this?" demanded the big man, taking notice of the girl still standing next to him. Chloe snapped out of her fog and felt the shock of panic flow through her veins as she thought desperately of what to say. She hadn't counted on speaking to anyone! She forced herself to open her mouth, realizing that suddenly, horrifyingly, everything hung on her answer.

"Uh . . ." She stopped, hoping the other servers would not hear.

"Yes? What is it, speak up, girl!" the man demanded.

Chloe pushed the words out of her unwilling lips. "Uh, well sir, these are special pies, baked . . . for our most honored guests."

"Special, eh?" said the big man shrewdly. "Well, well, and what makes them so *special*, might I ask?"

The table quieted, waiting for Chloe's answer. She did not know what to say. This was not in the plan. For an awful second it seemed the jig was up. She would ruin everything by giving the wrong answer. Oh, *why* did she have to use the word "special"? What could she possibly say *now*?

Out of the corner of her eye, Chloe noticed Mrs. Good-weather standing next to the head footman by the door to the kitchens. He was speaking to her angrily. As Chloe watched, stalling for time, Mrs. Goodweather said something to the footman, and they both turned and looked straight at Chloe. She saw the footman's face get very angry and he started toward her. Chloe knew she had only seconds before she would be removed. There was no time left.

She blurted out, "They are good fortune pies, sir, believed to bring the eater much luck and prosperity."

There was a long second's silence as the man looked stonily back at her. Chloe had a horrifying feeling that he saw right through her lie. The jig *was* up. The footman was almost upon them, and she braced herself for his angry grasp. She felt sick. Their plan had failed.

But the big man burst out laughing again. His red mouth opened even wider, he guffawed, he wheezed, and then he *roared* with laughter, slapping his thigh and spewing out more bits of food on the table. The guests around him nervously broke into their own hilarious peals of laughter mirroring his, at the same time watching him closely to know when to stop. There was a palpable tension in the smoky air as everyone waited to see what the big man would say.

"Good *fortune*, eh? Luck and *prosperity*? Well, ho ho ho, we could always use *more* of that, eh? Am I right? Hoo, hoo, hoo!"

The man leaned back in his chair for more room to laugh, and the table laughed along with him.

This was none other than Mr. Gog, and he pounded his meaty hand down on the table, tossing embers and ash on the cloth. His cousin Mr. Magog did the same, and then at the same time, they both reached out and snatched up a pie. Mr.

Gog reached out his other hand and snatched up another pie. He always wanted more than his cousin.

Chloe's heart seemed to stop as she watched in utter fascination as the man crammed an entire pie in his mouth and started to chew.

Mr. Gog's cheeks were puffed grotesquely with pastry. His cousin's were the same, and both men crunched down happily on Mrs. Goodweather's deliciously flaky crust. Mr. Gog finished his pie first, blueberry juice trickling down his chin as he swallowed, and he reached triumphantly for his goblet of wine.

"Delicious!" Mr. Gog cried, smacking his lips. "I feel luckier already!" He stuffed the second pie into his mouth.

The other guests were reaching for their own pies now, and taking bites. Chloe stared at them breathlessly, waiting to see what would happen. The angry footman was at her elbow, and was speaking to her, but she didn't hear him. He took hold of her arm and started to pull her away from the table. Chloe did not resist but stared back at the guests who were now almost finished with their pies. It didn't matter what the footman did now, the pies had been successfully served.

Mr. Gog stopped chewing. He had gone quite still, his eyes staring fixedly ahead, and his red mouth shut. Something very strange was happening, and the other guests at the table stopped chewing too, as all eyes riveted on him.

Mr. Gog looked odd. His clothes didn't seem to fit as well as they had. His tuxedo started to swallow him as his shoulders shortened, his head shrank, and his arms receded up his sleeves. Mr. Gog's collar rose up strangely to meet his cheeks, and the hand that reached to touch them was a boy's hand. His black mustache had completely disappeared, replaced by a soft downy fuzz that Mr. Gog stroked in wonder. He looked wildly around him, not knowing his bald head had sprouted thick, dark hair. As he sat dumbfounded and confused, Mr. Gog's cheeks suddenly bloomed with a bad case of acne. He still held his cigar, but dropped it when it burnt his small fingers, and then, confused and frightened, Mr. Gog began to cry.

Some guests sitting near him screamed. Others knocked over their chairs leaping to their feet to get away from this terrifying spectacle. Shouts of alarm rippled through the room as everyone realized Mr. Gog was not the only one transforming. Mr. Magog went through adolescence in a flash and was now a child of about three, sitting in a pile of his grown-up clothes. *All* of the guests that had eaten the pies were turning into children.

The footman released Chloe and they both watched in astonishment. When Mr. Gog started to cry, Chloe started to giggle uncontrollably. It was too absurd! She couldn't believe what she was seeing! Some of the guests had trouble seeing over the edge of the table! They were like children playing dress-up in their parents' clothes!

The ladies' wigs, hair pieces, and sparkling combs had slid grotesquely over on their child-sized heads, their fancy dresses puffed up about their ears. Mr. Gog's wife was almost completely lost inside her huge ball gown. Confused, she started to scream, but it came out the piping cry of a child, which frightened the child lady next to her, and she also started to cry.

The husbands wailed along with their wives, though it was clear to Chloe that they didn't know why they were crying, or even why they were sitting at this table in this crowded room. They looked hot and uncomfortable, and suddenly one said, "I want *cake and lemonade!*" Some of the other transformed guests began to bang their silverware on the table. Some decided they wanted to explore and got down from their chairs. A few tripped on their clothing and lay tangled on the floor, crying.

Mr. Gog was now about the age of two, and was standing on his chair, laughing with glee. He had kicked off his pants and stood bare-bottomed, his shirt like a long nightdress, and his silk cravat still hanging from his little neck. Mr. Gog clapped his chubby hands in delight at the chaos in front of him. He spotted a piece of chocolate cake on the tablecloth and started to crawl toward it.

The orchestra stopped playing abruptly, and the room erupted in panic. The other guests were flabbergasted and horrified by what was happening in front of their eyes, and they all stopped eating, looking at each other fearfully. What in the world was going on?

Chloe knew it was time to send the signal. The maids and footmen were frantic. They ran to the long table to try and clean up the spilled food and drinks, and to gather the squalling children, but it was becoming impossible. The other guests began to panic as the babies crawled toward them, and leaped up from their seats.

Chloe took the opportunity to turn and run to the door of the dining room, where she found Mrs. Goodweather waiting for her breathlessly.

"We've got to send the signal!"

They grabbed hands and ran down the stairs to the kitchen, and out the open back doors. Mrs. Goodweather held up a white tea towel and waved it in the direction of the tree house. They knew Lord Winchfillin had seen them for a large black crow immediately rose in the air, and flew away, cawing loudly.

Chloe's heart was hammering in her chest with excitement as Shakespeare, who had concealed himself behind some bags of flour, jumped out to join them.

"Shakespeare, my darling," Chloe said, stroking the white rat's head. "Go now, go find Celeste. You know where she will be waiting, if she can. She will be looking for you. Bring her safely back to us. Go now, my sweet friend! And good luck!"

Shakespeare squeaked reassuringly at the girl and leapt down from the barrel to race out the door, and into the night.

Chloe and Mrs. Goodweather stood panting against the wall. They could hear screams and breaking glass coming from the dining room.

"I've got to go save those babies," said Mrs. Goodweather, shaking her head.

"*What*? Why?" asked Chloe in surprise. This was not part of the plan. "They will be fine, the other people will pick them up, surely!" she argued.

"Well . . . maybe not," said Mrs. Goodweather, looking grim. "It's very dangerous in there, and people are panicking. They might get injured! Trust me, I didn't anticipate this, but I feel kind of . . . responsible for them."

Before they could move, or say anything else, a screech and a roar in the driveway distracted them. An ambulance blowing huge clouds of smoke skidded to a halt outside the doors, its silver body scorched, broken, and mangled, but somehow still driving. The dented doors flew open and two men leaped out. One was small, with greasy hair sticking out from under a dirty cap, the other tall and thin and covered in filth.

Chloe, hidden in the shadow of the doorway, almost screamed at the sight of her hated uncle, Blake Underwood. He looked more terrifying than ever, his once-white uniform blackened and torn, and splashed with different shades of red —some dark and old, some bright and fresh.

The two men slammed their doors and lurched up the stairs of the hospital. Uncle Blake called out drunkenly, "Oy! We're *back*! And just in time for the party! YOU!" he called to a footman rushing past. "Get us some wine!"

The footman ignored them and hurried on, toward the dining room.

Bings and Uncle Blake, totally unaware of the growing crisis inside, hung on to each other to keep from falling, bitterly complaining about the footman's disrespect. Chloe and Mrs. Goodweather shrank back farther into the corridor, and the men stumbled by without seeing them.

The noises coming from the dining room were louder now, and people were running in and out of the room, shouting and calling for someone to call the police, call the fire department, call anyone! But there was no one to call, even if anyone had heeded the words. The police and fire department had long since been overrun by the ambulance drivers. There was no one to come help. They were on their own.

"What the . . . ?" It was finally dawning on Blake and Bings that something was wrong. They halted uncertainly in the doorway, Blake clinging to the frame for support and Bings clinging to him. They were only feet away from where Chloe and Mrs. Goodweather were hiding.

"What in the heck is going on here?"

The men reeked of alcohol and sweat, and Chloe held her

breath to keep from choking. She looked at Mrs. Goodweather in horror. They hadn't expected this!

A great sound of breaking glass made everyone jump. Bings and Blake lost their hold on the doorway and, cursing loudly, fell on the floor. While they struggled to rise, the noises inside increased. It sounded as though the dining room was being torn apart.

"I should get back in there!" whispered Mrs. Goodweather.

"But we must wait for Brisco and the Artist!" said Chloe, scanning the sky and hillside for any sign of the animals and men.

There was nothing. The hill and the skies remained dark and motionless. Behind them the gala was dissolving into a riot. Screams, more breaking glass, and a lone siren had started from somewhere.

Suddenly Mrs. Goodweather gave a gasp. "*Oh no!*"

Chloe whirled around and screamed at the gruesome sight of her Uncle Blake's filthy, blood-spattered face staring into her own.

"Why, if it isn't my dear little niece."

CHAPTER TWENTY-EIGHT

*C*AW! CAW! A HUNDRED PAIRS OF EYES TURNED
to the sky at the sound.

An excited murmur broke out in the trees, spreading
quickly to the clearing below.

"Is it time?"

"Do we go now?"

"Is it the signal?"

All eyes turned from the crows to the two men standing at
the edge of the trees, and a tense silence hung over the meadow.
Brisco anxiously looked to the north, but the sky there was
empty. The eastern sky was the same. There was no sign of
Silas. They could not wait for him; they had known that from
the start. There was no time to lose, the signal had come, and
they had to move *now*.

Brisco turned to the waiting crowd of animals. He opened
his mouth, but could only get out the word "NOW!" before the
rest of his words were drowned out by the animals as they
leaped to their feet and cheered. *At last!*

"The signal has come!"

"Onward! Onward! To the hospital!"

This rallying cry unleashed the pent-up tension in the meadow like a bomb. With a collective roar, the animals surged forward, jumping over each other in their frenzy. Brisco and the Artist were quickly swept up in the throng and could barely keep their feet as the hundreds of animals poured down the hillside toward the hospital.

Afra and her people led the charge, with more deer and elk joining them in wild bounds, flashing their white tails like flags to show the way. Mai and the wolf pack came next, silently and effortlessly loping alongside the deer, their ancient history of predator and prey forgotten, suspended in the truce that comes with a common goal.

Rabbits and mountain lions, foxes and mice, all side by side in this strange, new alliance flooded down the hill together. Remington led the rabbits like the old war hero he was, his scarred ears standing up straight and true, his old eyes clear and fearless. He was a ruthless leader and slashed at the haunches of any rabbits that hesitated. Some of the younger ones were driven nearly mad with fear, and would veer crazily into the crowd, causing others to stumble and fall. It was pandemonium, but the line never faltered.

After the rabbits came other burrowing animals, running as fast as their shorter legs could take them. A hundred raccoons skittered through the trees, a battalion of squirrels followed, chattering at the top of their lungs, and even the Badger moved purposefully through the brush, leading a large contingent of his own people. The foxes, the otters, chipmunks, mice, and voles swarmed forward together, forming a brown-and-red carpet of fur and fangs. The birds filled the trees and sky, their cries carrying the battle cry.

"Onward!"

"To the hospital!"

The bears brought up the rear. Auberon and his people were the mighty guard that would surely finish the grisly job. They would not fail. No matter what happened, even if they should ultimately lose the war, the bears knew this would be the hour of their revenge. Nobody would stop them. They would fight to the death to get it, and they were determined to take as many humans along as they could. Their eyes gleamed red with the desire to fight, to tear, to rend. King Auberon pounded his heavy paws on the ground as he ran, creating a war beat that reverberated through the legs of every creature, and made them run even faster.

This was a herd like no other on earth, and every heart within it beat hot and wild, determined to take back what was theirs.

CHAPTER TWENTY-NINE

*U*NCLE BLAKE LUNGED TOWARD CHLOE, but Mrs. Goodweather blocked his way. Cursing, Blake grabbed the woman instead and started to choke her.

His red eyes looked mad as he croaked, "Why, as I live and . . . hahaha . . . *breathe, it's . . . little . . . Clothilde!*"

Chloe screamed, "Let her go, Uncle!"

Bings danced drunkenly from foot to foot, watching this scene. "Want me to grab the kid, boss?" he asked Blake.

Uncle Blake tightened his grip on Mrs. Goodweather, and hissed at the girl, "I had a bad feeling that I might see you again. I *knew* that good-for-nothing Artist would let you go. He was a *sap!* A *wimp!* I should never have let him get away from that poker game alive!" Blake bitterly spat out these last words.

"But I have learned my lesson!" he continued with a nasty smile. "I won't let you or your old lady friend here"—he choked Mrs. Goodweather a little more—"get away this time. BINGS!" Blake shouted over his shoulder to the little man who hurried forward. "Get the mask!"

"No!" yelled Chloe.

Mrs. Goodweather gave a sudden squirm and managed to free an elbow, which she promptly shot back, punching Uncle Blake squarely in the nose and producing a spurt of red blood.

He fell back, yelling in pain and holding his nose. He pulled his hands away and looked with shock at the blood on them.

Mrs. Goodweather shot her foot straight out, kicking Blake right between the legs with her pointed black shoe. Uncle Blake went dead silent, his grimy face white under its black smears, and he fell to the ground with a thud. Bings backed away slowly from Mrs. Goodweather, and then ran from the room.

Mrs. Goodweather winked at Chloe and said cheerfully, "I played kickball when I was a girl, and I was as good as any boy."

The sound of breaking glass reminded them where they were. They saw a weird, orange glow coming from the dining room, and they smelled smoke. Fire!

"What should we do?" cried Chloe.

"I'm going back to the dining room!" said Mrs. Good-weather. "You stay here, child, and wait for the Artist and Brisco! I'll be back as soon as I can!"

Just then they felt the ground tremble. A growing rumble beneath the earth made the two women look out the back doors in alarm. The trees above the hospital were shaking, bits of earth falling from the hillside. Was it an avalanche? A landslide?

It was an avalanche indeed, but not like any they had seen before. No, this one was a wave of animals that poured down the hill and spilled out into the hospital drive. Chloe and Mrs. Goodweather, standing at the doors, saw the plunging forms of deer, the gray faces of wolves, a flash of yellow mountain lions, and a general blur of fur that was hundreds of smaller animals, all racing toward them.

King Rei and his elks led the charge, bugling as they ran, their gleaming antlers with pointed tines as sharp as knives. The elk clattered onto the hospital driveway. Then, as Mrs. Goodweather and Chloe watched in amazement, the wolves followed, leaping nimbly across the drive, then wave upon wave of smaller animals, all collecting in a great mass outside the doors, which quickly became a dangerous place as the larger animals stepped on the smaller ones.

Another little earthquake announced the arrival of King Auberon and his people. Chloe gasped as the giant bears charged out of the trees and crashed into the drive. They came swiftly to the doors, but Auberon halted in front of Uncle Blake's broken ambulance. Chloe screamed as the enraged bear swiped the car aside with one swoosh of his massive paws, sending it end over end to land upside down against the hospital wall.

Chloe clung to Mrs. Goodweather, who clung to the doorway, as the animals collected in a swirling, growling mass in front of them. What would happen now? Where was Brisco? Where was the Artist? They looked frantically for the men.

"Chloe!" They heard the Artist's voice and finally spotted him and Brisco running toward them.

"Artist! Brisco!" Chloe embraced them both, and Mrs. Goodweather said frantically, "In the dining room!"

"The pies are working!" screamed Chloe. She looked around, over the animals' heads. "But wait, where's Silas?"

"He's on his way," said Brisco.

"We can't wait for him!" said Mrs. Goodweather.

"No, we can't wait!" agreed the Artist. "Are we ready, Brisco?"

For answer Brisco turned to the animals. "Inside! Inside! To victory!" he called out. The animals roared.

Chloe and Mrs. Goodweather stepped aside quickly, and Brisco dashed through the back doors, followed by a surge of animals. The noise was deafening as elk, wolf, fox, badger, cougar, and mouse all climbed the steps and crammed through the kitchen, destroying everything in their path.

"I had no idea there were so many!" shouted Chloe over the din.

"It's a real army, that's for certain!" hollered back Mrs. Goodweather, holding her arm protectively around the girl as they stood in the relative safety of the corner of the kitchen.

"Look out!" screamed Chloe.

Auberon's massive head poked through the door, and he growled. It appeared that his shoulders were too large to enter. With an angry roar, the great bear muscled his way through, breaking a hole big enough for his body to follow.

❧

UNCLE BLAKE PULLED HIMSELF PAINFULLY TO A SITTING position from where he lay on the floor from Mrs. Goodweather's well-aimed kick. *What is this nightmare?* he whimpered to himself. *Has someone let a whole zoo go free?* From behind a cupboard Uncle Blake watched as the last of the animals passed by and the kitchen finally emptied. He tried getting up from his cramped position. He had to get out of here—this was sheer madness! Uncle Blake got to his feet shakily, turned to the doorway, and froze.

He was face-to-face with the furious red eyes and dripping jowls of Auberon. The bear was looking through the back door of the kitchen, and he chuffed dangerously at the man, spraying Blake's coat with bear snot. Auberon could smell everything about the man, and it sickened him. He smelled the man's sweat, and the tangy smell of fear. He smelled the blood on his coat, on his face, under his fingernails. Auberon had had enough. He shoved his way through the door. Plaster bits and chunks of wood exploded and rained down on the countertops. Auberon's huge black shape pushed in and rose to tower over Uncle Blake, who made a weak, strangled scream, and fainted dead away.

❧

MRS. GOODWEATHER AND CHLOE WATCHED FROM THE doorway as King Auberon shoved Uncle Blake's inert form to the side with his paw, smashing him up against the kitchen cabinets. The bear then continued through the kitchen, stepping over the rubble, and disappearing up the stairs to the dining room.

Mrs. Goodweather held Chloe's shoulder and said earnestly, "Now is your chance, dear. Run and find your mum, and look for that nice Mr. Avery too, for Celeste. I will check on the others and then come and find you. I don't think you'll be noticed much in all this bedlam."

She gave Chloe a gentle shove in the direction of the hospital patients' wing. "Through those doors at the end, I believe. Now go on, child, look around, stay hidden if you are able—I will come for you just as soon as I can!"

CHAPTER THIRTY

*C*HLOE DIDN'T NEED URGING. SHE COULD NOT wait to go look for her mother—she had been waiting so long! She dashed toward the doors, calling back over her shoulder, "Bring the Artist with you!"

"I will, child. We will both come!" Mrs. Goodweather assured her.

Chloe ran to the doors and turned to look back, but Mrs. Goodweather had already gone. She took a deep breath and pushed open the doors.

She found herself in a white, brightly lit hallway lined with more doors. The hallway sparkled and gleamed, not a thing out of place, but was strangely quiet compared with the sounds coming from the other side of the hospital—distant crashes and screams, and that ongoing siren blaring its unheeded warning. Here all was still. Not a soul moved in the corridor. Where were the patients? Where were the doctors and nurses? Had they *all* run to the dining room? The hallway gleamed quietly in front of her, neatly stocked carts against the walls, their chromed sides winking in the new electric lights.

Chloe moved slowly forward down the corridor on silent feet, hardly daring to breathe. *I can't be seen. I can't be captured!* she thought, anxiously scanning the corridor ahead. Chloe tiptoed up to one of the doors and looked through the little window. Inside the room there was an empty bed, and some sort of electric instrument next to it. She moved farther down the hall and looked through another window. Another empty bed. And another. All the rooms were empty. There were no patients here! Where *was* everyone?

Chloe reached the end of the corridor and went through yet another pair of doors. Now she was in a larger room with several tables, lined up in a row. Each table had straps hanging from it. Chloe stared at the tables. *Why would you need straps on the tables?* she wondered. *Unless you were trying to hold someone down . . . and they were trying to get up?*

Shuddering at what that could mean, she tried not to look at anything else except for the door leading out. She suddenly did not want to know what went on in this room, and she couldn't wait to get out of it. Chloe finally spotted the exit at the far side of the room and crossed quickly, still running on her toes as if afraid to put her whole foot on the floor, her feet light with fear.

But when she pushed against the door on the other side of the room, Chloe found it was locked. What would she do now? She had to get out of here. Should she go back the way she had come? Just then her attention was caught by some noises coming from the other side of the locked door.

Chloe went still to listen, but could not quite make out what the noises were. She heard some bumps, a muted clang, and then . . . *voices*! Chloe pressed her ear against the door.

Listening intently, she could tell there were several people on the other side, and they seemed to be doing something strenuous. There were several curses, and the sound of something heavy being moved; she could hear a scraping sound, and the clang of metal against metal.

A vision of that horrible door Brisco had showed her the other day suddenly rose before her. Could *that* be the door on the other side of this one? Were the people out there moving bodies out of the door *right this minute*?

Suddenly Chloe felt terribly alone, and frightened, here in a dark room designed for what purpose she could not, *would* not, imagine. She wished Mrs. Goodweather and the Artist and Brisco would come. She was only twelve years old—what could she do alone?

Tears came to her eyes and she started to breathe faster. Chloe knew she was starting to panic and that it was the worst thing she could do. Mustering all her strength, she took a deep breath to calm her nerves. She could not fall to pieces now! She would think of something; she *had* to!

Chloe looked up, and noticed a window above the door. She jumped up, excited. If she could find something to stand on, she might be able to see who was on the other side, and what they were doing! She quickly looked around the room, but there was nothing to stand on except the tables. The ones with the straps. Chloe swallowed. Well, there was nothing for it; she would just have to do what she had to do.

She pushed the table over to the door and under the window. Carefully Chloe climbed up on the table, balancing precariously. Her knees shook, which made the table wobble, and she moved excruciatingly slowly to keep from making noise, or from falling. Chloe pulled herself to her feet, and held on to the transom window to steady herself. Gingerly raising her eyes up over the edge so that only the top of her head was visible, Chloe saw something that made her gasp and jerk backward. The table immediately rolled away from the wall with a *crash* and threw Chloe to the floor. All activity on the other side of the door halted abruptly at the sound.

Chloe lay on the floor, horrified. Her heart nearly stopped when she heard the voices shout, "Open that door! Open that door or we'll open it for you!"

CHAPTER THIRTY-ONE

RS. GOODWEATHER HAD TO HURRY. So much time had already been lost, and they only had this one chance to take control while chaos still reigned in the dining room. She hoped the animals were doing their job. She had to grab the babies. And she had to grab them first! Mrs. Goodweather dashed past a nurse holding off a badger with a bedpan and into the dining room.

Inside was complete mayhem. Screaming people and animals ran about in confusion and fear. Here and there strange combinations of man and creature were locked in combat, making it a surreal sort of battlefield. Maids and nurses were running from the room, pursued by a mountain lion and two foxes. An ambulance driver fought off an elk with a silver candlestick, and an entire battalion of squirrels ran down the middle of the tables, hurling silverware at anyone within range.

Mrs. Goodweather saw the Artist standing on the table at the end of the room. He brandished a broom at two white-coated orderlies who grabbed at his legs. Next to him Brisco struggled with a footman. It looked as though he had already suffered a black eye, but even as she watched, a flock of crows descended on the footman's head, scratching at his face and beating him with their wings until he let go of Brisco and fell back.

A crash beside her made Mrs. Goodweather jump aside just in time to avoid being crushed by an elk who had fallen to the floor. She backed away as the huge animal scrambled to its feet and with an angry blast lowered its antlers and rejoined the fray. Smoke began to filter into the room, and the lights flickered overhead.

Mrs. Goodweather hurried toward the big table, her eyes searching for the children. There was no sign of them at the big table, only the remains of the overturned food and broken dishes, and she felt a stab of fear that some harm might have come to the little ones.

After all, they were no longer the greedy, evil individuals that they had been. The truth was they were now wiped clean, a fresh slate, and it really wouldn't do to let any harm come to the little tots. In fact, Mrs. Goodweather had spent some time thinking that with the right upbringing they might even grow up to be very good adults, who might even do something in the future to mend the harm they had caused in the past.

That was the future, however, and this was the present. None of that would come to pass unless she found the babies *now*. Mrs. Goodweather moved to the end of the table and looked around wildly. She didn't see the children, but she did see one of her own pies left uneaten on a tray. Without thinking Mrs. Goodweather scooped it up and put it in her pocket. Then she heard a child's cry and, looking down, spotted the white flounce of a nurse's apron peeking out from beneath the table, as well as the heels of two black shoes.

Mrs. Goodweather bent down to look under the table. There were all the babies, gathered together and hidden with two young nurses. All of them, even the nurses, were crying.

"Ach, there, there," said Mrs. Goodweather kindly, pulling her hanky out of her pocket and handing it to one of the nurses. "Don't you cry, dear. Let's get these babies out of here."

She pulled one of the babies into her own arms and managed to pat the nurse comfortingly on the shoulder at the same time.

"But *how?*" sniffled the nurse fearfully. "There are *bears* and . . . and . . . *wolves* out there! Where did they come from?" She began to sob again.

"Bears? Wolves? Pish posh, what's the big deal?" said Mrs. Goodweather airily. "They won't be a problem, I promise." She winked at the nurses. "They're friends of mine."

Incredulous, the nurses gaped back at her, but their sobs subsided.

"Hold on to those babies now, and follow me." Mrs. Goodweather picked up another baby, a large one with a wide red smile and two white teeth in the middle of it. He was quite heavy, and as she stood up, Mrs. Goodweather adjusted him awkwardly on her hip. With a baby in each arm, she looked back at the two nurses peeking out from under the tablecloth.

"You've got the others?" she called down over the din. "OK, then let's go!"

The nurses stood up from under the table, each holding two babies.

"Now!" cried out Mrs. Goodweather, spotting a break in the fighting, and the three women moved as quickly as possible across the dining room with their heavy load.

All around them, the fight raged on. The fire was now licking up the front wall of the room. More hospital workers had come from the other side, and a battalion of ambulance drivers had brought in gas canisters and masks. They were having a hard time getting close enough to the wild animals to use them, however. It is one thing to overcome a human being, especially one in cumbersome clothing, but it is quite another to grab a spitting, clawing, slippery, powerful mountain lion and put a mask over its face.

Even as they realized their masks were almost useless, the ambulance drivers began using the canisters as cudgels, swinging as hard as they could and crushing whoever got in their way. They threw the heavy metal cans at the swarms of small creatures that surrounded them, and although most of the rabbits and mice, rats and otters were nimble enough to dodge these dangerous projectiles, a few were not.

They may have had some advantages, but the animals were in no way winning the fight. They were in an alien, unfamiliar environment full of strange objects, and slick surfaces they couldn't easily navigate. The elk's cloven hooves slipped on the slippery marble floor and many fell, only to be beaten where they lay, helpless to get up.

"This way!" Mrs. Goodweather called back to the nurses, leading them along the side of the room toward the door. The babies were hard to carry; they were frightened and they struggled. Mrs. Goodweather's arms felt like lead, but she pushed on. They had almost reached the doors to the kitchen.

"Ahhhhhhhhhh!" screamed one of the nurses.

A white-coated driver had grabbed her. Another driver yanked one of the babies from her arms.

"No!" screamed Mrs. Goodweather, lunging toward them, but she was hindered by the two heavy, squirming babies in her arms. She looked around desperately for something, *anything* that might help, and spotted a she-bear standing nervously nearby. Mrs. Goodweather made a desperate whistle, hoping to get the bear's attention.

The bear had an injured paw and looked confused. When she heard Mrs. Goodweather's whistle, the she-bear looked toward her with eyes red from the smoke. As their eyes met, the bear seemed to sense a friend.

The she-bear looked as though she had had enough of this madness. She stood, shaking herself, and moved toward the drivers. They took no notice and continued to drag the young nurse and the baby away, so the she-bear attacked. Roaring her rage, she moved so fast nobody even saw the mighty swipe of her paw that deftly knocked the drivers away from the nurse and child. Unharmed, the nurse ran back to Mrs. Goodweather, who pulled her quickly to safety. Pausing at the door to the kitchen, Mrs. Goodweather looked back and made a low whistle to the bear. The bear turned away from the prone figures on the floor and followed her. Mrs. Goodweather hurried, her arms nearly numb from the weight of the heavy babies. She had an idea of where to hide them, and then she *had* to find Chloe!

Mrs. Goodweather led the nurses to the silver pantry, where she had taken the silver tray earlier in the evening. It already seemed a lifetime ago—had it only been a few hours since she and Chloe had played their little ruse on the unsuspecting footman? Little had he known what that little prank would cost him.

"Stay in here," she ordered the nurses, handing her babies to them. "You should be safe, at least for the moment."

"I will post a guard outside this door, and I promise I will be back as soon as I am able!"

The frightened nurses nodded tearfully, and held the squirming, squalling babies close.

Mrs. Goodweather stepped out of the pantry and closed the door. She said to the bear who was waiting in the hallway, "I have another favor to ask you."

The bear growled softly.

"I must ask that you guard this door. Don't let anyone in or out until I come back. Do you understand?" The bear seemed to understand what it was the woman wanted, and accepted the task with a toss of her head.

"Thank you," said Mrs. Goodweather gratefully, smoothing her skirt and tightening her apron strings. "For everything. You are a very kind bear." The she-bear just looked back at the woman and said nothing.

Mrs. Goodweather hurried away from the silver pantry. She had to go to Chloe, but she didn't want to go alone. They would need more help than one old woman could provide, and that meant going back to the dining room to find Brisco and the Artist.

The dining hall was still a war zone, and it was still unclear who was winning. There were casualties on both sides. All around the vast room, men and animal alike lay in piles, dead and wounded. Many had been felled by flying medical instruments used as weapons or knocked to the ground by the big silver canisters. The fire had spread upstairs, and was so hot that windows were shattering, and the crashes could be heard coming from the rooms above. All the while, the alarm sounded on and on, calling nobody, and only added to the mayhem. Screams of animals and of men rose over the siren, and the floors were slippery with a mixture of water, wine, and blood.

A flash of something white caught her attention, and Mrs. Goodweather saw Afra, the great doe, fighting off half a dozen ambulance drivers who threatened her with canisters and clubs pulled from their waistbands. Afra flashed out her sharp hooves fiercely, catching the drivers' coats and ripping them to shreds, sometimes catching the flesh underneath it, as was evidenced by the red stains that appeared.

King Rei appeared at Afra's side, easily tossing a driver into the air with his sharp antlers. Mrs. Goodweather crouched down, hoping desperately to catch a glimpse of her friends. She had no time to waste! Chloe needed them now!

From her place behind the pillar, Mrs. Goodweather saw a curious medical unit made up of field mice, shrews, rabbits, and squirrels who ran out to the injured, and did their best to drag them to safety. The small animals pushed and pulled and dragged whatever animal they could to the relative safety of the wall, where they administered first aid. The animals too large to move remained where they were, while the bravest of the small ones stayed with them and provided what care that they could.

Mrs. Goodweather couldn't see the Artist or Brisco anywhere through the smoke and chaos. A huge crash over her head made her scream and duck, and she was showered with silverware and utensils from a cart hurled by a bear. Mrs. Goodweather thought in a panic they might be losing the battle. They needed help. *Where* was the Artist? Where was Brisco? And *where was Silas?*

A wolf howled in pain, and Mrs. Goodweather saw that it was held down by two drivers, who were preparing to place a mask over its face. As she watched fearfully, a small, furry form flew out to the wolf, followed by others. It was Remington and a band of his rabbits. The old hare screamed a rabbit's battle cry and led his group toward the drivers, surging between their legs, tripping them, scratching them, and biting them wherever they could. With his teeth, Remington himself grabbed hold of the leg of the driver holding the mask and held fast. The driver screamed in pain and jumped around, but the old rabbit prince held on.

The room was becoming more and more choked with smoke and flame. It was difficult to see anything clearly, but Mrs. Goodweather finally spotted the Artist. He was on the staircase leading to the landing where the orchestra had been, and he was fighting off several drivers. For such a peaceful man, the Artist was a very good fighter. Despite his gray hair, he was strong—his outdoor lifestyle had toughened him—and he easily fought off the men below him on the stairs. It didn't even look like he was breathing hard as he handily swung a broomstick, dislodging two of the drivers and sending them tumbling down the stairs.

The third driver was a good fighter too, however, and he pushed back hard against the Artist, forcing him to retreat backward up the stairs, until he had reached the landing, long since abandoned by the musicians, and had nowhere else to go.

Mrs. Goodweather saw two more drivers climb the stairs. It would only be a few minutes before the Artist would be overcome. Desperately, the Artist threw chairs at the advancing drivers, but was forced backward until suddenly he was pushed up against an abandoned cello, which made an unexpectedly loud *squawk*!

"*Now* is not the time to play a tune!" called a jolly voice from nearby.

Brisco Knot stood only twenty feet away on another landing facing the Artist. He held a cable that hung from the ceiling. As they all watched transfixed, the carpenter leapt into the air. The cable caught him and swung him gracefully over the distance to the Artist's landing, where he dropped nimbly beside him.

"But you never could resist a good song!" Brisco laughed.

The Artist laughed with him. The two men faced the drivers with nothing but their fists to defend themselves.

"You take that one, I'll take this one!" called the Artist to Brisco, and he darted to the side, confusing his driver and getting a good solid punch to the man's jaw. Brisco did the same thing and his driver fell stunned to the ground. The other drivers moved in, several carrying knives picked up from the dining tables.

Caw! Caw! Caw!

A cloud of screaming crows flew through a broken window, and descended on the men fighting on the landing. They had seen their beloved Brisco in trouble. The crows fought viciously, pecking the drivers with their long, pointed beaks, beating them in the faces with their powerful wings, and ripping their clothes and skin with their sharp talons. The drivers stood no chance at all against this flying foe. They fell to the ground with their hands over the heads as the birds descended on them in a black, flapping heap.

The Artist and Brisco ran back down the stairs to where Mrs. Goodweather was crouched behind the pillar. Breathlessly the three friends took cover behind an overturned table against the wall and held a quick conference.

"Where is Chloe?" gasped the Artist.

"She is looking for her mother!" answered Mrs. Goodweather. "I must go help her! Can you come with me?"

⚹

Just as Mrs. Goodweather and the Artist were about to leave the dining room, a great cry was heard—a surprisingly loud cry, as if from a hundred throats—coming from just outside the hall. It was a swelling sound made of many voices, but not the voices of animals. It was a different sound, familiar, but strange. And so powerful! All those that fought inside the hospital heard the sound reverberating through the walls and the broken windows. *What could it be?*

It was the townspeople from Fairfax. They were breaking into the hospital. Sick and tired of being shunted outside, waiting for days in the line, hidden behind the wooden barrier, they had decided to finally take action. When the first screams could be heard, and the sound of breaking glass, the people had all looked at each other in fear. What could be happening inside? Then, when flames appeared in the windows, the line finally broke, and the people surged in one great mass to the doors, broke them open, and poured into the hospital.

Panicked by the sight of the flames, fearing that their loved ones would surely be killed by the conflagration, the throng of angry, frightened citizens shoved their way through the waiting room, picked up the front desk, and threw it aside. The stony-faced nurse had long since left her post, and there was no one to stop the crowd, so it continued its headlong flight through the double doors and into the hallways of the hospital.

The people ran swiftly through the hushed, white tiled hallways, looking through the doors and small windows for their loved ones, looking for anyone. But the rooms and halls were empty. The crowd continued its race through the corridors until it reached the east wing of the hospital, and the dining room, where it joined the already furious fight in progress.

It was hard to tell who was fighting for whom. It was no longer man against animal, now it was also man against man. Fishermen struggled with drivers, some of the women of the town stood throwing dishes, cups, champagne bottles—anything they could find—at the doctors. Some of the townspeople were so shocked at the sight of the animals they could not fight at all, but stood stock-still in horror, making them easy targets for the gas masks. It was still anyone's fight, and as the throng poured into the smoke-filled room, the Artist and the others fought and pushed their way out.

Down the stairs they ran, pausing only to gulp the fresh air that came in through the open back doors. Outside a great struggle was going on as several ambulances were trying their best to get away and a great wall of bears was preventing them. King Auberon had his great shaggy arms wrapped around the front of one ambulance, and both drivers were hanging out the front windows screaming as he lifted the entire front end of the car above his head and squeezed it, crumpling it as if it were a toy. The other bears were rocking the other ambulances back and forth, back and forth, until they flipped them completely over on their sides.

Mrs. Goodweather filled her lungs with the blessed fresh air and turned to go back inside, to find Chloe. She was halted by a tug on her arm, and she looked at the Artist who was now pointing up, toward the hill.

Squinting her eyes to peer through the smoke, past the bears and the ambulance drivers, Mrs. Goodweather saw something. Something was coming.

CHAPTER THIRTY-TWO

*T*HE HILL OVER THE HOSPITAL WAS DARK, THE pines silhouetted against the midnight-blue sky. Something was moving down the hill, but it was impossible to see what it was. Mrs. Goodweather anxiously scanned the blackness.

There. There over the trees, a silver glow.

A growing white light danced from beneath the dark trees, lighting up the forest as it approached the hospital. The brush beneath the trees began to shake and a rolling vibration made the ground tremble. Breathless, Mrs. Goodweather clutched the doorway for support. *What in the world . . .*

BESIDE HER THE ARTIST AND BRISCO WATCHED IN fascination. The forest was illuminated, and a rush of wind came blowing down the hillside, making all the tree limbs dance, and sending the last autumn leaves swirling in clouds down to the hospital where they fell thickly around the back doors.

Silver forms appeared in the light under the trees, and as the friends watched from the door, the forms became horses.

Horses! Silver horses! Iridescent in the light of the moon, a vast herd of shining horses galloped down the hill. Long manes and tails flowed together like quicksilver, making them seem like liquid pouring down on the burning hospital.

"FOR THE NORTH!" A familiar voice made the men's eyes light up, and the Artist cheered.

It was Silas! The Stargazer sat astride Greybelle, who ran at the head of the herd. The mare was utterly transformed from the horse who used to pull Uncle Blake's carriage. Her head was high, her ears laced back, and her brilliant eyes wild as she led the great herd of silver horses to the door. Silas's white hair was unbraided and swirled about him like the horses' silver manes. He rode the mare without bridle or saddle and seemed a very part of her as they raced down the hill and across the drive, skidding to a halt in front of the open back doors.

"At last!" cried the three friends at the sight of the old man and the silver mare.

"We came as soon as we could!" called out Silas from Greybelle's back.

Greybelle wheeled in an excited circle, pirouetting on her hind legs. She whinnied joyfully at the sight of her friends and looked around anxiously for Chloe. The herd of horses from the north circled nervously, eyeing the bears who had stopped rolling the ambulances at the sight of the horses.

A final clatter on the drive announced the last arrival, who was none other than Old Raja. The old gelding hopped awkwardly down the embankment and stood on his thin, trembling legs, head held high, and his eyes bright with happiness at the sight of the Artist. He whinnied loudly, and the Artist went to him, petting his old comrade's sweating neck.

"There, there old man," he said to the horse. "You made it!"

"Tell us where to go!" urged Silas from Greybelle's back.

"In there! In the dining room!" said Mrs. Goodweather pointing into the kitchen. "And take them with you!" She gestured to the bears who had gone back to happily mashing the ambulances.

Silas raised one arm as Greybelle half reared. "To arms, my friends!" he called.

The herd of silver horses answered him, their whinnies like a thrumming, melodic chord struck on strings. Greybelle reared again and Silas beckoned to the bears. "To arms! To arms! In the name of your ancestors! In the name of the north!"

Greybelle galloped up the stairs of the hospital with Silas on her back, and into the fight. Kicking and screaming, the mare fought as hard as she could, throwing drivers and doctors to the right and to the left. Behind her raced a silver wave of destruction. Driven by a hatred and distrust that ran back for centuries, the horses from the north took their vengeance on the men. They knocked them down, then bit and struck at the men with their silver hooves, cleaving their skulls and breaking their bones.

But the most chilling thing of all for the men was that the horses were *talking* as they wreaked havoc upon them. To the drivers' complete and utter horror, they could hear the horses *speak* to them as they came down in a deadly deluge. And, like their predecessors so long ago, the men could not accept this, and so they went insane, even as they fell.

Silas rode Greybelle into the battle. His long gray hair mingled with hers, and they were a silver blur as they rode through rows of drivers and doctors, mowing them down like toys. The old man had not raised a hand in anger for a century, but he didn't hesitate now. Sure-footed as a deer, Greybelle carried him where he was needed, and they joined the silver herd on the front line of the fight.

⚶

A NEW CRASH WAS HEARD AT THE DOORS OF THE hospital. The northern bears had arrived. After rebuilding the Bridge of the Gods, King Arthur and his people had followed the silver horses across it, and to Fairfax. Now they came down the hill to join their southern kin for the first time in three hundred years. The huge bears tore into the room like armored tanks. The ambulance drivers didn't stand a chance against this terrifying onslaught and ran screaming from the talking horses and bears.

Slowly, brutally, the tide finally began to turn, and the wave of animals began to turn back the men. The remaining elk, King Rei among them, formed a line, their heads lowered and their antlers making a deadly wall. They advanced on one of the last groups of drivers and forced them out of the hall.

Several foxes and the only mountain lion still alive worked together to take down two more orderlies, grabbing the gas canister out of their hands and chasing them from the room.

"All for one and one for all!"

There was Lord Winchfillin, making his first appearance astride Old Raja. The earl had been detained by a bear that had taken a dislike to the little man, and had held him captive outside, holding him to the ground with one great paw. Finally, King Arthur himself had ordered the bear to free "the small friend of Silas," and Lord Winchfillin had gotten up angrily, dusted himself off, and spied Raja, who obligingly came when called and allowed the earl to mount.

Now, finally inside and astride the old gelding, Lord Winchfillin was ready for battle. Coatless, wigless, and smeared with dirt, the little lord held a broom in one hand like a sword, and he raised it over his head as the old horse plunged forward. Raja's eyes flashed fire as he began knocking down ambulance drivers, and Lord Winchfillin looked the picture of a battle-scarred cavalryman as he rode the old gelding masterfully, using his broom to sweep aside the enemy. Raja galloped this way and that, biting at the drivers that got in his way. The old horse reared up on his spindly legs in triumph, looking for a split second almost like a magnificent warhorse, his thin red mane whipping straight up in the air.

The animals cornered the last of the drivers and forced the rest of the men out of the room. The scene they left behind was an inferno. The roof of the hospital was almost completely engulfed in flames. One end of the dining room had been reduced to rubble, the windows shattered, and holes broken through the walls by the northern bears. Crushed and broken ambulances were strewn about where the bears had thrown them. Bodies of both men and animals lay everywhere, some still groaning. People still ran here and there, trying to find their loved ones. The medic squirrels and small creatures were kept busy treating the wounded.

The west wing of the hospital had not yet been touched by

fire, and black shadows could be seen at the windows as the people searched frantically inside. A curious green light appeared at the far side of the building, pulsing in the darkness over the ocean. And though it wasn't visible from the front of the hospital, from the west side it was clear that a door was slowly starting to open.

CHAPTER THIRTY-THREE

CHLOE HEARD THE DOOR HANDLE TURN. THE people on the other side were coming through. She had nowhere to hide, and nothing to defend herself with. She backed into one of the rolling tables, frightened of who might come through that door, and not sure what she would do when they did. Chloe almost jumped out of her skin when the door *behind* her flung open instead, and a crowd of angry townspeople ran into the room.

"Where are they?" screamed one woman, rushing forward and grabbing Chloe by the arms. "Where is my daughter?"

The others swarmed forward, crushing up against the front door and inadvertently preventing it from being opened. Once the crowd heard indistinct shouts from the other side of the door and realized that there were people there, they went crazy. A collective cry of rage went up, and the mob rushed forward, wrenching at the handles themselves. As the big door crashed back, it revealed a group of doctors and drivers grouped around rows of gurneys holding unconscious patients. The doctors and drivers were armed with masks and canisters.

"Get them!" screamed an ambulance driver.

The white coats raced forward to attack. The two groups clashed, and Chloe ran past them, into the west room. All around her were gurneys holding unconscious patients. Were they unconscious? Or were they dead? Chloe began to panic as she ran back and forth, looking for her mother. She saw that some patients were still alive and taking shallow breaths, but all had been made unconscious by the gas, and they lay completely inert, their faces pale. Chloe went from gurney to gurney, trying to see if one of them was her mother. She wasn't there.

A missile flew past her head, and Chloe ducked. She tried to push the gurneys out of the way of the fighting, but there were too many. Chloe ran to the open west door and looked out. She could see the boat down at the dock. Two white coats stood on its deck, looking up at the hospital. They were waiting for the patients.

Maybe they already have patients onboard. What if my mother is already on the ship?

Chloe ducked behind the wooden chute leading from the hospital down to the dock. Scanning the path, she could see a way to get to the boat undetected if she hid under the wooden supports of the chute. Gathering her courage, she slid underneath the wooden contraption, and quickly began her descent.

A huge *BOOM!* shook the earth, and Chloe shrieked. The white coats on the dock yelled and pointed up at the hospital. A gas canister had exploded and had set the corner of the building on fire. People screamed and ran away from the door, some spilling out onto the path to the dock.

Chloe began running. She leapt down the hill under the

chute and stumbled, scraping her knee badly. She made it to the edge of the little dock and hid behind a pile of barrels. Another huge *BOOM!* punched the air and she heard breaking glass as a large window blew out from the hospital above. The two guards moved forward for a better look at what was happening. Now was her chance.

Chloe moved swiftly onto the boat and toward the door leading down to the hold. She turned back once to glance up at the hospital and saw the fight had only intensified. She had very little time. The guards could decide to cast off and drive the boat away any minute.

Chloe looked fearfully into the dark hold. It was pitch black and ice cold. She couldn't see a thing, and her heart hammered so loudly she thought surely the guards would hear it, even over the noise of the battle. But she *must* go into that cold, dark place; there was no other option. Chloe gathered her courage and entered the hold, dreadfully afraid of what she would find there.

She stood at the bottom of the stairs, letting her eyes adjust to the darkness. Though she was momentarily blinded, her ears still worked perfectly, and she could hear steady breathing. A few more seconds and Chloe could make out two rows of bunks lining the hull of the ship. In each one lay a person. She heard soft moans coming from some of them, as the gas began to wear off.

"Mother?" Chloe called out softly, barely daring to hope.

"Mother? Eleanor Ashton . . . Are you here? It's me, Chloe!"

"Chloe?" said a *man's* voice.

Chloe turned in confusion. *Who could that be?*

"Chloe . . . Ashton?" said the voice.

Chloe recognized the voice. She had only heard it once before, but she knew now who it was. It was Avery Hart, Celeste's brother!

"Oh! Mr. Hart!" said Chloe eagerly, running to his side.

Avery Hart lay in his narrow bunk, weak and pale. His face was lean and stubbled, and his worried eyes softened with relief as the girl approached and shyly took his outstretched hand. Chloe had the strange feeling that comes when you grasp hands with someone you've hardly met, but that you feel you already know very well.

"It's *very* good to see you, young lady!" said Avery smiling weakly.

"And you, Mr. Hart!" said Chloe sincerely. "Celeste has told me so much about you."

"Celeste?" Avery gasped, his pale face brightening. "Have you seen her? Is my sister all right?"

"She's fine!" cried Chloe. "And she will be overjoyed that I have found you!"

Chloe clasped Avery's hand again, thinking of Celeste's happiness when she heard the news. But they weren't safe yet. Both felt a rumble beneath them as the little boat's engines throbbed louder.

"I must find my mother!" Chloe looked around anxiously at the dark hold full of people. "Have you seen her?"

"I haven't seen anyone, I'm sorry to say, Chloe," said Avery. "I just woke up the minute I heard your voice. But I will help you look."

Avery tried to sit up but was far too weak and fell back on his bunk with a groan.

Chloe put a reassuring hand on his shoulder, and bade him stay where he was for the moment.

"Mother?" she called out again softly. There was no answer.

A bump from above made Chloe flinch, and she cowered in the dark, wondering if someone would enter the hold. Just then another big bump came from directly over her head, followed by a terrible racket as someone fell down the steps, landing in a heap at the bottom. Chloe leapt backward and tried to hide. To her absolute horror, she saw Uncle Blake get clumsily to his feet. He immediately saw Chloe.

"Stop, girl!" Blake lurched toward her. He looked worse than ever. A red stripe of blood was splashed across his drunken face, and his clothes were torn beyond all recognition, and he was having trouble standing. Chloe moved backward, her heart pounding. Would he *never* go away?

Suddenly, she had had enough. She had come too far to give in to her uncle now. Chloe's fear melted away, replaced by a glowing, righteous anger. She was not the same girl she had been when he took her from home and sold her to the vagabonds! She was much stronger now, and Chloe realized that Uncle Blake was no match for her.

The girl faced him squarely, put her hands on her hips, and said as forcefully as she could, "No! *You* stop!"

Doing this made Chloe feel ten feet tall and far more powerful than her sniveling, whining, *pathetic* uncle. She blasted him again. "You tell me where Mother is, Uncle—*right now!*"

Blake flinched, suddenly seeming very afraid of this angry girl. As the boat rocked, he felt sick to his stomach, and before he knew it, he began to cry. "I don't know, I tell you! And how could I know? I've been terribly mistreated! I've wrecked my car, I've been chased by monstrous bears, I've been kicked by that horrible old woman's pointy shoe, and now I've fallen down the stairs! I'm bruised and I'm scraped and now you're screaming at me—well it's just too much!"

Chloe let him sob for a few minutes, and then she said simply, "You're disgusting. I'm *glad* all that happened to you, Uncle—it's the very least you deserve! Now tell me—what have they done with Lady Ashton? Where is my mother?"

Blake whimpered, looking very sorry for himself, "I don't *know*! I have no idea where your mother is!"

"I'm here."

A weak voice spoke from a corner of the ship. A woman's voice.

"*Mother?*" Chloe started violently, and whipped her head around, looking for the speaker in the dark.

"*Clothilde?*" said her mother from her corner of the ship.

Chloe ran to the cot which held her mother lying pale and wan, but moving, speaking!

"My dear, my dear! My darling child!"

Chloe wrapped herself in Lady Ashton's weak embrace. They both cried. It was a miracle—in the shadowed corner of the ship's hull, Chloe had found her mother. Thin and white as the sheet that covered her, Lady Ashton hugged her daughter as tightly as she could. After that first, fierce embrace, Chloe pulled away a little so as not to crush her.

"Are you all right, mother?" she asked anxiously.

"I will be, I think," said Lady Ashton, her eyes bright and soft as she looked at her daughter. "Are you all right, my darling?"

"Oh yes, mother! I'm fine!"

They both laughed at the word *fine*. They had never been less fine in their lives!

"Watch out! He's getting away!" Avery called to them from his own bunk. Uncle Blake was crawling up the stairs.

"Wait here!" said Chloe to her mother and dashed after him.

Coming out of the hold, she saw her uncle's muddy coattails disappearing over the rail of the ship, and the two guards still standing on the dock, watching the hospital. A horrible, orange glow lit the sky behind it, and black smoke billowed up into the night sky. The silhouettes of white coats, animals, and village folk could be seen running from the building.

Uncle Blake ran up to the two guards and grabbed onto one of their sleeves, yelling something and pointing toward the hold. The two guards looked back, but Chloe hid in the shadows. Uncle Blake gestured again, and the guard impatiently shook him off. They had more important things to worry about.

BOOM! A ball of orange fire went up into the sky, followed by another and another. The gas canisters, consumed by the spreading fire, were exploding like bombs. The hospital workers ran down the path to the ship, abandoning the gurneys full of patients. They yelled to the guards to cast off and get ready to sail. The guards bent quickly to unwind the ropes holding the ship.

Chloe knew she had to do something. In just a few seconds those doctors would be on the ship, and they would be sailing out to sea. She would not be able to save her mother and Avery. She had not come all this way and found them both alive—just to be stopped now.

Desperate, Chloe put two fingers to her mouth and whistled. She made the animal's call as best she could. Long, long, long, slooooooooow. Long, long, long, slooooooooow. She didn't know if anyone would hear it, but it was possible—one of the animals, or perhaps even Brisco, or Shakespeare. *He* would certainly recognize Chloe's call. Chloe kept calling, as loudly as she could.

The fleeing white coats from the hospital reached the dock and clattered down its length to the boat. They climbed aboard, and Chloe was forced to stop whistling, and duck down again, but not before one of the white coats spotted her, and ran to her hiding place, pulling her roughly out by her arm.

"Let me go!" screamed Chloe, struggling.

The boat's motor chugged to life, and it began to pull away from the dock, making them lurch to the side. Chloe kicked and tried to break out of the white coat's arms, but he held her arms fast.

"Get this tub out of here!" the guard yelled.

The ship rocked to the side again, and the engine throbbed and whined as it tried to pull away from the dock. Another *BOOM!* lit up the sky and sent flames into the air. The explosion was followed by a roar of voices. The people had taken over the hospital and now they were running down to the dock. Villagers running with torches, their faces scratched and bleeding, and all the animals that could still fight raced toward the little boat.

The white coats looked at each other, fear on every face. It was over, they were outnumbered. The engine whined and belched black smoke in its effort to pull away.

Chloe struggled hard against the white coat's arms. She succeeded in giving him a sharp jab in the ribs, making him grunt and curse.

"UNHAND THAT CHILD!"

Chloe looked up in shock. She knew that voice!

CHAPTER THIRTY-FOUR

*I*T WAS MR. MASON! THE OLD BUTLER WAS leading the charge to the dock, looking wilder than he ever had in his life. In his shirtsleeves, torn and dirty with his thin white hair standing straight up, Mr. Mason was almost unrecognizable as he led the entire staff of Ashton House down the hill.

"Let her go!" the old butler shouted, and surprising everyone, he magnificently jumped the few feet of water between the boat and the dock, neatly landing on the deck of the struggling ship.

The white coat holding Chloe was caught completely off guard by this crazy old man, and staggered back, dropping the girl's arm in order to fend off the old butler.

The other servants from Ashton House followed Mr. Mason onto the dock. They were all there—Mrs. Eames, Britta, Mr. Darby the gardener, and a small platoon of maids and footmen from Ashton House, all trying to board the boat to save their Chloe.

Mr. Darby bravely followed Mr. Mason's example and

made the leap onto the deck where he lost no time in flinging the ropes to the others. Several footmen caught the rope and lashed it to the dock.

The boat strained against the rope, but the rope held, and the engine began to whine horribly over the grinding gears. A loud *pop* and a *hiss* emanated from the engine room, followed by a great cloud of black smoke. The engine was dead.

With a cheer, the servants from Ashton House and the townspeople who joined them swarmed on board. The white coats tried to run, but there was nowhere to go, and they were soon in a fight for their lives.

Mrs. Eames, red-faced from her run down the hill, was angry as a wet hen. She proved to be a formidable adversary with her rolling pin, and Mr. Mason was no slouch either. Unbeknownst to most, he had been a lightweight boxer in his youth. To tell the truth, he hadn't felt this spry in years, and the old butler threw up his dukes to confront the guard that had held Chloe. The guard moved forward to finish off this tiresome old man, but before either of them could do anything, Mrs. Eames, a whirling dervish of destruction, cracked the guard on the head with her pin, knocking him out cold.

"Sorry, Mr. Mason!" she said, spinning off. "Couldn't help it!"

"Look out!" Chloe cried out to the butler.

Mr. Mason spun around to face Uncle Blake, who stood leering menacingly in front of him. Uncle Blake laughed out loud at the sight of the skinny old man with his hair on end, circling with his puny dukes up. He *hated* Mr. Mason, had hated him the first day he arrived at Ashton House, hated the way the old man looked at him, spoke to him, and treated him like some unwelcome, unworthy person to be only tolerated. He would enjoy beating him.

Blake snarled at Mr. Mason, and moved toward him, intending to throw him to the ground. Blake never got closer than two feet from the old butler. In a move too fast for the eye to see, the old man shot out one of his "puny dukes," popping Uncle Blake right in the nose. Blood spurted out in a geyser, and Uncle Blake dropped like a stone to the ground. He was done.

The battle above at the hospital raged on. The fire had taken hold of the roof, and it was an apocalyptic scene of red-and-orange flames, punctuated by explosions from the gas canisters.

Suddenly, a great whirring sound rose up behind the hospital, and a great wind blew down on the flames, and the fighting. A powerful jet of water came out of the sky, drenching the fire, and knocking over the people below. As everyone looked up to see what it was, Chloe laughed out loud in delight.

It was Brisco, riding in a wooden flying machine he had built out of hospital parts! The ingenious machine swooped in and around the flames of the roof, and Brisco managed to hold a hose shooting a great deal of water at the flames while he flew it. With a huge grin on his face, Brisco flew the machine all around the battle, putting out the flames and apparently deriving great glee from blasting the remaining white coats with his hose. Within minutes the remaining hospital workers were overwhelmed, and completely subdued.

The servants from Ashton House and the people of Fairfax took over the ship, and went through the hold, finding lost loved ones, and helping the wounded back on land.

Chloe ran forward to be embraced by her dear old friends from Ashton House. She hugged Mr. Mason fiercely, and they both had tears in their eyes.

"Oh, Mr. Mason!" cried Chloe. "How I've missed you!"

Mr. Mason wiped his eyes with a huge white handkerchief he pulled from his vest pocket. He was so overcome he couldn't say a word and just blew his nose loudly in reply. Everyone laughed, and Mrs. Eames wrapped Chloe in such a tight hug she could hardly breathe. Britta crowded around, and Thomas the stable boy, and all her old friends and companions from home. They were family to Chloe—she had known them all since the day she was born.

Celeste was there, too. She stood shyly by as the old friends were reunited, and Brisco stood next to her, his shoulder touching hers. Clearly smitten, the carpenter watched Celeste closely as she told her part of the story. It was she who had gone to Ashton House to get the servants' help, upon Chloe's suggestion. It had been a dangerous trip—there were still many ambulances patrolling the road. Once there, it had been no trouble at all convincing the servants to come to her aid. The entire staff at Ashton House had cheered when they heard the plan, and nothing could stop them from arming themselves with shovels, rakes, gardening tools—anything and everything they could find—and coming with her to help Lady Ashton and Chloe.

Shakespeare had been waiting for them on the road. The rat had quickly led them to the hospital, as planned. Once there they had not been able to find the child until Shakespeare heard Chloe's call from the dock. He had led the servants to the ship, and Mr. Mason had taken over from there.

Shakespeare was delighted to be back with his best friend and jumped onto Chloe's shoulder to nuzzle her cheek affectionately.

After that it was all over in a matter of minutes. Mr. Mason and some of the men from the village gathered all the white coats onboard the ship and tied them to the mast.

Chloe grabbed Celeste's hand and squeezed it.

"Let's go get Avery," she said, smiling.

"*Avery?*" gasped Celeste, her eyes disbelieving. "He's ..."

"He's here!" said Chloe joyfully, and pulled Celeste toward the door of the hold.

The two women descended the steps. Avery spotted his sister immediately.

"Celeste!" he cried out from his bunk.

With a joyful sob Celeste ran forward to embrace her brother. Chloe went quickly to her mother, and the other patients lying in their bunks broke out in weak cheers of relief.

They were saved!

CHAPTER THIRTY-FIVE

THE EFFICIENT SERVANTS OF ASHTON HALL quickly organized rescue operations, helping all the patients out of their bunks and onto the deck. Warm blankets were handed around, and a wagon was sent for, to carry the patients back up the hill. There were tearful reunions as old friends recognized each other, and loved ones were found.

Chloe could not stop hugging her mother. "I was so afraid for you, mother," she said, pressing her cheek against Lady Ashton's. "Tell me, what happened that night you disappeared? Mr. Mason said you were taken away. Was it in an ambulance?"

"Yes, darling," said Lady Ashton sadly, smoothing her daughter's hair from her face. "I hadn't been feeling particularly well that day. I hadn't been feeling well for a lot of days my dear, since your father died . . ." Lady Ashton's voice trailed off.

"I know, Mother," said Chloe. "It was a terrible time for you."

Lady Ashton's eyes focused and she sat a little straighter. She held Chloe at arm's length and looked directly into her daughter's eyes. "Darling . . . it was a terrible time for *you*. I am so sorry I did not see how this all affected you. I was so blinded by my own grief, and . . . oh my child, I am so sorry!"

Chloe cried and hugged her mother, saying "Mother, please don't be sad, I'm just so very grateful that we're both all right, and together, and isn't it wonderful, Mother—Uncle Blake has been caught, and he won't ever harm us again!"

"Yes, my darling," said Lady Ashton said with a tinge of sorrow. "It is truly wonderful."

Chloe then introduced her mother to Celeste and Avery Hart, and Lady Ashton pressed their hands and kissed their cheeks in gratitude for their help and concern for her daughter. Mr. Mason and Mrs. Eames were hailed as heroes of the day for their timely and surprisingly effective arrival. Chloe hugged them all, tears streaming down her face. She had longed for this moment for so long.

More wagons were sent for, and gradually all the patients were taken back up the hill. The white coats tied to the mast of the ship—including Uncle Blake—were loaded into a separate wagon, still roped together. Their faces were pale, and they looked terrified. They had seen the bears and the wolves, and their imaginations took a terrifying turn as they bumped back up the road to the hospital.

The hospital itself was still burning in places, but Brisco had managed to douse the worst of the fire. Fairfax had no fire department, but some of the bears had found hoses and were clumsily holding them on the remaining hot spots. Their aim wasn't great, but they managed to extinguish a good portion of the remaining flames. The bears were aided by small flocks of crows, owls, and jays that carried cups of water in their claws and dumped them on the embers. Soon the fire was extinguished and only the charred walls remained of the east side of the hospital. Where an hour before a splendid gala had taken place in an immaculate new facility, there now was only a blackened, smoking ruin.

Everywhere people and animals milled about, the uninjured helping the wounded. A group of nurses had come over to their side and were doing what they were trained to do. The nurses had never approved of how the hospital was run but had been forced to work and threatened with gas if they did not obey orders. When Chloe and her friends and all the animals descended on the gala, the nurses had happily joined the fight, hoping it would finally bring an end to all the cruelty they had seen.

Now the kind nurses were helping man and animal alike. The medic units made up of small creatures worked alongside them, and soon they had a triage area set up on the lawn for the worst cases. Using undamaged medical supplies that had escaped the fire, the small animals and nurses carefully cleaned and bandaged wounds, found water and blankets for everyone, and handed out cocoa to whoever wanted it.

Seeing the nurses reminded Mrs. Goodweather of the two nurses she had left in the silver pantry! Telling Chloe that she would return in a moment, Mrs. Goodweather dashed back into the hospital, down the steps to the kitchen, and to the silver pantry. When she threw open the door, both the young nurses looked up sleepily from where they had been curled up on a blanket with their charges. They had slept through the entire end of the battle, and their first question was "Did we win?"

Mrs. Goodweather assured them that they had, and that it was safe to come out. She took one of the babies in her own arms and led the little group out to where the others were gathered.

Lady Ashton was surrounded by the servants of Ashton House, who were making her as comfortable as possible, and arranging for a wagon to take them all home. They were all so happy to see her ladyship, so sorry about all that had happened, and they swore never to let her out of their sight again, and woe unto that rogue Mr. Underwood if he should try and come back into Ashton House! They would know what to do!

Chloe's mother smiled, and Chloe's heart sang at the sight. She hugged her mother again, holding her thin hand against her cheek.

"I'm so happy, Mother!" she whispered.

"Oh, my darling," whispered Lady Ashton, tears in her eyes as she caressed her daughter's hair. "I am too."

"Mother . . . I love you."

"Oh, my darling, I love you too, so much. We must change everything at home," said Lady Ashton brightly to her daughter. "We must make it a happy place once again! A place your dear Papa would have been proud of!"

"Yes!" cried Chloe, clapping her hands. "We will put it all back, even better than before! Oh, mother, we can have a big welcome-home party to celebrate! *Oh*, we're going home, we're going home!" The girl danced around her mother's chair, unable to contain her joy.

Ashton House. Chloe absolutely could not wait to get home to the great house and its beloved gardens. With her awful Uncle Blake gone, it would be the home she remembered, and now she could bring her new friends there, too. Chloe looked around anxiously for any sign of the Artist or Brisco or Mrs. Goodweather, and then she suddenly remembered—*Silas*! Had Silas come? Where was he? And where was Greybelle?

CHAPTER THIRTY-SIX

ILAS THE STARGAZER WAS STANDING ON A log on the hill behind the hospital. He was thanking the animals that had fought so bravely. A line of creatures filed past him, each dipping a head or paw in respect to the old man, who in turn would give each one his solemn thanks. Some of the animals began to disperse into the woods, away from the battle site. They did not want to linger; they had survived the war, and it was time to return to their dens, nests, and families.

The silver horses from the north pranced nervously at the edge of the hospital drive. Their mission accomplished, they were uncomfortable remaining so far south and were very anxious to return home. Greybelle stood with them, nickering gently to these long-lost family members, who felt like a dream come to life. A dream her mother had told her many times as a foal. She did not want them to go, when she had only just discovered them.

Paloma, a dappled cousin of Greybelle's, said, "Cousin, you are bleeding."

Greybelle looked down at the red stain on her leg and lifted it carefully. It seemed fine, only a shallow scrape.

"I'm all right, thank you. Dear cousin," Greybelle nickered gratefully, "what would we have ever done without you?"

Paloma tossed her mane and said, "No, Greybelle, the question is, what would *they* have done without *you*?"

The silver mare pointed to the other animals with her nose. "It was *your* presence with Silas, at the Bridge of the Gods, that convinced us to come. It's been three hundred years since anyone has crossed into the southlands, and we certainly had no desire to do so. If you had not accompanied the old man, and we had not heard of it . . . we may not have come at all."

Greybelle was overjoyed. She had helped her family and helped herself, and she had kept her word to Chloe. From the vagabond camp in the forest to the victory at the hospital, Greybelle had kept her promise to help the child, and now they had both come home.

The mare whinnied, looking around for Chloe. *There*! Chloe was there! Greybelle saw the girl, walking across the driveway. But wait . . .who was that with her? *Mr. Mason?* And Mrs. Eames, too?

Greybelle snorted in surprise at the sight of the servants she remembered well from Ashton House, coming toward her with Chloe among them. The mare trotted eagerly forward, and Chloe squealed in delight at the sight of her dear friend.

"Greybelle!" She ran forward to throw her arms around the silver mare's neck.

"Dear Chloe! I'm so glad you're all right!" whickered the mare into the girl's hair.

"We've done it, Greybelle!" cried out Chloe joyfully. "*You've* done it!"

"We've *all* done it, my dear!" answered the mare fondly.

"And it looks as though you found some old friends to help!"

Greybelle laughed out loud at the expression on old Mr. Mason's face at the sound of the mare talking. More introductions were made as the Artist, Brisco, and Lord Winchfillin joined their little group. Besides a few bruises and scrapes, everyone seemed relatively uninjured for which they were all very grateful.

Behind them, Silas stood on top of the log and held his hands up for attention. He cleared his throat of the soot and dust and fight of the battle, and then called out to all that could hear him, "YOU!"

The crowd went quiet.

"*You* have won a great victory today!"

"Huzzah!" screamed the animals, rejoicing.

The old man's eyes were shining. Silas looked wild and fierce, and very proud as he stood on the log, his hair standing out wildly around his head. He raised his arms high.

"You have saved the land!" he cried out joyfully.

The hospital drive and surrounding area erupted in cheers. Everywhere, the animals stopped what they were doing, laying down whatever they were holding in their paws or claws, and cheered and clapped and flapped and thumped on the ground as loudly as they could.

The wounded cheered too, as well as they were able. The Badger raised a bandaged paw from where he lay, being treated by the nurses. A group of wounded foxes yipped in a chorus, waving their crutches.

"You have truly outdone yourselves!" called Silas from the log. "You are all brave warriors, and you have won the day!"

"Hip, hip, hooray!" cheered the crowd of people and animals together.

There would be peace in the land. Everybody began talking, and dancing and laughing. New friendships were instantly forged as man and animal celebrated together, right where they were. Everyone began to think about food, and drink.

Behind the hospital, the horses from the north prepared to leave. Whirling as one, their manes and tails flying together in a silver wave, they whinnied impatiently to Silas.

Silas jumped down from the log and came over to where Chloe and her friends were standing. He patted the mare fondly on the neck. "I must go north. Now that the bridge is open, there is much to do."

He turned to Chloe and put out his hand. "I am very glad to finally meet you, Chloe."

Chloe reached out to shake the old man's hand. It felt remarkably smooth and soft, and warm.

"And I you, Mr. Stargazer, sir," she said respectfully.

"Silas, please, dear girl. Call me Silas. I know we will be great friends. I have heard much about you, and I would like to know more. Perhaps we will talk someday."

"I'd like that very much sir . . . er . . . *Silas*," Chloe said bashfully.

The old man gestured to Paloma, who came near him and dropped her shoulder toward the ground, offering him an easy climb to her back. Silas swung himself up, and the silver mare danced in place, happy to carry the Stargazer.

"I will send word to you, this spring," he said to the little group. "I want to call another meeting."

Lord Winchfillin groaned. "Another meeting! Does it have to be up a mountain, old chap?"

Everyone laughed.

"Not this time, dear Lord Winchfillin." Silas chuckled. "And it certainly will not be a council of war. No, I see a high summer meeting, deep in the cool Valley of Bree. It should be very pleasant. I hope you all can come."

Silas moved Paloma down the drive. "My friends!" he called to the remaining animals as he went. "This day will never be forgotten! We will write songs about this day, and we will sing them this summer!"

The animals cheered again.

"You must all come north this summer!" Silas called. "We will have a great celebration, and you are all invited!"

A huge hooray came from a large group of field mice, recovering under the trees.

"Until then my friends, goodbye!"

Paloma reared and snorted and Silas waved goodbye from her back. The beautiful silver herd wheeled and galloped up the hill, away from the hospital, and into the cool cover of the trees. As they went, the silver horses called back in musical tones, "Goodbye! Goodbye! Until we meet again!"

Greybelle stood for a long moment after her family disappeared, her head held high, and her ears pricked forward to hear the last sounds of their departure. The mare's sensitive nostrils fluttered, reaching for the last scent of her family, and when they were completely gone, she whinnied a long, loud call—full of longing, and of love. The faint, musical notes of her answering family came floating back on the wind to her, and then they too, were gone.

The Artist and Chloe came up to her and draped their arms around their old friend's neck.

"You have the most amazing family in the world!" said

Chloe. "I've never seen such beautiful horses in my life. Well, except for you, of course!" She hugged her dear friend, and the mare whickered back.

Lord Winchfillin came up, limping on one shoe, his eyes streaming with tears. When they looked at him questioningly, he began to cry in earnest and, barely managing to get out the words, sobbed, "Ra . . . Ra . . . Raja is dead!"

CHAPTER THIRTY-SEVEN

THE LITTLE LORD WEPT, BURYING HIS FACE IN a torn, sooty handkerchief, his small shoulders shaking.

Raja, dead! How could it be? The old gelding had been fighting like a hero the last they had seen him, the earl on his back like a tiny Napoleon, fending off all foes. When had it happened? *How* had it happened?

"He . . . he was charging toward the west door, bravely going to help where he could, when . . . wh . . . when . . . he was hit by an ambulance!" sobbed Lord Winchfillin.

The Artist stood still, his face white. "Take us to him."

Lord Winchfillin led them to a dark shape lying in the road on the side of the hospital. Old Raja lay there, his eyes closed and an ugly wound visible in his side. The Artist laid his head down close to Raja's heart, listening for any sign of life. When he gently touched the old horse's throat for a pulse and found none, he was forced to accept that his dear friend lived no more. Overcome with grief, the Artist laid his head on Old Raja's cheek and cried.

It was a somber gathering that collected in front of the hospital that night. The joy of reunion and the thrill of victory were dampened by the tragic losses, which were considerable on both sides. The nurses and animal medics were hard at work, sorting the wounded from the dead. They worked quietly, quickly, and very efficiently to guide the wounded back into the undamaged wing of the hospital for *real* treatment. No masks, no gas, and everyone was welcome to accompany their loved one into their rooms and stay as long as they liked.

Mr. Mason and the servants of Ashton House took it upon themselves to arrange the burial of the dead. The Badger, with a bandage over one eye, called in all the burrowing animals, who immediately set to the sad work of digging graves. The Badger called out orders and encouraged the others to "make it a good and fitting bed for their fallen comrades."

Mr. Mason volunteered his services as chaplain. "I was a captain in the British navy when I was a younger man," he explained. "And that makes me as good as a chaplain, at least in the eyes of the law."

A simple, heartfelt service was said for all the fallen that night. Everyone stopped their work and gathered at the gravesites, where man and animal laid bowers of wild flowers, and the nurses brought out a few candles that survived the fire to light the sad service. All those who could walk or stand or be carried along came to pay their respects. Lady Ashton was there, wheeled in a chair by a nurse and holding Chloe's hand. Avery Hart stood on his feet with the aid of a cane and his sister Celeste's arm. Brisco Knot was there, as was the Artist, who stood with his arm around Greybelle. Lord Winchfillin, who had grown extremely fond of Old Raja, sat on a log and wept into his filthy lace handkerchief, and Mrs. Goodweather did her best to comfort him.

Mr. Mason waited until everyone was assembled and stepped forward into the flickering candlelight. The old butler stood over the graves, his white head framed by the stems and blooms the animals had brought to honor their dead.

"Here lie great heroes," Mr. Mason began softly.

Not a soul moved. Not a whisker twitched. Everyone listened intently to the old man's surprisingly eloquent words.

"This has become hallowed ground," Mr. Mason continued. "Our friends and loved ones have consecrated this place by their great sacrifice. But the blood that has been so tragically spilled here has not been spilled in vain."

All of the animals and people gathered there took a deep breath and nodded their heads in agreement with the old butler.

"For their sacrifice has brought us all freedom. Their courage and bravery has brought peace to the land. Our children are safe, our families are safe, and we owe it all to them."

The field mice made a small, sad cheer but were quickly shushed by the Badger.

Mr. Mason bowed his head. "Now, we relinquish our dearly departed to the heavens. May they be called home to a place where there is no fear, no pain, and no death. We will never forget them. We will think of them every day. And we will look forward to one day meeting them again."

There was a general sigh in the crowd. The Artist stepped forward and pulled his flute from his coat pocket. His eyes were wet with tears.

"Allow me to play a song for my friend, Raja," he said softly. "Many was the time on the road when I would play it and he would nod his head along in time with the tune. It was always one of his favorites, and I think he'd be glad to hear it now."

The Artist closed his eyes and raised the flute to his lips. It was an old song, and some of the people gathered knew it well. They softly started to sing the words, swaying back and forth in the candlelight.

Tell me the tales that to me were so dear,
Long, long ago, long, long ago,
Sing me the songs I delighted to hear,
Long, long ago, long ago,
Now you are come all my grief is removed,
Let me forget that so long you have roved.
Let me believe that you love as you loved,
Long, long ago, long ago.

Do you remember the paths where we met?
Long, long ago, long, long ago.
Ah, yes, you told me you'd never forget,
Long, long ago, long ago.
Then to all others, my smile you preferred,
Love, when you spoke, gave a charm to each word.
Still my heart treasures the phrases I heard,
Long, long ago, long ago.

The last notes of the song floated up and away into the dark sky. Everyone was exhausted. Slowly the gathering began to disperse back to the hospital. There was much to do before they could leave. Everyone who needed a bed, or a shower, was welcomed into the undamaged wing of the hospital. Mrs. Goodweather, Mrs. Eames, and Britta the kitchen maid retied their aprons and got to work in the partially scorched kitchen with the squirrels helping, making a simple, nourishing dinner for everyone. Brisco and the bears began to clear the yard and drive of debris and damaged ambulances. The maids and the footman from Ashton House made themselves useful and helped the nurses change the sheets and get everyone tucked in as comfortably as possible. Lord Winchfillin proved himself quite proficient at getting the younger wounded animals to settle, telling them stories which they listened to with wide eyes, as the nurses bustled about.

Finally, everyone was taken care of at the hospital, and Lady Ashton insisted that all of Chloe's friends come home to Ashton House. Everyone readily and gratefully agreed. It would be wonderful to bathe properly, eat a home-cooked meal, and sleep in a comfortable bed. Lady Ashton assured them that they must stay as long they liked to recuperate, and when they were ready, and had quite recovered, she wanted to discuss the future.

But first they must address the present.

CHAPTER THIRTY‑EIGHT

LL THE REMAINING DOCTORS, ORDERLIES, and ambulance drivers were still tied up in the wagon that had brought them up from the docks. They were being guarded by bears, who were having a wonderful time playing a game they had just invented called "Swat the White Coat." The white coats *hated* this game, and they cowered in the back of the wagon, cringing out of the reach of those claws. Uncle Blake was one of them. He screamed every time a bear took a swipe.

"Swat *that* one hard!" growled Livermore, a half-grown black bear who had had enough of Blake's irritating shrieks. "I'll give you three points!"

"Just a minute there!" called out Mrs. Goodweather, appearing with Chloe, the Artist, Brisco, and the others. The bears looked annoyed at being interrupted, but the same bear who had guarded the silver pantry—whose name was Ursula—recognized Mrs. Goodweather, and told the other bears to stop. They did so, growling nastily at the white coats.

The people approached the wagon.

"What should we do with them?" asked the Artist.

"We can't let them go," said Brisco. "They'll be back up to their old tricks in no time at all."

"I have an idea," said Mrs. Goodweather. She reached into her pocket and pulled out the blueberry pie she had picked up from the dining room.

"This ought to do the trick."

She broke the pie in half, and then nodded at Brisco and the Artist. The two men understood her at once and moved forward to grab Uncle Blake by the head and shoulders, holding him fast.

"What are you doing?" Uncle Blake hollered. "Let me go!"

He watched as Mrs. Goodweather slowly approached him with the pie. Uncle Blake squirmed fearfully in the men's arms.

"I don't want that! I won't eat it! You can't make me!" Blake locked his jaw closed defiantly.

"Oh yes, you will!" said the Artist, wrenching Uncle Blake's head back.

"Oh yes, we can!" said Brisco, forcing his fingers into the side of Uncle Blake's mouth. At the same time Mrs. Goodweather rushed forward and smashed the half pie against his lips.

"Mmph . . . mmmphph . . . GAH!"

Uncle Blake couldn't breathe and was forced to gasp for air whereupon Mrs. Goodweather shoved half of the entire pie right into his mouth. Brisco squeezed Blake's cheeks so hard he could not open his mouth to spit out the pie, and finally he was forced to swallow or suffocate. When he swallowed the pie, Brisco let him go.

Blake began to change. His hard, pinched-looking face

softened, rounded, and filled out at the cheeks. His greasy hair shrunk back into his head and became silky-soft, curly locks. His beard growth disappeared, his neck shortened, and Blake's red-rimmed, watery eyes grew round and bright as a child's.

Uncle Blake *was* a child. His skinny frame absorbed the power of the pie almost instantly, and he zipped through adolescence in a matter of seconds. Within a few more seconds he was a very small child, and an angry one. His short legs collapsed on the ground, and he immediately threw a tantrum, squalling and beating the earth with chubby fists. Celeste took pity on him then, and moved forward to help him to his feet, but the transformation was not yet complete. Even as Celeste reached toward the child, he shrank to an infant. Uncle Blake's angry cry became the hungry cry of a tiny baby, who wanted nothing more than to be fed.

Celeste stooped down and gathered tiny baby Uncle Blake into her arms. She looked kindly down at his little pink face and jiggled him gently up and down. Uncle Blake giggled happily. His thoughts were those of an infant, and his anger had completely melted away, replaced by a sweet smile and an adoring expression as he gazed up at this nice woman holding him.

Ursula the bear came up, intrigued by this strange transformation, and peered over Celeste's shoulder. The bear made a funny face at Blake who cooed in delight and broke out in a peal of baby laughter.

The other half of the pie was divided between the remaining white coats. Brisco and the Artist made them all eat the pieces, with the help of the bears. There wasn't enough pie left to change them all into babies, but it was enough to make

them teenagers, which wasn't ideal, but besides a sullen atti-
tude and a lot of eye rolling, they became harmless enough.
Mrs. Goodweather said if they didn't behave themselves she
would make more pies in a jiffy and turn them into toddlers,
which seemed to adequately subdue them.

Baby Uncle Blake and the teenagers were taken to the
hospital nursery where they joined Mr. Gog and the others
who had been transformed earlier, and were being tended to by
the kind nurses. Two of the bears had taken quite a fancy to
the children and wanted to help. King Auberon reluctantly
gave his permission for them to stay for a while and help
babysit, before returning to the woods. The bears proved
themselves surprisingly gentle with the babies. They loved to
gently poke their tummies and make them laugh. The babies
in turn loved to crawl on top of the bears and pull their long
hair. The bears were remarkably tolerant, and merely squashed
the tots gently flat when their antics got out of hand.

CHAPTER THIRTY-NINE

*T*HE NEXT MORNING WAS ALREADY UPON them. The sky in the east turned golden, and the overnight fog disappeared, leaving behind dew that sparkled over the land in the rising sun. As the minutes ticked by, the sun rose higher, its golden fingers gently gilding every tree, every rock, and illuminating the ruins of the hospital.

The crows had never gone to sleep, and now they rose one by one from the damp trees, circling in the rose-colored sky, and calling to each other.

"A new day!"

The crows were joined by a chorus of other birds, all the birds who had helped win the battle, and all of their family members. They rose from the trees and flew out over the ocean to be met by gulls, who flew higher and higher over the cliffs of Fairfax, calling down to the sea.

"A new day has come!"

In front of the hospital people were moving about, loading their loved ones into wagons and carts, and slowly beginning to return to their homes. The Fairfax police had been found lost in the woods, and were now helping to restore order.

The bear Ursula and her sister Nita donned aprons and caps, and were busy wheeling patients in and out of the hospital. Whitestone and Nettle the squirrels had also elected to stay behind and help wherever they could. They had been instrumental in getting messages back and forth during the battle, and would continue to do so until the telegraph lines started working again.

Chloe and her mother were gathered around the wagons from Ashton House, come to take them all home. All her friends were there, and the servants. Chloe was exhausted, but so excited to finally be going home she hardly noticed. She climbed into the carriage Mr. Mason had sent for and settled in cozily next to Lady Ashton. Shakespeare poked his head out of her pocket and climbed out onto her lap. Lady Ashton had already met the white rat, and found him to be completely charming.

"Oh, mother, I can hardly believe we're going home!" Chloe sang out, petting the rat happily. "My dear, dear Shakespeare, we are going back to Ashton House! We shall have such lovely, fun times again!"

Lady Ashton waved her handkerchief out of the window as the carriage pulled away down the drive. "Goodbye!" she called to the nurses and the bears on the lawn. "Goodbye and thank you!"

Everyone piled into whatever wagon they could, and set off down the road, away from the hospital, the tree house, and the forested hills behind them, toward Fairfax, and finally to Ashton House. It was a jolly journey with all the servants singing, and the Artist playing his flute. Brisco led them on a round that had everyone confused and laughing as they rolled down the road. When they arrived at the doors of the great house, everyone piled out and immediately went to their rooms to rest and wash up for dinner.

Ashton House became a merry place once more. Over the next few days, the servants went into a flurry of cleaning. Every window in the house was opened, and washed until it sparkled, every floor was vigorously swept and mopped, and all the doors flung wide to the fresh, sea air. For days, dust rags and mop ends could be seen shaking from doors and windows as the maids gave everything a good going over. All the curtains and linens were taken down, washed, and hung to dry in the orchard, so that for one whole day it was a magical place, the trees swathed in multicolored fabrics that billowed in the wind, and made wonderful tents for Chloe and Shakespeare to play under.

Mrs. Goodweather stayed on to help the family settle and to exchange cooking tips with Mrs. Eames. The two ladies struck up a solid friendship, and enjoyed strolling through the gardens of Ashton House, picking vegetables and discussing different ways to prepare them. Together they cooked up many delicious meals for everyone, and the kitchen stove never cooled. The aromas wafting through Ashton House carried the most delicious smells of rich and savory gravies, baked bread and rolls, and the sweet and sugary smells of pies, cookies, and cakes. Everyone ate as much as they liked, and nobody complained about the dishes. It was so wonderful to be home again, no chore seemed difficult or tedious. Every moment was a pleasure.

Avery and Celeste Hart had each been given rooms, and Lady Ashton had generously offered them a place to stay for as long as they liked. She was so grateful to them for trying so hard to help her daughter that she said they could consider Ashton House their home forever if they chose to do so.

When she heard this, Chloe jumped up and down and begged the Harts, "Oh, please do! Please do! Nothing would make me happier!"

Avery and Celeste looked at each other, and then Celeste looked quickly at Brisco. There was an awkward pause as everyone suddenly looked at each other, and then Avery broke the spell and laughed. "Well I can't speak for my sister, dear Lady Ashton, but for my part I'd like to thank you from the bottom of my heart for your kind offer. I would love to stay, at least until I am fully recovered, and then we can see."

Celeste and Brisco looked slightly uncomfortable, and Lady Ashton broke in kindly to save any embarrassment. "Perhaps it is a little too soon to be making such big decisions. I think I'm getting ahead of myself. You must all stay or go as you please, of course! I only hope you will all stay as long as possible."

The Artist refused a room in the big house and chose instead to stay in the airy rooms above the stable. There he was quite comfortable, and spent long afternoons with Mr. Darby the gardener, cleaning up the grounds and gardens. When the work was done, the Artist painted the portraits of anyone who would sit for him, and they all took turns posing.

Chloe was delighted to have the Artist at Ashton House, and she spent special afternoons showing him all her favorite places. She took him to where she had fallen in the creek, and first seen the Illuminata flowers. She showed him the otter's den, and the place near the house where the rabbits had nodded at her, and one windy day she took him to the same cliffs where the gull had smiled. Inside Ashton House she showed him her reading nook where she first met Shakespeare, during the storm.

Everything seemed even more beautiful to her now, than it ever had been before. Knowing how easily it all could change made Chloe relish every moment with a profound kind of gratitude. Now everything seemed to sparkle, even the most ordinary things—*especially* the most ordinary things—and a song was always on her lips. She was home again.

The town of Fairfax itself was recovering from the war. What remained of the hospital was quickly rebuilt into a small clinic, run by the nurses, and by the bears. The rubble was cleared away and the walls repaired and painted. King Auberon had reluctantly given his permission for Nita and Ursula to stay on as long as they liked. Mrs. Goodweather had gone back to the hospital for a little while to help the nurses and the bears put in a large, organic garden. They planted corn and lettuce, tomatoes and beans, peas and spinach, and they planted fruit. Berries and melons were planted, and Mr. Mason and Mr. Darby the gardener promised to plant a large fruit and nut orchard behind the hospital in the spring. Chloe looked forward to the plums and apples and hazelnuts they would yield.

One beautiful day Chloe took her friends up to the cliff where she and Mr. Mason had picnicked together. They brought their own picnic, packed in several baskets by Mrs. Eames and Mrs. Goodweather. They all spread out blankets on the grass and enjoyed the feast immensely. After lunch, they packed everything away and stood together at the edge of the cliff, gazing out at the ocean and listening to the waves pounding below. The gulls danced on the air around them, their soft cries soothing, and no one felt the need to say a word. When you've been through so much with someone, you can sometimes speak without talking, and at that moment they all felt the same thing—that their friendship would last forever, and indeed, that it had only just begun.

CHAPTER FORTY

*I*T WAS CLEAR THAT OTHER BONDS HAD been forged over the last few days, as well. While the others picnicked, waded in the sea, played badminton on the great lawn of Ashton House, and danced to the Artist's merry tunes, Brisco and Celeste were often seen together, walking under the trees, and quietly talking. Everyone noticed, but no one remarked upon the shy glances exchanged between the two, and the blushes that bloomed on Celeste's cheeks when Brisco stood near her. Before long they began holding hands on their walks, and soon they hardly left each other's side.

The days passed happily, until one morning the Artist suddenly put down his mug of tea and quietly announced, "It's time for me to move along."

Chloe put down her own mug with a thud. "What? No! You can't leave!" She hadn't even considered the Artist might leave!

"But I must, child," said the Artist kindly. "I make my living on the road, and back to the road I must go."

"But you don't *have* to make a living anymore!" cried Chloe. "You can live here, with me and Mother!" She looked anxiously at Lady Ashton, who nodded her head, yes indeed.

"But I *like* to make my own living, and I like to travel," the Artist said simply. "I wouldn't be happy in one place all the time."

Chloe looked down sadly. If she were honest, she had known somewhere in the back of her mind that the Artist might move on again, but she had hoped it wouldn't be so soon.

"But I will be back, certainly!" assured the Artist. "I will make a special point of it, my dear! But just now the road is calling me, and further adventures await." He winked at Chloe, who tried her best to smile back.

She asked him sadly, "Where will you go?"

"I thought I might go north," said the Artist. "Silas has very kindly invited Greybelle and I to visit as soon as we are able."

"Oh! Greybelle too?" cried Chloe in despair. "Is *everyone* leaving me?"

"Now, now, my dear child," said the Artist kindly, patting Chloe's hand. "Greybelle wants to visit her family, you can understand that."

Chloe felt ashamed. Of *course* she could understand. She realized she was being selfish, and Greybelle had been the most loyal friend a person could have. Of *course*, she should go north as soon as possible and be with her family! Chloe sniffed back her tears, and smiled despite them at the Artist's next words.

"Don't forget, my dear, the summer meeting in the north! Shall we go together?"

"Oh, Artist, I would love to!" said Chloe, her tears forgotten.

What could be more wonderful? she thought, as she imagined crossing the Bridge of the Gods, and of meeting Greybelle's beautiful family again, and hearing them all speak! And they would see Silas again, and . . . well, who knew what other wonders awaited them there?

Chloe nodded her head vigorously, drying her tears and laughing at herself. "You're right, as usual, dear Artist," she said, squeezing his hand. "I will look forward to that very much!"

Lord Winchfillin sighed wearily, from the other end of the table. "Well, *I'm* not going north, not now and not in the summer," he said decidedly. "It's all very nice of course, but it's *much* too far and much too cold! No, I must return to my poor, ruined chateau and see what I can salvage from it. I am also anxious to see if any of my old servants are about and need assistance, the poor dears. Yes . . ." Lord Winchfillin had a faraway look in his eyes. "I want to do things a bit differently from now on, perhaps spend less, work more, live a little more simply."

The Artist stifled a laugh into his beard at the vision of Lord Winchfillin living frugally.

Brisco said jovially, "Well, when you get it all fixed up, you ought to throw a party! We'll all come!"

Lord Winchfillin looked delighted. "That's it!" he exclaimed, clapping his hands. "I'll throw you all a party! Come to my house in the autumn. That ought to give me enough time, and it will be after your summer meeting, too. By September I'm sure it will be a whole new place! A new dining hall, a dancing hall, perhaps a pool, a gazebo of course, and a new stage? Oh, it will be wonderful, I assure you! The best food, wine, musicians, and plays . . ." His eyes glazed a bit as he imagined the wonderful party he would throw in his new chateau. The notion of a simpler life had completely evaporated.

"Wouldn't miss it for the world!" said the Artist, clapping his friend on the shoulder.

"Nor I!" said Chloe, excited at the prospect of a journey west to Lord Winchfillin's house in the autumn.

Everyone agreed to meet at Lord Winchfillin's house in September for the party. Just as they were all rising from the table, a *clip clop clip clop* was heard outside the open kitchen door.

Mr. Mason rose to go see who it was. He was back in a moment with a mysterious sparkle in his eye as he said, "There is someone outside to see you, miss Chloe."

"Outside? Why outside?" asked Chloe, excitedly getting up from her chair. "Why don't they come in?"

She rounded the corner to the open front door, and there, sitting on a fat black pony, was Faron the stable boy from Hotel Nell!

"Faron!" squealed Chloe. "What are you doing here?" She ran over to the boy on the back of the pony and grabbed his hands. Laughing, Faron slid down from the pony's back. "I came from Tillamook Town, of course," he said, laughing. "I heard about the trouble here, and came to help, and now I see you made it home safe and sound!"

Chloe gave her friend an embrace and answered, "Yes, isn't it wonderful? And the Artist is here, too! And Lord Winchfillin!"

"That's what they told me in town," the boy said.

They were interrupted by a happy gasp from the doorway as Mrs. Goodweather spied the new arrivals.

"Why it's Blossom!" cried out Mrs. Goodweather, running to embrace her old pony. "Whatever are you doing here? How did you get here, my dear?"

Blossom could not tell Mrs. Goodweather that she had followed the oily scent of that awful machine her mistress had driven away in, and it had led her to Fairfax. There she had been found by this boy, and coincidentally had been ridden straight to her own destination!

Mrs. Goodweather was overjoyed to see the cantankerous old pony and embraced her warmly. Blossom snorted and tossed her mane, more interested in a large bag of oats than anything else.

Chloe and Mr. Mason ushered Faron into the house to join the others at breakfast. The boy dug into the delicious food ravenously, while Mrs. Goodweather accompanied Blossom to the stables where she was fed a large ration of oats and fragrant hay.

Chloe told Faron all that had happened since she had last seen him, while the boy ate his fill of pancakes. He listened, raptly, his eyes bulging as she recounted the battle at the hospital. He was particularly impressed by how fearless she had been to go on that horrible boat, and that she had found Lady Ashton there.

"And surely *you* can stay here now, Faron, can't you?" asked Chloe hopefully as the boy finished his last bite and pushed the plate away with a satisfied sigh.

"Well, no, actually," Faron answered. "I have to return to the hotel, pretty soon now that I know you're all right."

"*What?* Back to Hotel Nell!" said Chloe. "Why would you want to return to that horrible place, Faron? You could stay here at Ashton House! You don't need to go back to a place that makes you work so hard and sleep in the stable!"

"Well, actually, Chloe, I do need to go back, in fact—I want to!" said Faron. "You see, as it turns out, Mr. Nell is my father."

"Your *father*?" gasped Chloe. "How do you . . . when did you . . ." She stopped in confusion.

"It turns out the baby that turned up on Hotel Nell's doorstep so long ago—that would be me—was his *own son*! My mother left me with him, knowing he was my father but afraid to tell him, and then she died. He didn't know, before, and now he's dreadfully sorry about everything. He says he wants to change everything. He wants me to take over the business, and he's promised to stop selling stolen goods. He says he never knew how much he counted on me, and it's time he showed it to the world. Chloe . . . I have a *dad*!"

Faron's eyes were so bright, and his face so lit with joy that Chloe's heart melted, and she forgave Mr. Nell his past reprehensible behavior, and congratulated her friend wholeheartedly.

The mood was bright and festive all that morning, after so many surprises and promises of good times ahead. But it wasn't over yet—there was still another surprise to come.

CHAPTER FORTY'ONE

*I*T WAS OBVIOUS TO EVERYONE THAT BRISCO and Celeste were in love. And the same morning that the Artist announced his intentions to go north, and Lord Winchfillin declared his desire to return home, Brisco and Celeste came forward to announce their engagement to be married. The entire company was truly delighted, including Avery. He beamed as he raised his glass to toast the happy couple, pronouncing Brisco to be the best brother-in-law he could ask for, and the perfect husband for his dear sister. Celeste for her part looked radiantly happy standing next to the dashing Brisco, who could not have been prouder of his kind, beautiful, and courageous bride.

No one could leave before the wedding, so they decided to have it the very next day. Neither Celeste nor Brisco wanted a huge affair and were more than contented at the thought of a small wedding at Ashton House with their new friends.

Instantly the house went into preparations for the nuptials. Mrs. Eames and Mrs. Goodweather started baking a multitiered wedding cake. Britta and her fellow kitchen maids organized the buffet. Mr. Mason would officiate, and he went off to clean his best black coat and practice the service. Chloe and Celeste and all the house maids gathered flowers by the armload from the gardens, and hung them everywhere, outside and in. Every vase, urn, and jar held a bouquet, filling the house with their sweet, fresh scent. They created an arched bower of blooms for the couple to stand under, and the footmen hung lights and lanterns in the trees and in the orchard, which danced in the breezes.

The next day's dawn was radiant. It was one of those wonderful mornings where there is no dew or damp, no clouds, no chill breeze, just the fresh feeling of promise and possibility from the moment the sun rises. The morning light touched the tops of the pines, and the uppermost windows of Ashton House caught the rays and sparkled like jewels.

The wedding was to be that morning, and nobody stopped for breakfast. There was a table with coffee and juice in the hall, and everyone stopped by for a fortifying cup on their way to their duties. Upstairs everyone splashed their faces with water and carefully dressed in their best for the wedding.

This morning they were all extra-splendid in fresh attire. The Artist looked quite dignified in a black broadcloth suit and white shirt. Instead of his old blue silk scarf, which had been burnt in the fire, he had a new red scarf tied jauntily around his neck. His gray hair and beard were brushed as smooth as they could be, but soon fluffed up again in the morning breeze.

Faron looked only slightly uncomfortable in a new pair of trousers and jacket. His face was fresh-scrubbed (Mrs. Eames had seen to that), and he smiled ruefully at Chloe as she admired his appearance.

Lord Winchfillin was almost his old self again as he made an entrance down the stairs, wearing a black velvet suit of Lord Ashton's that Lady Ashton had thoughtfully had altered for the little lord. Now, Lord Winchfillin made his stately way down the stairs in the fine-fitting velvet, a fresh white lace cravat at his throat and lace at his cuffs. Somewhere he had found a walking stick, and Chloe was reminded of her first sight of him at his house, at the top of his stairs with his silver-headed cane. She was glad to see the little earl so happy again.

Mr. Mason stood under the arched bower hung with flowers. Brisco stood at his side, dressed in a deep red velvet suit with black suspenders. He had a white magnolia in his buttonhole and his fine mustache was freshly groomed. Brisco's handsome face beamed with joy at the sight of Celeste making her way down the aisle toward him.

Celeste was beautiful. Gone was the faded purple dress she had worn so long, and in its place Lady Ashton's own wedding dress, made of the finest French lace. Its long sleeves and narrow waist were trimmed in ribbon, and a long veil trailed down the back. Celeste carried a simple bouquet of white roses and ferns, and seemed almost to float toward Brisco. As she took Brisco's outstretched hand, Mr. Mason said the words that bound them together and pronounced them man and wife.

Brisco and Celeste kissed, and the company burst into applause. Mrs. Eames, Britta the kitchen maid, and Lord Winchfillin all cried and wiped their eyes with handkerchiefs.

"To the bride and groom!" said Mr. Mason.

"To the bride and groom!" cheered the company and the celebration began.

Champagne was poured, and footmen circulated with trays

of filled glasses. The Artist struck up a lively tune, joined by one of the stable boys who played the fiddle, and one of the footmen who banged on a drum. Everyone danced while the tables were set, and after an hour or so, they all sat down to a delicious supper out on the lawn. Many toasts were made to the health and happiness of the bride and groom, and to everyone present, and to everyone everywhere. It had been a wonderful day—the best day Ashton House had seen in a long time.

As the sun began to sink and the shadows to fall across the fields, the lanterns hanging in the trees were lit, and the fireflies began to dance across the lawn. Everyone was very full and starting to feel sleepy. Some had celebrated a bit too much, and here and there a footman lay snoring off the champagne under the trees. A few guests were still dancing slowly to the Artist's mellow tune.

Brisco kissed his new wife and stood up from the table. "I'll be right back, darling," he said.

A few minutes later Brisco returned, driving a carriage that had been decorated with flowers and ribbons. Everyone exclaimed in pleasure at the charming sight and walked over to it. Brisco scooped Celeste up in his arms and carried her to the carriage, placing her gently inside. Then he climbed into the front seat and chirruped to the horse.

"Follow us!" he called out to the company, and everyone fell in behind the carriage as it rolled slowly down the road toward the sea. The evening was beautiful, the sky a golden apricot as the sun began to set. The maids began singing and everyone took up the tune as they all walked contentedly down to the shore.

Once there Brisco led them to a little wooden dock where there was piled an enormous heap of all kinds of things. There was wood stacked high, and scraps of metal, and sheets of glass. There were nuts, bolts, and wooden pegs. There was a great mound of folded canvas and piles of rope. Everyone gathered wonderingly around the piles on the dock. What was Brisco up to now?

The carpenter turned to face the company, and laid his finger slyly against his nose. He winked at Chloe. Then, once again Brisco was a blur. Once again he zipped here and there, taking from the pile of goods and beginning to build . . . what *was* that he was building . . . no, it couldn't be . . . yes, it was! It was a *ship*!

Beneath his flying fingers, a beautiful wooden ship began to take shape. Brisco was building a schooner for two, and it was truly a masterpiece. A tall and graceful hull formed quickly, growing a high, shining bow before their eyes.

Oohs and aahs came from those watching as the craft emerged under Brisco's skilled hands. Polished and shining, the slender masts stood tall and proud, and even now the sails appeared and caught the rising wind, ballooning until they stood smooth and full. Emblazoned on the sails was a green-and-gold rose that Brisco had chosen as a crest for his bride. Long, fluttering flags flew from the top of the masts, unfurling and snapping their tails in the wind. Before ten minutes had passed, the beautiful schooner was finished and sat bobbing in the waves next to the dock, pulling impatiently at her ropes, waiting to take her crew of two off on their honeymoon.

Brisco helped Celeste on board the beautiful schooner, and the company cheered as the couple prepared to cast off. Everyone waved goodbye, Avery blew his sister a kiss, the maids waved their hankies, and Mr. Mason waved his napkin, which he had forgotten to take off from around his neck. The schooner slowly sailed away from the dock, toward the setting sun. A line of gulls followed the ship away from the shore, swooping over and around the tall masts and fluttering banners. No one was sad about the couple's departure, for they would be back in three weeks' time. They planned on sailing to visit some friends of Brisco on an island he claimed had the clearest water and softest sand found anywhere in the south. After that the couple planned to return to Fairfax and settle down.

After the boat disappeared, the crowd of well-wishers walked or rode in the carriage back to Ashton House where they spent the rest of the evening around a crackling fire in the backyard, singing songs and telling stories until everyone was too tired to sing and tell any longer, and went to bed.

CHAPTER FORTY-TWO

*T*HE FOLLOWING MORNING WAS BOTH wonderful and terrible. The wonderful part was the delicious feeling Chloe had from waking in soft, clean sheets, freshly bathed, with the promise of a delicious breakfast ahead of her, and the memories of a beautiful wedding dancing in her mind. After all she had been through, Chloe would never take clean sheets for granted again. But the terrible part was that now the wedding was over, everyone was going to leave.

By midmorning the various carts and wagons had assembled in the front drive of Ashton House. Mrs. Goodweather was there, in a new hat, pulling on her gloves and speaking to Blossom who stood grumpily in the traces, waiting to go.

"Now you just wipe that look off of your face, Blossom dear," said Mrs. Goodweather, not unkindly. "We have a long way to go and you might as well get used to the idea now and save us a lot of trouble along the way."

Blossom tossed her head and snorted indignantly.

Mrs. Goodweather turned to everyone assembled on the steps and opened her arms to Chloe who ran into them.

"Goodbye, my dear."

The woman kissed the girl's head tenderly and smoothed her hair. "We mustn't be sad, for it won't be for long. I expect a visit from you and your mother just as soon as possible. And you too, dear Mrs. Eames, I must show you my garden!"

The cook smiled back. "I wouldn't miss it for the world, dear Mrs. Goodweather!"

"Do you *have* to leave?" asked Chloe one last time.

"Yes, dear, I do." Mrs. Goodweather gathered up the reins and climbed onto the seat of the cart. "I have people back at home counting on me to get their pies, cakes, and cookies! I mustn't disappoint them, you know. It will be good to get back to my own house and my own garden. Why I'll wager that even cranky old Blossom here would like that!"

The pony whinnied her agreement and everyone laughed.

"Wait for me! Wait for me!" Everyone turned to see Lord Winchfillin hurrying down the steps, carrying a valise and waving a parasol.

"Don't worry, your lordship, we said we would give you a lift, and we wouldn't leave without you!"

Mrs. Goodweather reached down and offered Lord Winchfillin a hand. He hopped into the little cart with a bounce that made Blossom snort, and popped open the parasol to shade them from the sun. The popping of the parasol frightened Blossom, and she leaped ahead before they could say their final goodbyes.

"Goodbye, my dear!" Lord Winchfillin called back to Chloe, blowing her a kiss. "And goodbye, my lady!" he called to Lady Ashton. "Don't forget! Look for my invitation! I will see you all in September! Au revoir, my dears!"

The little lord's goodbyes died away as the cart rounded the corner and was gone.

Then, it was the Artist's turn. He put his arm around Chloe's shoulders, and she buried her face in his new soft coat.

"Oh, dear Artist!" she sobbed. "What should I ever have done if you hadn't won me in that poker game!"

"That *was* a lucky night," he agreed. "For me, too. For all of us, I'd say."

The Artist turned to Lady Ashton and said to her, "Thank you, ma'am. Thank you for your kindness and generosity to all of us. I want you to know that I think as highly of your daughter Chloe as I have ever thought of anyone in this world. She is truly a special girl."

"That she is," agreed Lady Ashton, reaching out for Chloe's hand and squeezing it. "And, dear Mr. Artist, it is *I* who should thank you. You saved my child. You saved me. You all saved our town!" Lady Ashton leaned forward. "I give you my heartfelt, eternal gratitude, and I hope you know you will *always* have a home here at Ashton House."

"Thank you again, your ladyship," said the Artist. "That surely is good to know. Although I am a man of the road, I will be back, you can count on that."

The Artist put his fingers between his teeth and gave a low whistle. Greybelle trotted up to the Artist and tossed her silvery mane, whickering softly. She wore no bridle, needing no other direction than a spoken word, but she had a soft blanket spread over her back and several bags tied across her shoulders, holding supplies to see them both through on their journey north.

Greybelle went to Chloe and nuzzled her cheek, blowing

apple- and hay-scented breath against her hair. "It's only for a little while, my dear. We'll soon see each other again. And when we do, I will introduce you to my family! My *family*, Chloe, isn't it wonderful? I'm going to the Valley of Bree!"

Chloe hugged Greybelle fiercely and said, "I am so happy for you!"

Faron came up just then, and the Artist asked him, "Are you ready?"

"Ready for what?" asked Chloe. "Are you leaving now too?"

"Yes, the Artist offered to take me back to the Hotel Nell on his way north," he explained. "I've got to get back and help my father. Things will be picking up at the hotel now." He held out his hand and Chloe shook it.

"Remember, you've got to seek he keeps his promise to stop selling stolen goods!" she said to the boy.

"I will!" said Faron, laughing. He climbed up into the cart beside the Artist and turned back to Chloe and Lady Ashton. "You'll see, I'm going to fix the whole place up, and we're going to change the way things are done around there. If you ever come to Tillamook Town, you'll be welcome at the Hotel Nell as my special guests!"

Chloe and Lady Ashton promised to come visit the hotel, Faron, and his father, Mr. Nell, just as soon as they could.

It was time for them to go. Chloe buried her face one last time in Greybelle's soft, warm neck. "Goodbye, Greybelle," she said. "Safe travels, and I'll see you in the summer!"

The mare whickered gently into the girl's hair, and said softly, "It's not for long. Goodbye, my darling Chloe!"

"Goodbye!"

"Good luck!"

Everyone called out to their departing friends and waved them off down the drive. The Artist struck up a song, singing loudly, and encouraging Faron to join him.

Our anchor we'll weigh,
And our sails we will set.
Goodbye, fare-ye-well,
Goodbye, fare-ye-well.
The friends we are leaving,
We leave with regret,
Hurrah, my boys, we're homeward bound.

The Artist, Greybelle, and Faron were the last travelers to depart and the last set of hooves to clip-clop down the long drive of Ashton House. When the sound and the song died away, the servants and Chloe and her mother turned to go back into the house. The air seemed too quiet with all the people that had made the place so lively gone.

But with the stillness came the room to take notice of other things. A single note of a warbler fell on their ears, and Lady Ashton's hand brushed Chloe's as they walked up the steps. Chloe turned to look at her mother and in that look they shared was all the love and tenderness and understanding that they had not been able to express in the past. Lady Ashton reached down and took her daughter's hand.

"I'm so proud of you, darling," she said to Chloe. "You are so brave and so strong. You did things I could never do. I think you are the bravest girl in the world!"

Chloe felt herself blush. "It wasn't just me, mother. It was my friends too—without them I couldn't have done any of it."

Shakespeare, who as usual had been riding in Chloe's pocket, poked his head out and squeaked as if to say, "I'm one of those friends, don't forget!"

"Oh, how could we possibly forget you?" Chloe said, laughing. "You are a hero, my dear Shakespeare! A hero of a rat!"

Shakespeare secretly agreed with the girl. A delicious smell of cooking tickled their noses and made them turn hungrily toward the house. With Shakespeare sitting on her shoulder and her arm around her mother's waist, Chloe walked back up the steps and into the house, where Mr. Mason greeted them warmly and closed the door gently behind them.

EPILOGUE

W Y'EAST WAS RADIANT IN THE MORNING
sun. His happiness sparkled over the land
from his snow-covered peaks and lit up the
valley below him. The great mountain could not contain his
joy—Wy'east had woken his sleeping mountain love, Loowit.

When he helped rebuild the Bridge of the Gods, the fierce
rumbling and crumbling of boulders and stone, rocks and
earth, had woken his beloved. Blinking back the sleep of three
hundred years, Loowit's gaze met that of Wy'east, and as their
eyes locked, Wy'east's angry heart melted. Loowit saw her
beloved's face and it revived her. She raised her beautiful white
head and stood proudly, returning his love with all her heart.

All the land felt the two mountains' happiness, and with
the melting of Wy'east's heart came the melting of the deep
snows. The rushing of the waters could be heard for miles as
mountain springs and rivers burst forth, and all of life for
miles around seemed to sing out with joy.

Far away, across the long valley, the white-capped Klickitat
watched the reunion of lovers and sighed deeply, causing the

three thousand birds perched in his trees to take sudden flight. It was obvious that Loowit preferred his brother, but Klickitat wished them no harm, and accepted the truth gracefully.

At the new Bridge of the Gods, a migration of sorts was happening. For the first time in three hundred years, the animals were crossing from the south to the north, and vice versa. The smaller animals were the first to venture forth, tentatively crossing the great stone span, and soon the larger animals followed.

King Rei the elk was there, taller than the rest of his people who followed him eagerly across the bridge. His antlers had been damaged in the fight and were missing a point or two, but he still sported a huge rack of gleaming points that looked for all the world like a magnificent golden crown. The bears came next, running swiftly across, and Mai the wolf silently slipped across with them.

Silas was there, too. As the little old man placed his bare feet onto the bridge, he was joined by a massive black shape that stepped along with him, matching its huge steps to his small ones. King Auberon growled gently at Silas, and bumped up against him affectionately, nearly causing the old man to fall. Silas recovered himself and reached up to pat the huge bear.

Once on the other side, Silas turned to wave to the mountain, and Wy'east rumbled his reply, sending small avalanches of sparkling snow down his sides that dissolved in the crisp mountain air, showering the highest pines with twinkling ice diamonds.

"Go in peace, my friend," said Silas to the mountain, and, in the shadow of Auberon the bear king, crossed the Bridge of the Gods, and walked into the hazy morning mist of the magical northern lands.

Award-winning author and illustrator Diane Rios lives and writes in Portland, Oregon. Her debut novel, *Bridge of the Gods*, won the 2017 silver Moonbeam Children's Book Award for Pre-Teen Fantasy, was a finalist for the USA Best Book Award in Children's Fiction, and was a finalist for a 2017 Oregon Book Award for Children's Literature. A long-time Oregon artist and musician, Rios wrote and illustrated the picture book *Dizzy's Dream*. Rios spent three years working at the world's largest independent bookstore, Powell's Books in Portland, where she greatly increased her own children's book collection and was inspired to write the Silver Mountain Series.

SELECTED TITLES FROM SHE WRITES PRESS

She Writes Press is an independent publishing company
founded to serve women writers everywhere.
Visit us at www.shewritespress.com.

Bridge of the Gods by Diane Rios. $16.95, 978-1-63152-244-4. An
evil is rising in the land. The country is under attack, and all creatures,
man and beast, must hide. As twelve-year-old Chloe struggles to
survive, she discovers an ancient magic that still exists deep within
the forests—and learns that friendship doesn't always come in human
form.

South of Everything by Audrey Taylor Gonzalez. $16.95,
978-1-63152-949-8. A powerful parable about the changing South
after World War II, told through the eyes of young white woman
whose friendship with her parents' black servant, Old Thomas, initi-
ates her into a world of magic and spiritual richness.

The Same River by Lisa Reddick. $16.95, 978-1-63152-483-7. As
Jess, a feisty, sexy, biologist, fights fiercely to save the river she loves,
Piah, a young Native American woman, battles the invisible intrusion
of disease and invasive danger on the same river 200 years earlier—
and the two women mysteriously begin to make contact with one
another.

The Afterlife of Kenzaburo Tsuruda by Elisabeth Wilkins Lombardo.
$16.95, 978-1-63152-481-3. As he stumbles through an afterlife he
never believed in, scientist Kenzaboro Tsuruda must make sense of
his life and confront his family's secrets in order to save his ancestors
from becoming Hungry Ghosts, even as his daughter, wife, and sis-
ter-in-law struggle with their own feelings of loss.

The Wiregrass by Pam Webber. $16.95, 978-1-63152-943-6. A story
about a summer of discontent, change, and dangerous mysteries in a
small Southern Wiregrass town.